A Hole in the Universe!

The gaudy colors of the phenomenon writhed forward, its outermost tendrils just brushing the pockmarked, cindery surface of the inner planet. The planet seemed to waver, becoming almost transparent, and then it vanished from view as the time/space rip enveloped it.

Spock swung about in his chair and looked at Kirk. "All readings have ceased. Scanners show only the meaningless readings associated with the phenomenon. For all intents and purposes the planet no longer exists."

"But where has it gone, Mr. Spock?" Scotty murmured.

"Into wherever *that*," he pointed at the aurora that danced and sparkled across the screen, "leads."

Look for STAR TREK Fiction from Pocket Books

THE TEARS OF THE SINGERS

MELINDA SNODGRASS

A STAR TREK® NOVEL

POCKET BOOKS

New York   London   Toronto   Sydney   Tokyo

Another *Original* publication of POCKET BOOKS

POCKET BOOKS, a division of Simon & Schuster Inc.
1230 Avenue of the Americas, New York, N.Y. 10020

STAR TREK is a Registered Trademark of
Paramount Pictures Corporation.

This book is published by Pocket Books, a division of
Simon & Schuster Inc., under exclusive license from
Paramount Pictures Corporation.

ISBN: 0-671-67076-X

First Pocket Books printing September 1984

10 9 8 7 6 5 4 3 2

POCKET and colophon are trademarks of
Simon & Schuster Inc.

Printed in the U.S.A.

THE TEARS
OF THE SINGERS

Prologue

An ice green sea lapped softly at the sparkling sands and crystal cliffs of the strange, silver-lit world. Along the length and breadth of the glittering beach played the junior Singers. Cubs, perhaps, although the adults resting in their crystal grottos showed no parental interest in the small furry youngsters who tumbled, hummed, chirruped and warbled on the beach below them.

The hunters stepped carefully, yet uninterestedly, through the gamboling packs of silver white creatures. The little fellows were cute enough, with their pale blue eyes and ingeniously smiling faces, but the money lay with the adults. Long and sleek they reclined in their grottos, unmoved by the icy wind that whipped off the whitecapped ocean. Their eyes had darkened to the profound midnight blue of adulthood, and they seemed to be staring into a place beyond time as they blended their strange siren voices into an intricate and never-ending song.

It behooved a man not to look into those eyes when he fired

the electric current that stilled yet another voice in the mighty chorus. Those who had, described it as looking into eternity, and they didn't seem like men who had enjoyed the sight.

So they learned to do their work cleanly and efficiently, concentrating only on the rewards to be gained when the crystal tears were marketed back on Earth or Rigel, or any of a hundred other Federation worlds where men and women adorned themselves.

The creatures made no move to escape or even acknowledge their destroyers. They merely continued their particular harmony as the humans laboriously climbed the treacherous cliffs, and placed their shockwands at the base of a Singer's skull. One of the hunters fired, and a discordant cry pierced through the perfect harmony of the song. The creature rolled ponderously onto its side, its eyes secreting a viscous blue substance. The "tears," as the humans had dubbed them, soon solidified into the gleaming gems so prized on civilized worlds.

The man swept the seven crystals into a soft leather pouch. Something caught his attention, and he fished back the last jewel. He held it up to the diffuse light, and frowned when he noticed a minute flaw in the crystal. A bit of sand had become embedded in the gem, warping its perfect symmetry and color. Grumbling, he tossed it down the rock wall, where it shattered with the sound of a thousand bells. It was an eerie and melancholy sound in the frigid air.

Chapter One

James Kirk was bored. This was an unusual state for the captain of the U.S.S. *Enterprise,* but one which was all too common when he found himself trapped at a star base for routine maintenance.

He fiddled with his desk communicator, and debated about calling that attractive maintenance engineer he had met yesterday when she had been poking about the computers, much to Spock's irritation.

He dismissed the notion with a quick shake of his head. He wasn't in the mood for groundside company, however attractive. What he really wanted was the companionship of his own people, and God alone knew where they had gotten to. He supposed he could make a circuit of the more exotic saloons, and no doubt stumble across McCoy or Scotty or both, but even bar crawling had lost its allure.

With a sigh he poured a drink, flipped on the reader and tried not to think about the four days still remaining before they could leave. He had barely found his place among Nelson's strategies at Trafalgar when his door page chimed.

"Come," he called eagerly, and snapped off the reader. In his present mood it didn't matter who was outside so long as they took him away from his own company, and the nineteenth century.

"Captain," Uhura said as she stepped through the door. "I'm glad we caught you in." Her slender body was swathed in a wrap of gold material which left one dark shoulder provocatively bare. Long golden earrings swung from her lobes, and tinkled softly with each step she took. Spock followed her through the door, his hands clasped characteristically behind his back. Uncharacteristically, he was wearing his dress uniform.

Kirk raised an eyebrow in unconcious imitation of his first officer, and a smile tugged at his lips. "You two are dressed to the nines. What's the occasion?"

"I fail to understand what the numeral nine has to do with the lieutenant's or my choice of attire, Captain."

Kirk swallowed a sigh. "Old Earth phrase, Spock," he explained. Spock nodded slowly, and seemed to withdraw into that Vulcan space he inhabited so much of the time.

"I had a feeling you might be getting itchy, so we came to see if you'd like to attend a concert with us," Uhura said.

"Concert," Kirk said somewhat dubiously. Music was not one of his favorite pastimes although he did enjoy listening to Spock and Uhura's impromptu performances aboard the *Enterprise*.

"It is highbrow, Captain, but it's really worth hearing. Guy Maslin is here for two days only, and he'll be performing Chopin, Rachmaninoff, Weston, S'urak, and several of his own works as well." She gave him a pleading look.

"The bad boy of classical music, eh?" Kirk asked, tugging at his lower lip.

"He might better be described as this century's Mozart or S'urak," Spock stated.

"However, his interstellar temper tantrums are of more interest to a tin ear like myself, Mr. Spock," Kirk said with a twinkle in his hazel eyes.

"I managed to beg an extra ticket from Commander Li," Uhura said. "And it would be nice if you would join us."

"How about you, Spock? I don't want to horn in on you and the lieutenant," he said with a teasing glance to the beautiful communications officer.

"Hardly, sir. The lieutenant and I merely share an interest in classical music. Your presence would offer no intrusion."

Kirk spread his hands in a gesture of surrender. "What can I say to such a generous offer but—I accept." He left his friends and officers waiting while he quickly changed into a dress uniform.

Kirk was enjoying the concert. Maslin really was a virtuoso pianist, and the beauty of the outdoor concert hall, with its surrounding umbrella trees silhouetted against the night sky, diamond-hard stars and form-contouring chairs seemed to ease the jitters he had felt earlier in the evening. The Star Base 24 symphony orchestra wasn't precisely the Terran Philharmonic, but they were certainly enthusiastic, and Kirk had a feeling that Maslin's talent and presence could have made a jug band sound good.

The lights dimmed for the second half. Spock slid into a half-meditative state while Uhura sat bolt upright on the edge of her seat, hands clasped tightly about the program, eyes riveted on the still-empty piano stool.

Kirk leaned in to her and whispered, "Are you about to develop a crush, like ten thousand other women on a hundred other worlds?"

Uhura gave him a decidedly insubordinate look, and turned back to the stage. There was a ripple of applause as Maslin strode into view. He took his place at the piano and, with an impatient gesture, brushed back his falling black forelock.

Kirk had just settled back into his seat when there was a light touch on his sleeve. He looked up to find a young ensign standing nervously in the aisle next to him.

"Sir," he whispered under the rising opening chords of the orchestra. "I have an urgent message from Commander Li. He requests that you report to his office at once, sir."

Kirk leaned across Uhura to touch Spock on the arm. Instantly he was the focus of the Vulcan's attention. "We've got a problem upstairs, and I think I'd like to have you along."

Spock nodded, and followed the captain into the aisle. Uhura rose to accompany them, but Kirk pushed her firmly back into her seat. "Stay and enjoy for us. I'll let you know if I need you."

"Yes, sir," she said gratefully.

Kirk and Spock trailed the ensign out of the hall as Maslin joined the orchestra with a brilliant allegro run that marked the entrance of the piano in his *Concerto for a Dying World*. Spock paused briefly to listen, then gave a nod of satisfaction and stepped into the courtyard lobby of the outdoor concert hall.

Commander Li's office was on the top floor of an immense skyscraper at the edge of the spaceport. The commander's desk was framed by a floor-to-ceiling picture window which overlooked the shuttle landing area. Li rose from behind his desk, hand outstretched; and Kirk wondered, as he stepped forward, why all base commanders had similarly situated offices. It was either a bureaucratic mandate from Star Fleet or a way for now-deskbound captains to get closer to the stars they had lost.

Li's office was, however, less austere than most. Several fine Chinese scrolls hung on the walls, and a celadon bowl rested on the broad desk. Spock picked up the fragile bowl, turning it almost reverently between his long fingers.

"Tang dynasty," Li said with a proud smile. "A fine piece, isn't it?"

"Exquisite would be more accurate, Commander."

"Thank you, Mr. Spock." Kirk took a chair, and declined one of the thin, maroon-colored Beleteguese cigars that the tall Chinese commander affected, to the ruination of the atmosphere in any room.

"Sorry to pull you out of the concert. I would be there myself if this problem hadn't arisen. My wife is still there, and probably cursing me with every breath for deserting her." He paused to puff the cigar to life.

"I take it from your call to Captain Kirk that this represents an off-world problem requiring a starship's assistance?"

"Correct." Li pressed a button on his desk, and a large viewing screen slid over the window. "A week ago the freighter *Wanderlust* sighted a strange spatial effect near the Taygeta V system. The freighter was returning to pick up some hunters which it had dropped on Taygeta, which is the only planet of any interest in the entire system. It was then that it noticed the phenomenon.

"They radioed us for instructions, and we requested they take a closer look. Apparently something happened to the *Wanderlust* during that investigation, for all that remained to be found by one of our patrol scouts was their jettisoned communications buoy."

"No debris?" Kirk asked.

"None. It's as if Captain Ridly realized he was in trouble, jettisoned the buoy, and then vanished—he and his ship with him."

"This phenomenon?" Spock prodded gently.

"Oh yes." The commander flipped another switch on the desk console. The room darkened, and the holograms taken by the *Wanderlust* in its last moments flowed across the screen. Captain Ridly's voice maintained a running commentary under the swirling images.

"It's like nothing I've ever seen before. It's almost as if the granddaddy of all aurorae boreales had been rolled up and moved to this remote corner of the galaxy. We're coming in for some buffeting now, and . . . wait. . . ." Ridly gave a nervous laugh. "An insane sensation . . . I just *tasted* music." There was a long pause while the incandescent lights played and rippled across the screen. "We're all beginning to experience strange sensory hallucinations. People are feeling colors, tasting and smelling sounds. It's weird—no, wait! Something's beginning to happen to the ship!" A babble of voices rose over Ridly's rapidly hysterical commentary. "Taru!" they heard him shout. "Taru! Jettison buoy! Jettison buoy!"

The screen went dark.

Kirk felt the air gust from his straining lungs, and he realized he had been holding his breath during the death throes of the *Wanderlust*. There was an almost subliminal shivering along his nerve endings, and he felt suddenly cold even though the room was a comfortable seventy-two degrees.

He realized that he could have dealt with the loss of the freighter more easily if there had been a blast of destructive force that had left debris and rubble in its wake. This sense of nothingness, of a ship and her crew helpless in the face of something they could not understand, filled him with disquiet. That could have been *his* ship. The emotion passed as Kirk pushed away his foreboding.

"So you want the *Enterprise* to check out this phenomenon?"

"I'm afraid we have no other choice. Computer analysis by the scout ship indicated that the space/time distortion is spreading outward from the Taygeta system. I know it pulls you off your assigned course toward the Romulan neutral zone, but I've cleared it with Star Fleet. They agree this should take precedence over brandishing the big stick."

14

Kirk smiled at Li's sally, and cocked an inquiring eyebrow at Spock. "Any questions, Mr. Spock?"

The Vulcan shifted in his seat, and steepled his hands before his face. "I would question whether there is anything peculiar to this area of space, the local star or surrounding planets which might account for this effect."

Li shook his head. "We've had computer analyses of the star and the surrounding area drawn from the data banks of the survey craft which listed the system. As for the planets, aside from Taygeta they are lifeless balls of rock or gas giants."

"And Taygeta?"

"The area has only recently been opened to exploration, and the only point of interest would be to exobiologists or zoologists. Unfortunately there hasn't been enough money to mount an expedition to Taygeta."

"And what's on Taygeta that the Federation would want to?" Kirk asked.

"The planet is inhabited by a strange mammalian species."

"Intelligent?"

"One hopes not, since the planet has become a mecca for fortune hunters." Kirk looked puzzled, and Li enunciated two words. "Crystal tears."

"Oh," Kirk said. "I see."

Spock broke in. "Forgive me, Captain, but I do not see. What are crystal tears?"

"The galaxy's newest and most costly craze," Li explained. "My daughters are all hounding me for a tear. So far I've been holding them at bay since the cost is astronomical."

"I gather that these tears are garnered on Taygeta?"

"Not from Taygeta, Mr. Spock, rather from the inhabitants of Taygeta. The tears are formed by an eye secretion emitted at the moment of a Singer's death."

"Singers, Commander?" Spock repeated, sitting forward attentively.

"The name that's been given to the creatures who dwell on Taygeta. The beasts seem to sing constantly. Not like any human or humanoid music known, but a very definite and complex song. That's one of the questions an expedition would have answered, along with how the creatures maintain themselves, since they never seem to feed."

"I am disturbed by this failure of Federation policy. The evidence of such complex behavior would argue against the nonsentience of the creatures. If such were the case the Federation's action in allowing the hunters access to the planet may be destroying an intelligent species."

Li spread his hands. "As with all governments, Mr. Spock, there are failures and oversights. The present issue before us, however, is not the inhabitants of Taygeta, intelligent or otherwise, but with this strange warp in space." He shifted in his chair, and looked back to Kirk. "Captain, how soon can you be ready to leave dock?"

"As soon as I get to the *Enterprise* I'll cancel all shore leave. With Scotty back on board we ought to be able to get the inspectors off in a matter of hours."

"Good, and if we need to fudge a bit on any inspection certificates just let me know."

"I like a man who knows how to cut through red tape," Kirk said with a smile. He rose, and shook hands with Li. Spock politely inclined his head to the base commander, and they left the office.

Spock hesitated in the hall rather than following Kirk toward the lifts. "Captain, with your permission I would like to delay my return to the *Enterprise* by perhaps as much as an hour."

"Why, what's this, Spock? Are you beginning to pine over the loss of a shore leave?" Kirk teased.

Spock drew himself regally erect. "Hardly, Captain! I merely wish to pursue a possible line of investigation while I have the libraries of a star base at my disposal."

Kirk paused and looked thoughtfully at his first officer. Sometimes Spock's logical or intuitive leaps seemed far-fetched, but Kirk had learned not to question them. Many times Spock's seemingly outlandish lines of research had provided the solution to a particular knotty problem. If Spock wanted to go off and study a species of singing aliens there was, no doubt, a very good reason for it.

"Request granted, Mr. Spock. But see to it that it only takes an hour. I want to be ready to pull out by morning."

Spock nodded. "Very good, Captain."

As Kirk thumbed the lift for the ground floor he noticed that the last trace of his boredom had vanished.

The crowd in the Green Room had begun to thin, and still Uhura waited. She was mentally castigating herself for foolish and adolescent behavior, but it didn't help. She couldn't bring herself to walk out of the room.

A tall woman swathed totally in gold-tipped Ssravat fur gave one final gushing comment, took her escort's arm and they swept toward the door, and Maslin stood revealed. He made a rude gesture toward the pair's departing backs, and then turned toward his dressing room. He halted after only a few steps, and looked back as if arrested by Uhura's close scrutiny.

Brilliant green eyes stared suspiciously out of a thin, pale face made even paler by the shock of jet black hair which fell across the man's high forehead. There was a world of exhaustion and cynicism in those eyes, and Uhura almost blanched when he said in an infinitely weary and sardonic tone, "I suppose you want an autograph too?"

Anger that her idol should possess such obvious feet of clay, and anger at herself for having waited literally at the stage door like some star-struck schoolgirl, swept away her embarrassment.

"Not anymore, thank you," she said coolly. "I did when I

walked in here, but I find that after a few minutes of exposure to your personality I've changed my mind." She crossed the room to the door, her head held high.

"Wait," Maslin said, eyeing her curiously. "You're not like these vapid socialites. What are you?"

She found it odd that he asked her *what* rather than *who* she was, but she ignored it, and answered, "I'm a Star Fleet officer assigned to the U.S.S. *Enterprise.*"

"Impressive, if one happens to be awed by that institution. But what's a technocrat like you doing at one of my concerts, Madam Star Fleet?"

"I'm also a musician, Mr. Maslin, and you're displaying an appalling amount of ignorance and bias in assuming that all Star Fleet personnel lack an appreciation or understanding of the arts."

Maslin walked slowly up to her, and Uhura noticed that he was a small man. They were eye to eye, and she was wearing sandals.

"What are you doing now?" he asked abruptly.

"Now? I'm going back to my hotel room."

"Why don't you come to supper with me? I may be a royal son of a bitch most of the time, but I pride myself on an open mind. I think I'd like to be lectured and corrected by you, Madam Star Fleet."

It was on the tip of her tongue to refuse, but there was a compelling power about Maslin when he dropped his prickly, sarcastic mien, and concentrated his not inconsiderable charm on a person.

"All right," she said at last. "But only if you ask my name, and stop calling me Madam Star Fleet. I'm owed that courtesy at least."

"I think you might be owed a good many others as well," Maslin retorted with an appraising look. "And what is your name?"

"Uhura."

"A powerful name for a powerful lady. Just let me change, and you can try to teach me some manners."

"That's too large an undertaking for a single evening, Mr. Maslin," she replied easily.

He mimed a touché, and suddenly smiled. The expression softened the harsh lines around his mouth, and made him seem younger. He vanished into his dressing room, and Uhura realized that she hadn't felt this giddy in years. She decided to enjoy the sensation and the moment for as long as they lasted.

When Maslin returned he had shed his formal attire, and wore slacks, a sweater and a long, knee-length jacket. Uhura noticed the height of his boot heels, and decided that Guy Maslin was not a man who lived comfortably with his size.

The composer held the stage door for her, and they stepped out into the warm night air. Capella was a lush and hospitable world, and Uhura breathed in the scent of citrus and alien fruit which was carried to her by the wind.

"Do you mind if I don't call a cab?" Maslin asked. "On a night like this I'd rather walk."

"Fine. It isn't often that I'm planetside, and I enjoy the feel of earth underfoot."

"How do you stand it?" he asked, thrusting his hands into his pockets, and striding along beside her.

"What?"

"Being closed in on a ship all the time."

She smiled at him. "A common misconception that people have. First, the *Enterprise* is one of the largest ships in the fleet, so I'm hardly cramped. Also, we have rec rooms, and gyms, and a botanical garden where a person can relax, and more importantly—I love it. My work is interesting, and you never know what new experience is going to confront you when you're on board an exploratory vessel like the *Enterprise*. I don't think I'd be as happy making a milk run between Earth and Vulcan, say."

"An adventuresome as well as a beautiful lady," he murmured with a sideways glance at her.

"That's coming on a bit too strong."

"I never pay empty compliments."

"And I wonder how many women have heard that line?"

"And she's also a lady who reads the gossip columns."

Uhura blushed with vexation. "I do not. Your reputation transcends even the gossip columns."

"Touché again." He stopped walking, and pulled a gold cigarette case from his coat pocket. He thumbed a tiny button on the side of the case, and a cigarette slid smoothly from the recesses of the case already burning. Uhura raised a brow at the expensive toy. He returned the case to his pocket, and studied her as he took a thoughtful drag on the cigarette. "How does a man get to you?" he finally asked.

"By not playing games with me."

"Fair enough. Okay, no more empty compliments, but you will permit me to buy your dinner, won't you?"

"Of course. You invited me."

They walked on in silence until they reached an awning-covered doorway.

Maslin indicated the bright blue canopy. "What passes for elegance on this backwater. I suppose I should be grateful that there is anyplace other than bars that is open at this hour," he added as he held open the door.

"I take it you've never been out to the frontier before."

"This is the first and the last time. I like my caviar to be Beluga, my champagne aged and my jumps between worlds to be short. And those amenities you only find in the settled areas."

"A luxury-minded and *not* very adventuresome man," Uhura murmured in imitation of his earlier remark.

"No, you are definitely not going to be easy," Maslin said in a low voice as they followed the maître d' to the table. The composer ordered quickly, choosing an elegant and expensive supper. When the waiter left he leaned back in the booth and studied Uhura. "You're the first Star Fleet type I've ever really talked to."

"Yet you seem to have formed some pretty strong opinions about us on the basis of little or no information."

He shrugged, and took a sip of champagne. "You represent a lot of things I don't like."

"Such as?"

"Discipline."

"You have to be disciplined to be a musician."

"That's self-discipline, not discipline imposed from outside."

"We're not precisely keelhauled if we step out of line, and remember we choose to join the service. There are no conscripts in Star Fleet."

"You said you were a musician," he said, switching subjects. "What do you play?"

"Not play, sing. I can handle the Vulcan lyrette, though Spock tells me my attempts are feeble at best."

"I'm surprised you tackled it at all. It's a difficult instrument."

"I like challenges, Mr. Maslin."

"Guy, please."

"All right, Guy."

"And who's Spock that he sees fit to comment on your musical skill?"

"He's our half-Vulcan first officer. He plays the lyrette very well, and has given me a few lessons."

"After supper will you sing for me?"

Uhura felt her throat constrict at the thought. Maslin had performed with some of the greatest voices in the Federation. What was acceptable aboard the *Enterprise* became ridiculous when in the company of this man. She quickly shook her head.

"Come now, if you don't I'll think my original impression, that all Star Fleet personnel are technocrats, was the correct one."

She gave a laugh, and reached for her champagne. "When you put it that way I have to agree, if for no other reason than for the honor of the fleet."

"That's the spirit."

They were interrupted by an insistent beeping from Uhura's communicator. She pulled it from a fold in her gown, and flipped it open. Maslin watched curiously.

"Lieutenant Uhura here."

"Lieutenant," came the voice of her second. "I'm to inform you that all shore leaves have been canceled, and all personnel are to report aboard ship as soon as possible."

"Thank you, T'zeela. I'm on my way." She flipped shut the communicator, and looked at Maslin.

"I'm sorry, but I have to go. Maybe you can find someone else to share dinner with you." She rose and started away from the table when his hand shot out, and closed around her wrist. There was surprising strength in the long, slender fingers. She looked at him questioningly.

"Wait. That person said 'as soon as possible.' In this case I think as soon as possible means after supper."

"A nice try, but I can't agree. You don't know Captain Kirk. Soon for him means now."

"You're becoming all hard and military on me," he complained. "Where's that sensitive artist I saw looking out of those beautiful eyes?"

"She's moving aside for the officer, which is how it should be."

"We're talking about thirty minutes, maybe an hour tops," he pressed. "And this is probably the only time we'll ever spend together. Please say you'll stay."

She wavered, reminding herself of duty and responsibility; but that gay, carefree side that had surfaced during this evening reminded her of the inspections, and that they really couldn't leave until they were completed.

Maslin's hand was warm on hers as she sank back into the booth.

Chapter Two

The bridge hummed with quiet activity. Kirk paused just off the turbolift, and allowed that surge of satisfaction he always felt when he entered the command center of his ship to wash through him. There was polite acknowledgment of his arrival from the crew members at their various stations as he moved to the command chair.

Kirk realized after scanning the circular room that none of his first-line people was present. Lieutenant Riley held down the helm for Sulu, T'zeela occupied Uhura's seat and Scotty's pert young assistant worked at engineering. Kirk spent a moment admiring the way Lieutenant Bethany Wilson fitted her uniform, and he dubbed Scotty a sly dog for attracting her from life support to engineering.

The captain slid into the command chair, and a young yeoman brought him the day's paperwork. Kirk signed the sheets without really knowing what they contained. He knew it was a bad habit, but he had given up on reading the reports years ago when he had realized that their only purpose was to satisfy the paper pushers back on Earth.

The door of the lift hissed open. *Scotty,* Kirk identified from the sound and rhythm of the boot heels on the deck. He gave the yeoman a dismissing nod, and handed back the clipboard.

"Captain! I tell ya I canna stand it!" It was apparent that Scotty was deeply moved for his accent blurred all of his words instead of the few he considered obligatory.

"What seems to be the trouble, Mr. Scott?" Kirk asked, swinging around in his chair.

The chief engineer's round face was ruddier than usual, and his jaw worked for several seconds before he answered. "That damn Ssasenach inspector. He's driving me and my engineers crazy. He keeps crawling through my engines with that pinched and sour look of his even after I've *told* him everything is fine. At this rate we might be cleared to warp sometime next year."

"Show a little pity, Scotty. The fellow's probably a frustrated Star Fleet applicant."

"He's a damn bureaucrat! Him and his damn snotty ways, as if I don't know how to maintain me own engines!"

"Relax, Scotty. If I have to I'll call Li, and have him get this inspector off our backs. Besides, sometimes they do find something that needs overhauling."

The engineer gave a disdainful sniff. "Maybe on a lesser ship than the *Enterprise.*"

"Get back to your engines, Mr. Scott. When we *are* cleared to leave I want to be ready to go."

"Aye, sir." He paused at the door to the turbolift. "But I tell you, Captain, you best do something quick before I commit murder."

Kirk laughed. "Don't worry, Scott."

The engineer left, and Kirk settled back in his seat to meditate on the situation they were being sent to investigate. The phenomenon offered dangers of an unknown quality and quantity, but Kirk had other fears as well. This particular quadrant was one which both the Federation and the Klingon Empire were expanding into. Ultimately there would be a clash, new lines would be drawn and the uneasy peace would be maintained. But in the meantime it was up for grabs, and the two major powers would be battling by whatever means were available for territory. Kirk just hoped that word of the phenomenon hadn't reached Klinzhai, and that he wouldn't find any Klingon destroyers waiting at Taygeta. He leaned his head against the back of his chair, and wove contingency plans if he should find the Klingons holding the high ground, so to speak.

The turbolift hissed open again, and Sulu bounced onto the bridge. His dark eyes were sparkling, and there was a wolfish grin on his narrow face. He paused by Kirk's chair, and shook a fist in mock anger.

"Have a good shore leave, Sulu?" Kirk asked blandly.

"That's the problem, sir. It's hard to come back to reality when a man's been in heaven."

"Let me guess. You were at a fencing tournament?"

"She does fence, sir." Sulu moved down to the helm, and tapped Riley on the shoulder. "Okay, Riley. Move over and let the expert in the driver's seat."

"Whew!" The lieutenant pretended to reel away from Sulu's breath. "Didn't anyone ever tell you about drinking and driving?"

"Clown," grumbled Sulu. "I took a soberall before coming aboard. What are you trying to do? Upset the captain?"

"Oh no, never that, sir," called Riley to Kirk, and he executed a sloppy salute and headed to the turbolift.

"Someday," Kirk remarked, almost to himself, "we'll make an officer of that man."

"But never a gentleman," quipped Sulu, and began checking his panel.

Kirk waited several more minutes, but Uhura didn't appear. He decided that the bridge was for the most part in competent hands, and Uhura did have to change, he thought, justifying her tardiness. With a grunt he pushed out of the command chair and left the bridge. A dose of Dr. McCoy seemed to be in order.

McCoy was wandering through sick bay with a bottle of brandy clutched in one hand, a glass in the other and the overall appearance of a man who had misplaced everything. He whirled when Kirk entered the office, and blurted, "Now damn it, Jim . . ."

"Easy," Kirk said, holding up his hands. "It wasn't my fault."

"So whose dulcet voice was it on my communicator ordering me back to the *Enterprise* at *eleven-thirty* at night. Uhura?"

"No. Besides, Uhura isn't back yet."

"Smart lady. Wish I'd had the gumption to ignore such an asinine order. So when do we leave since you were in such an all-fired rush to call us back?"

Kirk gave a slight cough. "Well, I'm afraid we're going to have to delay departure until we finish the mandatory inspection, and the people seem determined to be difficult."

"Can you blame them? I bet you pulled them out of bed to finish those inspections."

Kirk looked a bit shamefaced. Then a small smile tugged at his mouth. "Actually, yes."

"And you enjoyed it too," McCoy accused.

"Again yes. These government bureaucrats seem to think we're here for their convenience, and when I think of all the round-the-clock alerts this ship has endured I decided it would do them good."

McCoy slowly smiled, and extended the bottle. "Have a drink."

Kirk poured out a small splash of the Saurian brandy, and took a seat across the desk from McCoy. "Actually, it wasn't just malice that made me roust the inspectors. We really do have an urgent mission, and we've got to get out of here. Li called me and showed Spock and me—"

McCoy held up a hand. "No. I don't want to know about it. Not until I absolutely have to. I still might be able to grab a few hours of sleep tonight, and I don't want to be disturbed by nightmares."

The communicator whistled through the sick bay. "Captain Kirk," came Uhura's velvet voice.

Kirk leaned over and snapped on the desk communicator. "Kirk here, what can I do for you Lieutenant?"

"Mr. Spock has just beamed aboard, and he would like you and Dr. McCoy to join him in briefing room seven."

"Thank you, Lieutenant. We're on our way. And, by the way, glad to have you back aboard."

"Yes, sir," Uhura murmured, and she sounded faintly embarrassed.

"There goes my sleep," muttered McCoy as he downed the last of his brandy.

Spock was seated at the briefing-room table when they entered. His hands played with a stack of computer tapes that lay before him, and his face was grave. To people who didn't know the Vulcan, his face always seemed uniformly impassive; but after years with his first officer, Kirk knew every subtle nuance that passed for expression on Spock's face.

"This better be good," McCoy growled as he pulled out a seat.

"Believe me, Doctor, I would not have disturbed you at this hour if I did not feel it were necessary."

"Just because you have a metabolism that can run without sleep—" McCoy began, only to be interrupted by Kirk.

"What have you got, Spock?"

"I ran a tape of the Taygetians' song through the central library computer. I instructed it to search for similar tonal patterns, and it produced three such examples."

The Vulcan slid a tape into the computer terminal on the

table, and sat back to listen. Soon a strange series of sounds, ranging from basso profundo roars to high-pitched squeals and clicks, echoed through the room.

"What you are listening to," Spock said over the din, "are the songs of the now-extinct humpback whales of your Earth. Fortunately a large body of their songs was preserved before their final destruction."

The sound switched, and they listened to a series of fluting trills. "This second recording is the communication of a large aquatic mammal found on Regulas V." The tape shifted for a third time, and they heard a long passage of wavering honks and squeals. "This final example is of a freshwater dweller from the lakes of Deneb." Spock paused and glanced at the two humans. "All three examples represent the communication of intelligent species."

Kirk gave a low whistle and leaned back in his seat. McCoy gave the other men a mystified look and, finally, plaintively asked, "Would someone mind filling me in?"

"I had assumed the captain had already done so."

Kirk gave the Vulcan a wry glance, and said quietly, "Occasionally I fall from perfection, Mr. Spock. I confess that Dr. McCoy and I were relaxing rather than talking business."

Spock gave him a look that said he knew fully well what "relaxing" entailed, then turned his attention to McCoy. In a few concise sentences he apprised the doctor of the situation, and it was McCoy's turn to look startled.

"So, it's likely that the critters on Taygeta are intelligent, but what has that got to do with this warp in the space/time fabric?"

"It is my opinion that the presence of the creatures on Taygeta and the appearance of the phenomenon are linked."

"Your evidence, Mr. Spock?" The Vulcan remained silent, and looked faintly uncomfortable. "Riding a hunch, eh?" Kirk added.

Spock raised an eyebrow. "The logic employed was somewhat complex, Captain, and I doubt I could explain it in simple enough terms."

"I see," Kirk drawled. He paused for several seconds, musing on what he had heard. "It's interesting that all four races are water dwellers."

Spock nodded. "Yet it does make a certain type of sense. By an evolutionary fluke these species have been denied manipulative appendages. Since they cannot build or write their only outlet would be in the area of pure mentation, and music falls easily within that category. Also it could be a way to preserve and pass on a body of philosophy, as is the case on Deneb."

"Could you translate any of the Taygetian song?"

"I regret to report, Captain, that I failed in the attempt. I believe it to be possible, but only by a more talented musician than myself."

"I never thought I'd live to hear it," muttered McCoy. "Spock admitting to a limitation."

"Recommendations, Spock," Kirk said hurriedly before the doctor and first officer could begin exchanging insults.

The Vulcan rested his elbows on the table, and steepled his hands. "We require a musician of extraordinary ability, one who can translate music into mathematics almost instantly, for all these songs have in common a strong mathematical base."

"Good God," broke in McCoy. "How do you expect to find someone like that out here on the edge of the Federation?"

"I made a computer search for such an individual, Doctor, and the machine returned five names. Of those, two are on Vulcan, one is on Earth and one is on Capica. The fifth, however, is present at Star Base 24."

"Guy Maslin," murmured Kirk.

"Precisely, Captain. I suggest we contact the gentleman. He would be of great aid in solving this problem."

Kirk pressed the communicator. "Lieutenant Uhura."

"Yes, Captain."

"Please locate Mr. Guy Maslin, and request that he come aboard the *Enterprise*."

Uhura looked startled, and Kirk thought that she blushed slightly. It was gone in an instant, however, and he decided he had imagined it. "Aye, aye, sir. When do you want him aboard?"

"As soon as possible. Have him escorted to briefing room seven."

"Yes, Captain." Her image faded from the screen, and Kirk swung back to face his first officer and chief medical officer.

"Once we have Maslin aboard all that's left is to get rid of the inspectors, and we're on our way."

"Somehow when you make things sound simple, Jim, they always seem to turn out otherwise," McCoy remarked.

"Faith, Bones. Our troubles won't start until we reach Taygeta."

It was Uhura who escorted Maslin and a fat balding man into the conference room instead of the usual security detail. She also remained in the room, taking an unobtrusive seat at the end of the table. Kirk decided to overlook this newest aberration by his communications officer, and turned his attention to the musician.

Kirk rose to shake hands with Maslin, and realized how small the other man was. The composer had an overwhelmingly commanding presence from the stage, but in person he stood no more than five feet three or four. Kirk became aware of a dull red suffusing Maslin's pale cheeks at the obvious scrutiny, and the captain hurriedly resumed his seat.

"I'm glad you could join us, Mr. Maslin."

"Did I have a choice?" Maslin remained tensely standing in front of the table.

The fat, nervous man tugged at the sleeve of Maslin's coat, and indicated a chair. "Why don't you sit down, Guy? It'll be better that way."

The composer crossly shrugged off the other man's hand. "Do stop fussing, Cubby. I'm fine."

Kirk eyed the fat man, and finally asked, "Excuse me, but just who are you, and why are you here?"

"I'm Mr. Maslin's manager, Harvey Cumberland." Stating his name and position seemed to give the man confidence. He stepped forward, rested his knuckles on the table, and leaned in on Kirk. "And let me tell you, sir, you had better have a pretty damn good reason for pulling us out at this hour."

"Since I don't recall inviting you, Mr. Cumberland, I'm not particularly concerned with your likes or dislikes. My business is with Mr. Maslin." The captain turned his attention to the small musician. "Won't you please sit down, Mr. Maslin, and hear what we have to say?" Maslin gave an abrupt nod, and took a seat opposite Kirk.

"The *Enterprise* has been assigned to investigate a strange phenomenon in the Taygeta V system. There is only one habitable planet in the system, and the life form inhabiting it is a seallike creature which seems to sing." Maslin had been looking bored, staring down at his hands, which rested on the table, but now his eyes flicked to Kirk's face. "Mr. Spock, if you would, please."

The first officer snapped in a tape, and the eerie vocal blending of the Taygetian song filled the room. Maslin closed his eyes, and leaned intently forward. There was a frown of concentration between his upswept brows. After a few minutes he opened his eyes.

"Large pieces of it are missing."

"I beg your pardon?" Kirk asked.

"Whatever these creatures are doing, their song has the scope and complexity of a Bach chorale, and the mathematical complexity to match. However, there seem to be places where the logical progression of the sound breaks down. My guess is that some of the creatures' sounds are ultrasonic."

"Fascinating," Spock murmured. "And how would you go about detecting these sections of the song?"

"You'd need a powerful CompuSynthesizer like the one I use for composition. How you'd obtain one out here I don't know."

Kirk gave a delicate cough. "Well, that rather brings us around to the issue, Mr. Maslin. My first officer holds the opinion that the space phenomenon which has already claimed one ship is somehow linked to the creatures' song. His recommendation is that we obtain a superior musician as expert advisor. A computer search turned up your name, and by good fortune you are accessible, unlike the other four."

"What exactly is it you're suggesting, Captain?"

"We'd like to have you accompany us to Taygeta V, and work with us on solving this problem."

"No," Maslin said crisply. He pushed back his chair, and headed for the door.

The Star Fleet officers exchanged stunned glances. "May I ask why?"

"You can ask," Maslin said indifferently.

Kirk felt a dull rage beginning to roil through his body. He clenched a fist beneath the table in an effort to calm himself. The manager, Cubby, seemed to sense Kirk's anger, for he turned back and helplessly spread his hands.

"Mr. Maslin is on a concert tour. He has commitments that have to be met. You know how it is."

"No, I don't," Kirk snapped, rising from his seat. "A concert date can be rescheduled, while we may be dealing with something that could threaten the Federation. That's hundreds of planets, millions of lives, and I would say that outweighs the wishes and desires of one person. Some things are more important than individuals. It's to just that sort of cause that the people aboard this ship have dedicated their lives."

Maslin turned languidly back from the door. "Good. Then you military geniuses figure it out. And by the way, save the stirring speeches for your crew. They might find it inspiring—

I don't." Maslin paused, and withdrew a cigarette. Taking a long drag on the cigarette, he eyed Kirk through a haze of swirling smoke, and added, "I've also never liked my tax dollars going to provide jobs for people who can't cut it in civilian life, and given that attitude I'm not about to donate my help to this institution."

"Now look here, Mr. Maslin," McCoy gritted, leaping to his feet. "This so called *institution* has stood between you and some pretty unpleasant people who would have made it real hard for you to tinkle on your piano if we hadn't been around."

"Bones," Kirk said quietly, and pulled the doctor back into his seat. Anger still smoldered in his eyes, but a slight smile played about his lips. His officers recognized that expression, and they knew that Kirk was holding an ace.

Kirk leaned back in his seat. "Mr. Spock, please assist me. Which section of the Emergency Defense Act am I trying to think of?"

For a moment Spock remained quiet, as if momentarily puzzled by Kirk's request. Then he gave a slow nod of his head. "I believe the section you are seeking, Captain, is article 9, section 5, paragraph 7 entitled 'The Civilian Emergency Mobilization Act.'"

"Thank you, Mr. Spock. That was the section."

Cumberland goggled, Maslin became even whiter and there was a faint, inarticulate sound from Uhura. She had been so still during the entire proceeding that Kirk had almost forgotten she was present.

Maslin at last found his voice. "Are you attempting to draft me, Captain?"

"Not draft, Mr. Maslin, mobilize, and I'm not attempting, I'm doing it."

"No, you can't!" Cumberland blurted, lurching toward the table.

"Oh, Cubby, do *shut up!*" Maslin snapped.

33

"And what is to prevent Captain Kirk from taking this action?" Spock asked, raising an eyebrow at the manager's obvious distress.

"Guy has Richart's syndrome."

"God *damn* you, Cubby!" Maslin exploded, and whirled away from the group.

"Guy must never be very far away from the most up-to-date medical facility—"

"He'll have that aboard the *Enterprise*," Kirk interrupted.

"It's not just the availability of medical care, Jim," McCoy interjected. "Richart's syndrome is triggered and fueled by stress. There's no known cure, and if the victim is subjected to sufficient stress and exhaustion he in essence burns himself out."

Kirk indicated to Spock and McCoy, and he led them out of the briefing room and into the corridor. "Recommendations, gentlemen?" He suddenly found Uhura at his elbow.

"Captain," she said urgently. "You can't require him to accompany us when it could cost him his life."

"Lieutenant, we may not have a choice. How about it, Spock? Can we bring in someone else?"

"Negative, Captain. The field of space/time distortion is widening at an alarming rate. We dare not delay."

"McCoy?"

"Oh, I've got the facilities to care for him, but it's a rare condition, and it can get away from you fairly easily. Also the more intense the personality the more difficult it is to keep it under control."

Uhura started to speak, then stopped herself. Kirk wondered what she had been about to say, but didn't have time to ponder on it. He rubbed a hand across his face, and gave a sigh.

"I see no alternative, gentlemen. We need an expert; Maslin is available, so we'll take him."

"The logical decision, Captain."

"And if he dies will it still be the logical decision, Mr. Spock?" Uhura asked in a low voice.

"A non sequitur, Lieutenant. A logical action once undertaken remains logical."

"I'll debate you on that," McCoy said. "But at some other time."

"Yes, let's get it over with," Kirk said.

They reentered the briefing room, and Cumberland read the decision in their expressions. His face seemed to melt, pulling down into a look of misery.

"Mr. Maslin, if there were anyone else to call upon, believe me we would do so; but such an option is not open to us. Therefore you are temporarily mobilized into Star Fleet with the honorary rank of lieutenant. If you could ready any equipment you will require we'll beam it aboard. We want to get underway as soon as possible."

Maslin's thin lips drew back in a sneer. "Do I have the right to file a protest with the commander of Star Base 24?"

"You have the right to file any protest you wish so long as you're back on this ship by 0300. I'll send two security guards to help you organize your equipment."

"Afraid I might try to bolt, Captain?"

"I'm going to assume you're a man of honor, and will adjust yourself to the realities."

"I'll try to use you for a model," Maslin said sarcastically.

Cumberland slumped in his seat, mumbling what sounded like a litany of dates and places. Maslin slapped him on the shoulder.

"Come, come, Cubby. Think of all the fun you'll have canceling and rescheduling all those performances. You might actually, for the first time in your career, earn your twenty percent."

Uhura stepped to Maslin's side, and tentatively touched his sleeve. "Is there . . ." she began, only to be interrupted by the musician.

35

"So there are no conscripts in Star Fleet, eh?" She retreated before the bitterness in his face. "I would salute you, Captain, but I don't know how. You must instruct me when I return. Come, Cubby." And the door hissed shut behind them.

Kirk sighed, and surveyed his officers. Spock looked thoughtful, McCoy was frowning at nothing and Uhura stood staring at the door with a deeply hurt expression on her beautiful face. Kirk sighed again, and pressed the heels of his hands against his eyes. They felt gritty from lack of sleep.

"So your troubles won't start until we reach Taygeta, huh, Jim?"

Kirk rubbed his forehead, and gave McCoy a sideways glance. "How about if we just hope they don't get any worse, Bones."

Chapter Three

Maslin carefully laid the violin case on the table in the center of the room, and threw his single piece of luggage onto the bed. It was a useless and petulant gesture, but it somehow made him feel better. He then folded his arms across his chest, and slowly surveyed his new quarters. In spite of his relatively low rank he had been assigned to a VIP room. Still, the stark military efficiency of the room grated on him.

He prowled about the chamber, locating the head and the swing-out dresser. Resting his arms on the top of the dresser he studied himself in the round mirror. The face that looked back was not encouraging. A heavy five o'clock shadow darkened his cheeks and chin, and his eyes seemed sunken into his head. Not since his halcyon days at Juilliard and the Rome Conservatory had he stayed up all night. With the onset of the disease, rest had become his god.

His first wild night in years, and by God, he was paying for it, he thought, feeling his heart hammering in his chest. He dug into his pocket, and pulled out a pill case. Shaking several of the small green pills into his hand, he swallowed them and waited for his heart to quiet its frantic fluttering.

He turned back to face the room, and suppressed a shudder. He wished now he had brought some of his own things to relieve the dull gray sameness of the quarters, but there hadn't been time. Most important had been his instruments, in particular the giant CompuSynthesizer which had required such care while beaming aboard. Kirk's time limit had hung over him like some statement of doom, so he had simply thrown together some clothes, escaped from Cubby's babblings and incoherent farewells and beamed aboard the *Enterprise*.

God, how he hated space travel, he thought as he moved to unpack. The vastness of space filled him with neither a sense of awe nor a sense of adventure. It made him think of eternity, and he lived too damn close to that state to enjoy it.

He finished unpacking and glanced at his watch. He had no idea what time the day began aboard this monstrosity, but he knew if he didn't get sleep, and soon, he would be spending his first day in the sick bay. He gazed longingly at the bed, and contemplated just throwing himself down on the glittering red coverlet fully clothed. He pushed away temptation, and forced himself to undress and change into a pair of Capellan-spider silk pajamas. He wasn't going to lose all of his dignity or forgo all of his lifestyle just because a latter-day Captain Bligh had impressed him into the service. It was his last concious thought before exhaustion claimed him.

The door signal took him off-guard and he jumped convulsively, spilling tea across his musical score. Cursing, he mopped at the pages with the sleeve of his robe, and finally shouted, "Come in."

Uhura stepped into the room and quickly assessed the situation. "I'll get you a towel," she said, and disappeared into the lavatory.

"I came to see if you wanted to join us for breakfast," she said as she helped him smooth and dry the pages of music.

"And are you the curvaceous bribe who's been sent to keep my spirits up?"

Uhura threw the towel down on the table, and stared at him coldly. "If you're going to be as much of a bastard as you were last night I'll leave."

"I thought I was quite charming last night."

"I'd say that was a matter of opinion. You had no right to make that remark to me about conscripts."

"Why? It's true, isn't it?"

"It's not the same situation, and you know it."

Maslin paused, and riffled nervously through the pages of his score. "Did you argue against my coming when all of you had that little meeting in the hall?"

"Yes, and I was out of line to have done it." She turned away, and began fidgeting with the hairbrushes and after-shave bottles that rested on the dresser. "More than that, I was out of line to have been there at all," she added at last.

"Then why did you do it?"

Uhura turned back to face him. "I don't know."

They stood in silence for several moments, then Maslin said in a low voice, "Would you mind if I told you I was glad you were there?"

She shook her head, and he wasn't certain if she was objecting or not. She walked back over to him, and asked, "What about breakfast?"

"No, thank you. Tea in my room and privacy. I loathe my fellow man before noon."

"There's at least one of your fellow men you'd better learn to tolerate," Uhura said. "Captain Kirk would like you to join him on the bridge as soon as possible."

"And as soon as possible means now."

"You're a quick learner."

"No, I have a good memory. Now, what about breakfast?"

"I thought you didn't want any, and if you don't you'd better deal with the captain first."

"Oh, all right." Maslin grabbed some clothes and vanished into the lavatory to change. "Did you get in trouble for reporting back late last night?" he called through the door.

"No, there were too many other matters to occupy people's attention."

"Are you going to escort me to the bridge?"

"If you'd like."

"I would consider it preferable to wandering aimlessly about this ship for the next two or three days," he replied tartly, as he stepped back into the room.

"I told you it was big."

"And ugly," Maslin added as they walked into the corridor.

"It's not a luxury liner, and you'd better not let our chief engineer hear you say that. You're likely to find yourself on the receiving end of a great deal of Scottish ire."

"I'll keep that in mind."

They passed a number of people on their way to the turbolift, and Maslin noticed that he received a good many interested stares. He wasn't certain if the interest was due to his lack of a uniform, or if his reputation had preceded him.

In the turbolift Uhura turned the control and murmured, "Bridge." The elevator whined into life, moving with incredible speed. They rode in silence, Uhura gazing thoughtfully at the floor. Maslin surveyed her classically lovely face, and wondered why he was so forbearing with this woman? She was a part of everything he despised, and should therefore be his enemy. Yet it was her presence which had made him take the attitude of unwilling guest rather than embittered prisoner.

The doors hissed open, and Maslin stepped onto the bridge. The moving star field on the front screen arrested him, holding him frozen with fear and wonder. On all luxury liners it was common to keep the screens dark or carrying images of pastoral landscapes for the comfort of the passengers. If you were an adventuresome soul there was a special space viewing room, but Maslin had never used one. He pulled his gaze away, and was careful not to let it wander back to the dangerously mesmerizing screen.

"Captain's Log, Star Date 3126.7: We are three hours out from Star Base 24, en route to the Taygeta V system and the mysterious phenomenon that is warping space and time in that sector," Maslin heard Kirk say from the command chair. "On board to serve as an albeit reluctant advisor is Guy Maslin, interstellarly famous composer, conductor and performer.

"I hope the man is worth the effort it has taken to include him in this mission. Invoking the Civilian Mobilization Act is not a thing I undertake lightly. Spock is convinced the man will be of use, but I have my doubts, given his attitude."

Uhura started to step forward as if to warn Kirk of their presence, but Maslin caught her by the arm, and forced her to wait. Kirk glanced to his right, toward Uhura's station, then gave a nod of satisfaction, and continued with his log entry.

"It is possible that the presence of Lieutenant Uhura aboard the *Enterprise* will provide a beneficial effect on Maslin's attitude. She seems interested in Maslin. I only hope she doesn't find herself torn between her duty and attraction to this man."

Maslin gave Uhura an ironic glance, but she refused to meet his taunting gaze. Her face seemed carved from ebony as she stepped swiftly to Kirk's chair.

"Captain," she said crisply. "Mr. Maslin is here."

"Thank you, Lieutenant." Kirk rose, studying her impassive face. "Did you just arrive?" he asked casually, tugging down his shirt.

"Several minutes ago, sir."

Maslin watched to see how Kirk would react to that, and his grudging admiration for the man increased when it didn't seem to faze Kirk in the least.

"Very good, Lieutenant. You may return to your station."

"Yes, sir."

"Welcome aboard, Mr. Maslin. I should have been on hand earlier this morning when you beamed up, but I had several Federation inspectors to get out of my hair. I trust everything went smoothly?"

Maslin accepted the outstretched hand. "Everything was fine, and I, the synthesizer and my piano are safely aboard. However, I am a man of strict habits. I'm accustomed to spending my mornings in quiet and privacy, so if you could be brief."

Kirk raised an eyebrow at the commanding tone. "Well, you may have to alter your habits somewhat, Mr. Maslin. We all must make our little sacrifices," he concluded with a half smile.

"I'd say I've made a hell of a big sacrifice, Kirk, so why don't you just get to the bottom line. Why did you call me up here? To impress me with the awesome power under your command? If so consider me impressed, and let's get on with it."

"You're a difficult man, Mr. Maslin."

"I could say the same about you, Captain. As I recall I'm the one who's been impressed."

"Okay, bottom line. I want to discuss the team that should be assembled to work with you, and who will command them."

"It's my effort. I'll command it."

"Out of the question."

"I am now, thanks to your gracious intervention, a lieutenant in Star Fleet."

"It's an honorific only. You are not, I repeat *not,* in the chain of command. You will obey any order given to you by a member of this ship's contingent, but you will issue no orders unless I have specifically placed a person or persons under your command. Is that clear?"

"Perfectly clear," Maslin muttered, tight-lipped.

"Good. Now what are you going to need in the way of personnel?"

"Well, since we're dealing with a musical puzzle it would be nice to have people around me who aren't tone deaf."

Spock removed the monitor from his ear, and stepped down to join the conversation. "Captain, might I suggest that I am the logical person to command the landing party. I have extensive musical training, and my ear is superior to a human's."

Kirk's lips twitched in an involuntary smile, and Maslin, following the captain's gaze to the Vulcan's elegantly pointed ears, found himself smiling also.

"Your suggestion is well merited, Mr. Spock. You'll command the landing party."

"And I want Lieutenant Uhura included in the party," Maslin said.

"Uhura is my chief communications officer. You'd be stripping my bridge crew if you took her as well as Spock."

"Uhura is also a singer, and *I* need her on the ground."

The two men stood rigidly squared off. Most of the bridge crew kept their eyes riveted on their panels, but Chekov risked a glance at the players in this interesting dispute. What he saw in Uhura's face made him give a low whistle.

"What is it?" Sulu whispered out of the corner of his mouth.

"Later, but I'll tell you now it is werry interesting," the ensign whispered back.

The doors of the lift opened, and McCoy stepped onto the bridge. Seeing that something was afoot he moved to the back of Kirk's chair, and leaned in to listen.

Uhura stepped down from her position at the com. "Captain, with your permission I would like to serve on the survey team with Mr. Spock and Mr. Maslin."

"It would seem logical, Captain. It is unlikely that there are large numbers of trained musicians aboard the *Enterprise,* and it would be best not to waste one of Lieutenant Uhura's abilities."

Kirk tugged at his lower lip, and surveyed the three people ranged before him. "All right, permission granted, Lieutenant. Now how will you fill the rest of your complement?"

"I'll hold auditions for those people who feel they can add some expertise or input to the shore party."

"You're likely to end up with four hundred and thirty people lined up on your doorstep, and all of them armed with jew's harps, kazoos, saws and anything else they can think of," murmured McCoy.

Maslin gave him a mirthless smile. "One taste of my auditioning techniques, and all but the stouthearted will flee."

"When do you want me to audition?" Uhura asked.

"That won't be necessary," Maslin said shortly.

"I disagree. You've never heard me sing, and it wouldn't be fair if I were accepted without having to undergo the same test as the others."

"The lieutenant is correct. Both of us must be included in the audition."

Maslin looked nettled at being corrected, but he agreed with a frown.

McCoy gave a chuckle. "Aren't you worried about failing the audition, Spock?"

Spock gave McCoy a majestic look. "Such a failure on my part is hardly likely, Doctor. In fact the odds are—"

"Oh yes," McCoy said to Maslin, interrupting Spock before he could get into full swing. "It's a good thing you turned up here. Saves me having to track you down. I think you better come down to sick bay where I can give you a going over. I want to know exactly what we're dealin' with here."

Maslin's hands clenched tightly at his sides. "Thank you, Doctor," he said sarcastically. "For thirteen years I have successfully kept my illness a secret from everyone but my doctors and Cubby. But now, between you and my manager, at least half the galaxy knows."

"And you know something else?" McCoy retorted. "Nobody cares. Now, if you'll come with me please."

"Is this one of those commands you were talking about?" Maslin asked Kirk.

"It certainly sounds like one."

"And you will learn that if you do not give Dr. McCoy a chance to practice what limited medical skills he possesses he will hound you ceaselessly until you do submit," Spock added.

Maslin gave Kirk a startled look. The captain laughed. "Don't worry. You're just hearing part of a long-standing and ever-continuing battle. Believe me, you're in good hands."

"That is perhaps being somewhat too optimistic, Captain."

"Spock, you're just beggin' for a physical. A *complete* physical," McCoy threatened as he herded Maslin onto the turbolift.

Kirk and McCoy strolled through the corridors of the *Enterprise* heading toward rec room C. The ship was three days out from Star Base 24, and proceeding toward Taygeta at warp six.

"This isn't going to be easy, Jim," McCoy said. "I can see why that manager of his was worried. We haven't even reached Taygeta, and he's already working too hard."

"You're monitoring him?"

"I'm having him come in every day for a checkup, which is making him madder than hell, but what can I do?"

"Nothing. After all the trouble we went through to get him we don't want to lose our star expert before we even reach the problem."

Before anything further could be said Scotty came hurrying past, his bagpipes clutched firmly beneath his arm, and an expression of anticipation on his round face.

"Why, what's this, Mr. Scott? Are you going to audition for Mr. Maslin?"

"Aye, Captain," he said proudly.

"I thought the goal was to communicate with these creatures, Jim. Let them get a load of Scotty on those pipes, and it'll scare 'em to death before we have a chance to explain."

"It's plain, Doctor, that ye have no appreciation of fine music."

"Oh, were we talking about music? I thought we were talking about bagpipes." Scotty glared at McCoy, and marched on down the corridor.

"Well, shall we go join the fun, Doctor? I understand Maslin has opened the auditions, and it's almost outdrawing Riley's betting pool."

McCoy nodded, and they moved on to the recreation room. It was Kirk's favorite, where he often played chess with Spock, enjoyed a cup of coffee and listened to Uhura sing. He also liked it because it was close to the bridge, and he could respond faster should an emergency arise.

The tables had been pushed back toward the walls to form a sort of stage near the far end of the room. The large table that held Spock's three-dimensional chess board was set horizontally across the room facing the stage area. The chess set had been relegated to the far end of the table, and Maslin sat at the table with papers scattered about him. Uhura was seated at his side.

Scotty was droning vigorously through "Scotland the Brave," while Kirk and McCoy took an unobtrusive position along one wall where they could watch the audition. Maslin kept his eyes riveted on the engineer, and his pen unconsciously beat time on the papers before him. Uhura was watching Maslin. Scotty concluded, and there was a swell of enthusiastic applause from the assembled crew members. Whether the listeners liked bagpipes might be in doubt, but they unquestionably liked Scotty, and they showed their support with a long and loud ovation.

"Do you read music, Mr. Scott?" Maslin asked while Scotty beamed at his public.

"Aye, sir. That I do."

Maslin and Uhura put their heads together, and conferred for a few brief seconds. "Mr. Scott, if you can be spared from your duties aboard the *Enterprise* I'd like to have you included in the landing party."

A slow grin split the engineer's face. "Aye, thank you, sir, and I'm sure it can be arranged."

"My God, I've lost another one," Kirk muttered as McCoy gave him an incredulous look.

"Why in the hell . . ." McCoy began.

"I haven't a notion." Kirk had thought he had Maslin's tastes figured out when the composer had accepted Spock, and had politely declined Riley's aid after hearing the lieutenant's dubious singing abilities, but now he had totally destroyed Kirk's careful construct by deciding to utilize Scotty and his pipes.

Maslin reached for his mug of tea as Lt. Donovan from biology began to tune his guitar. He gripped the cup, but his hand was shaking so badly that it slipped from his grasp. Uhura rescued the notes from the spreading tide of tea, then gently touched Maslin's shoulder as he sat slumped in his seat, eyes squeezed shut, and hands tightly clasped to prevent their palsied trembling. She said something to him which he reacted to with a vehement shake of the head. Uhura frowned in irritation, hesitated for a moment, then said, "That will be all for today. Mr. Maslin will pick up again tomorrow."

The crew members obediently filed out while Kirk and McCoy joined the couple at the table.

"God *damn* you! I told you I was fine!"

"You're not fine, and don't curse at me. I'm not one of your groupies, and I don't have to take it."

Her exasperated tone drew a reluctant laugh from Maslin. "No, you're a troublesome and bad-tempered woman," he said between short, painful breaths.

"Very likely," Uhura said calmly as she helped him from his seat.

"That's it. See if you can get him to behave, Uhura. God knows I'm not having any luck," McCoy said, perching on the corner of the table.

"The lieutenant has certain undeniable charms that you manifestly lack, Doctor."

"Stop sounding like Spock. One is bad enough," McCoy complained.

"Yes, do slow down, Mr. Maslin," Kirk said. "We're still four days out from Taygeta. You really can't solve anything until we arrive."

"I can perhaps get a head start by analyzing the one tape we do have of the Taygetian song."

"You yourself said the tape is incomplete since the survey team failed to capture the ultra and subsonics. Drop it for now. In fact I'm ordering you to take the remainder of the day off, and no working on that synthesizer of yours tonight. Dr. McCoy tells me you're not resting."

"Your concern is touching, Captain," Maslin drawled sarcastically.

"Touching, hell. I'm not worried about you except insofar as it might affect us to lose you before we reach Taygeta. What I'm really concerned about is if you come to grief on this mission. That, together with that protest you filed with Star Fleet Command, could make things difficult for me."

Maslin caught the mischievous gleam in Kirk's hazel eyes. He sighed. "Why is it that I'm constantly unable to silence you, Kirk?" He turned to Uhura. "So, am I to go to bed now, Madam Star Fleet?"

"No," said McCoy. "You've been hunched over that contraption of yours, or this table, for three days. Go take a walk—unwind. *Then* try to get some sleep. Have Uhura give you a tour of the ship."

"A daunting prospect."

Uhura slipped her arm through his. "Oh, come on. I still

have to show you why I'm never claustrophobic aboard the *Enterprise*."

Maslin suddenly smiled in capitulation. It was an expression of extreme sweetness, and Kirk was startled at how it softened the harsh angles of Maslin's thin face. Uhura smiled softly in response, and her fingers laced through the composer's. Maslin indicated the door, and they left the room.

"Well!" exclaimed McCoy. "What do you make of that?"

"Trouble," Kirk said shortly, a thoughtful frown between his brows.

"So where are you taking me?" Maslin asked as they strolled down the corridor. They were close, but not touching, yet Uhura was still aware of his incredible magnetism. "I hope it's not your botanical garden," he continued, "for I'll have you know that I find flowers boring."

"And why is that?"

"I get so many after every performance."

"Jaded cynic," she said. "No, I'm not taking you to the gardens, but to my solitary place. We all use it for that. It's a place to rest and find yourself, and we never infringe on anyone who's already there."

"Sounds intriguing."

They took the turbolift to deck five, level seven, where Uhura led them through a door and onto the observation deck. Wide ports, that could be shielded during battle, gave a giant panorama of the stars. Here the star field did not appear to be moving. It was as if the *Enterprise* had stopped her swift journey between the worlds, and hung suspended in the cosmos.

Uhura stepped to one port, and rested the palms of her hands on the clear plexisteel, absorbing the grandeur of a billion suns. Moments passed, and she realized that Maslin had not joined her at the port. She turned back to face him, and found him trembling uncontrollably in the center of the room.

"Guy?" she said questioningly, taking a few steps toward him.

"Too much," he finally forced between stiff lips. "How do you live so close to death?" he asked in an anguished whisper. His eyes stared unfocused at the stars, and even in the dim light of the observation deck Uhura could see that he had lost all color in his face. His question made no sense to her, but she could see that he was in great distress. She crossed swiftly to him, and without thinking wrapped her arms about his slender body.

He gave a moan of relief, and buried his face against her. Gently she stroked his hair, enjoying the silky touch of the strands against her fingers. Slowly the trembling subsided, and he stood quietly in the circle of her arms. He raised his head, and they gazed seriously into one another's eyes.

"I need . . . to know . . . life," he said disjointedly and, lifting his hand he cupped her cheek with it, and pressed his lips on hers.

She had fantasized about this moment, wondering if it would ever come, and how she would react if it did. Now it had arrived, finding her unprepared and off-guard. All of her careful objections to this man—his lifestyle, his many women, his dislike of her work—fled from her mind beneath the heady touch of his lips.

The embrace was long, and Uhura was shaken at the power of her reaction. She had had her lovers, but none had ever affected her so deeply with only a kiss.

Maslin released her, and took one step toward the port. The faint light in the room heightened the gauntness of his face and deepened the shadows beneath his eyes. He stared, fascinated, at the star field, and the look on his face was that of a man who has heard a distant call that lay far beyond the senses of mortal men.

Uhura felt fear, followed by a sense of furious denial at what she read in his face. She caught him by the shoulders, and jerked him around to face her.

"What do you want?" she asked in a low voice, her hands digging into his shoulders.

"To know I'm still living."

"Then I'll give you that, but damn it, don't you dare slip passively into that long night. I'll take no lost causes, no unresisting martyrs."

He smiled for the first time since they had entered the observation deck, and he lost some of that fey quality that had so frightened her.

"All right. No great sacrifices, I promise. And now I want you, Uhura."

She drew in a steadying breath. "Then you can have me." His hand was warm on her waist as they left the deck.

Chapter Four

"Captain's Log, Star Date 3127.1: We are within minutes of attaining the Taygeta system. I have placed the ship on standby alert in case we should find enemy vessels already present in the system. I hope my fears will prove to be groundless, and that we will be able to accomplish this mission without the added burden of dealing with the Klingons."

Kirk snapped off the recorder and leaned forward, intently watching the main screen. There was a brief moment of disorientation as they shifted from warp to sublight speed, and the stars seemed to rearrange themselves on the screen. The Taygetian system lay before them. They swept past a large gas giant. Several smaller planets loomed into view and faded behind them as they continued to move deeper into the system.

Suddenly they observed the phenomenon. It lay like an opalescent curtain between the ship and the sun. Uhura gave a gasp of wonder, and Sulu whistled tonelessly between his teeth. Kirk had to admit that it was an awe-inspiring sight. Brilliant colors danced and shimmered against the utter blackness of space, cutting off all view of the stars beyond. Arching tendrils from the sun's corona reached out and joined with the fulgent aurora, striking golden fire from the edge of the phenomenon. Its beauty was awesome, as was its deadliness, for Kirk could see that where the flares touched the space/time vortex there was a writhing maelstorm, and the flares vanished.

They made a slow pass by the edges of the eddying veil so Spock could take readings. Then Kirk leaned back in his chair, and said, "Take us on to Taygeta, Mr. Sulu. I think I've seen all I want to of this beast, and I certainly don't want to get any closer."

"Aye, sir."

The planet approached quickly, seeming to swell and blossom in the forward screen. Three small moons came chasing each other around the bulge of the mother planet. Silver white clouds swirled over the planet's face, but through occasional breaks in the cover Kirk could distinguish flashes of brilliant blue green. The clouds vanished, and a medium-sized continent came into view as the planet revolved on its axis.

"The larger of the two continents, Captain," Spock said from the science station.

"Orbit in three minutes, Captain," Sulu said, glancing down at the chronometer set in the navigation console.

The bridge door hissed open. Kirk glanced quickly over his shoulder. Maslin and McCoy stepped onto the bridge. Maslin's narrow face was white and tense as he watched the screen. He moved quickly to stand next to Uhura's chair, while McCoy drifted down to stand slightly behind Kirk's chair. He stared meditatively at the screen, and bounced lightly up and down on the balls of his feet.

"So, this is it," Maslin said softly to Uhura.

"Yes," she said, continuing to watch the screen while one hand delicately touched the monitor in her ear.

"When will we be heading down?"

"Probably an hour or so after we enter orbit. Spock will have to run a scan, and the rest of the ground party will have to—" She broke off abruptly, the fingers of her right hand playing rapidly over the communications console.

"What is it?" Maslin asked. She silenced him with a quick gesture.

"Captain, I'm picking up a coded transmission."

"Source?"

"Uncertain, sir. I had it for only an instant."

Kirk knuckled his chin, weighing what he had heard. Every person watched him intently, waiting for orders.

"Mr. Sulu, pull out. I don't want us trapped against this planet in case we should have company."

"Aye aye, sir."

The *Enterprise* began to swing away from the planet. Spock stood hunched over his scanners. Suddenly his head jerked up. "Ships, Captain! Two of them." He returned to the scanner. "And by their configuration they are—"

"Klingon," Kirk finished for him as he watched two of the Empire's battle cruisers appear from both sides of the planet. Spock turned slowly to survey the screen, and one mobile eyebrow quirked upward.

Kirk slammed his hand down onto one of the buttons set in the arm of his chair, opening the ship's intercoms. "Red alert! Battle stations! All hands to battle stations. This is not a drill!"

The alarm began whooping through the ship. Sulu brought up the screens, and readied the phasers and photon torpedos. Maslin placed his hand on Uhura's shoulder, gripping it tightly. Unconsciously she reached up and laid her hand over his. Her brown eyes were locked on the screen.

"The Klingons are holding their position some one hundred and fifty kilometers from the *Enterprise*," Sulu reported.

"Interesting. It seems they are as uncertain as we are." Kirk sat silent for several moments. "Lieutenant, open a hailing frequency. Let's see if we can find out why the Klingons aren't shooting first and asking questions later."

"Aye, sir."

The screen flickered, then settled into a picture of the bridge of a Klingon warship. A man was seated with his back to the *Enterprise* bridge crew. Slowly he swung about in his chair, and smiled ironically into the screen.

"Greetings, Captain Kirk. I knew your high command would send someone to investigate this phenomenon, but I never expected you. It has been a while, hasn't it?"

Kirk and Spock exchanged glances. "A long time, and a long way from Organia, Commander."

Kor smiled, his teeth gleaming whitely in his dark face. He reached up and lightly stroked at his thin, drooping moustache. "I'm surprised you remember, Kirk."

"It would be difficult to forget, Commander."

"I found it so myself. I still regret the Organian interference that kept us from our appointed duel."

"Are you suggesting that we pick up where we left off?"

"I would say that depends on you, Kirk, and that thing," Kor added, pointing off to his left, "which is eating away at the fabric of space."

"I'll get back to you, Commander."

"Don't take too long, Captain. There are some aboard my ships who would not be as forbearing as I am." The screen went dark.

McCoy released a pent-up breath. "Well, what do you make of that?"

"I make of it that he's worried about that phenomenon, just as worried as we are, and he doesn't want to risk his ship in a battle."

"I concur, Captain. At present the space/time warp represents a greater threat to the Klingons than it does to the Federation. They hold inhabited planets closer to this sector than we do. Kor has obviously been sent here to investigate the phenomenon. He will not willingly risk his ships even for the lure of a Federation starship."

"How the hell do you know what their willin' to risk, Spock?" McCoy exploded. "These are *Klingons,* for God's sake. They're about as trustworthy as a rattler."

"Maybe, maybe not, Bones. They've got a problem on their borders that's larger than the Federation right now. I think they may hold off."

"I hope you're right, Jim, but just in case you're not I'm going down to sick bay, and get set up for casualties." McCoy gave a nod for emphasis, and stomped from the bridge.

"What do we do now, Captain?" Sulu asked.

"Maintain red alert and wait. We'll let the Klingons make the next move." Sulu grinned, and turned back to his console.

"I hope he knows what he's doing," Maslin muttered. Uhura glanced up at him, noting that in spite of his dubious tone there was an expression of respect and grudging admiration on his face.

"He's always known before," she said quietly, and returned to work.

The conference room aboard the Klingon flagship was a scene of chaos. Kandi, captain of the second Klingon vessel, sprawled in a chair near the door, stared morosely at the toes of his high-topped boots and wondered if Kor had lost his reason. To have the *Enterprise* under the disruptor fire of two Imperial cruisers, and let the opportunity pass, seemed like madness. Apparently the other men in the room agreed, but they chose to be more vocal in their objections. Karsul, Kor's ambitious second-in-command, was holding forth the loudest, and drawing nods of approval from his listeners.

Kandi thoughtfully stroked his spadelike beard, and watched Karsul through narrowed eyes. Ambition was a good thing in an officer, but not when the officer served under one's best friend.

Perhaps it is time to suggest to Kor that we arrange a tragic accident for this one, Kandi mused.

The door hissed open, and Kor strode into the conference room. The hubbub died as the top officers of the two ships eyed their commander. Kor straightened the gold command sash, and dropped heavily into a chair at the head of the table.

"Recommendations?" he asked.

"Attack! Attack at once!" Karsul stated. He brought his fist down on the table for emphasis.

"Any other recommendations?" Kor asked mildly. There was a confused muttering.

"It would help if we had some idea about your own thoughts on the matter," Kandi drawled, rising from his seat and moving to the table.

"Clever, Kandi," Kor murmured to his old friend and companion. "Put me on record so that if my plan goes wrong there will be only one to bear the blame."

"I am not trying to trap you," Kandi replied in the same low tone. "But there are others who will," he added with a glance toward Karsul.

"I am aware of the situation, but this is not the time to discuss it." Kor lifted his head, and scanned the handsome, dark-skinned faces of his officers. "I admit it is difficult to forgo a tempting target like the *Enterprise*," he said in a normal tone.

"Then why do it?" Karsul demanded.

"For an obvious reason—the space/time rip. A computer extrapolation indicates that the rip is increasing at a terrifying rate. At its present rate of growth it will begin to offer a substantial threat to Imperial shipping in fifteen days, and a threat to nearby worlds in another thirty."

"So let us deal with the Federation ship, and then turn to the phenomenon."

"You make it sound as if we are dealing with a scout ship. This is the *Enterprise* . . . with Kirk in command. Even with two cruisers it is very likely that we would end up with both ships crippled or one destroyed. That would certainly hamper our investigation of the phenomenon."

"Kor is right. The *Enterprise* is the most powerful starship in the Federation fleet, and Kirk is no average Earther. He can fight like a Klingon when pressed to it." Kandi shook his head. "I would not willingly go up against him unless he were heavily outnumbered, and certainly not when we are faced with what could potentially be a greater threat than the Federation."

"What would you consider a sufficient number of ships?" Karsul asked. His tone was polite, but there was something in his expression that indicated that he thought Kor and Kandi were behaving like cowardly old men.

"Three at least," Kandi replied, refusing to be provoked.

"So what do we do?" Kaandal, Kor's aide-de-camp, asked. "Sit and stare at the Earthers until the phenomenon devours us all?"

Kandi cocked an eyebrow at Kor. "He has a point. I'm also not enamored with the idea of a standoff with the humans."

Kor folded his hands on the table, and carefully studied his fingers. "The humans are technologically superior in some areas to us Klingons." He cut off the babble of protest with a hard glance. "It serves no purpose to deny it. Their worlds are richer, and such abundance gives them advantages. It is possible that they have techniques, equipment that will allow them to solve the puzzle of this space/time warp faster than we could."

"So we sit back and let them do the work for us?"

"No. We work with them. It will increase our chances of success if we pool our resources."

"Work with humans?" Karsul spat out, his face twisted with anger. "Never!" He paced furiously away from the men clustered at the table. Kor's eyes narrowed in fury, and he rose and kicked back his chair with a booted foot. He walked to his second, and swung the younger man around.

"Is your answer still 'never' when I say this is an order?" The silence stretched between them. Karsul panted slightly with anger. "Think well, Karsul," Kor said softly. "The agonizer is an effective device for quelling even the hottest temper."

The younger man's jaw worked for several seconds, then he gave an abrupt nod. "If it is your order, Commander, I will work with the humans."

"A wise choice." Kor turned back to the other officers. "Kandi, get back to your ship. The rest of you return to your stations. We will see if Captain Kirk is willing to be reasonable."

Kandi paused at the door, and looked back over his shoulder. "And after we have dealt with the phenomenon?"

A small, almost mischievous, smile tugged at Kor's lips. "We can always attack the *Enterprise* then."

There was a gust of laughter from the relieved officers, and Kandi nodded slightly, indicating his approval of Kor's tactics.

Kor waved dismissingly to his junior officers, and fell into step with his old friend. The corridors were deserted. Everyone was at his post because of the alert which had been called with the arrival of the *Enterprise*. They reached a connecting corridor, and halted. Here they would have to part, Kandi to the transporter room to return to his ship, and Kor to the bridge.

"You are going to take vengeance on Kirk for the trouble he has caused you?"

Kor sighed, leaned against the wall and folded his arms across his chest. "I suppose so, although I would probably be better served by taking vengeance on those men at Fleet Command who reprimanded me. Kirk and I were merely victims of the Organians. No matter who had been in command on Organia the result would have been the same. I did not fail in my command," he concluded, and his expression was bitter.

"Not so loud," Kandi warned. "There are some on your ship who wouldn't hesitate to report such insubordination back to Klinzhai."

"You think I can't control my officers?"

"I don't think you are realistic about their capability for treachery."

Kor smiled faintly. "That just makes them good Klingons."

"And thwarting them makes you a better one," Kandi retorted. He clasped Kor on the shoulder. "I must go now. And remember—watch your back."

"I always do." Kor watched as Kandi strode quickly down the corridor, and felt bereft. He wished he could have had Kandi as his second. Then he would have known that his back was secure, but the younger man was too fine an officer to be left playing second fiddle to him. He deserved a ship of his own.

Kor continued to stare down the hall long after the lean, elegant figure of his friend had vanished. Then with a sigh he pushed away from the wall, and continued to the bridge. It did no good to repine. He would just have to guard his own back.

His bridge crew turned expectantly to face him as he entered. He waved them back to their stations, then paused by his communications officer.

"Get me Kirk."

"Yes, sir."

"Sir, we're receiving a signal from the Klingon cruiser."

"Put it on the screen, Lieutenant." Kirk gave a smile of satisfaction and leaned back in his chair, his fingers laced over his belly. Maslin moved away from Uhura to stand near the command chair.

"I apprehend that you expected this development, Captain," Spock said, stepping down from his science station.

"Quite true, Mr. Spock."

"May I know the reason, Captain?"

"The Klingons are obviously as concerned about the phenomenon as we are, and I find the fact that they sent two ships very telling."

"In what way?"

"Two ships? Two science teams? They obviously don't have much confidence in their ability to solve this mystery."

"I see. Then you believe they will propose a truce?"

"I think it highly likely."

"But can we trust them?" Maslin said abruptly, moving in to join the conversation. "I've heard stories about Klingon treachery."

"Beginning to be glad you're on a starship, and not on a luxury cruiser, Mr. Maslin?" Kirk asked with a teasing gleam in his eye. "But as for your not unfounded fears, this is Kor we're dealing with. He's a Klingon, but on Organia he seemed like a man who disliked senseless waste. I think he'll respond the same way in this situation. At any rate, we'll just have to—" He broke off as the Klingon bridge flickered to life on the screen.

"Captain Kirk, still waiting I see."

"Wouldn't miss it for the world, Commander. Besides, I have a job to do. Your presence here doesn't alter that fact."

"And I too have a job to do, Captain. However, since our jobs overlap, I suggest that we pool our resources. It may lead to a speedier resolution of the problem."

"I think that's an excellent suggestion, Commander. The rate at which this phenomenon is expanding makes it imperative that we act at once. I don't think either one of us has the time to indulge in the luxury of a battle." Kirk smiled, and Kor gave a wolf's grin in answer.

The Klingon made a sound of disappointment, and shook his head. "It's a pity that we are once more thwarted in our test of strength."

"That space/time rip may require all the strength we've got,

61

Commander." Kirk paused. "Then I take it we have a truce?"

Kor nodded. "What kind of surety do you want, Kirk?"

"We'll prepare a jettison buoy outlining our agreement, and voice printed under both our names. That may deter any treachery on either of our parts."

"You're a trusting man, Kirk."

"Hostages are more trouble than they're worth, Commander, and I'm sure you don't want humans on your ship any more than I want Klingons on mine."

"So, where do we begin?" Kor said, accepting the logic of Kirk's statement. "We have scanned the perimeter of the phenomenon, but the data is meaningless."

"My first officer is of the opinion that the root of the problem lies not in space, but on the planet below us."

Kor frowned. "On what does he base this conclusion?"

Kirk shot an ironic look at Spock. "Logical intuition," he replied dryly. "At any rate, I'm sending a landing party to the planet."

"In that case we will naturally wish to have one of our own present."

"I expected you would."

"It is only prudent, Kirk. We will ready our science team. Please let us know where you intend to beam down. We wish to be near—but not too near."

"A wise precaution, Commander. We wouldn't want to cause friction between our people. Until later." Kirk signaled Uhura, who broke connection.

He cocked an eye over his shoulder at Maslin. "Well, Mr. Maslin, how's this 'institution' doing so far in dealing with those threats that you made so light of when you first joined the *Enterprise?*"

"Not bad," Maslin said stiffly. "I suppose I didn't really expect to find Klingons."

"You never do, Mr. Maslin, you never do." The smaller man flushed slightly at the condescension in Kirk's voice.

Kirk leaned forward in his chair. "Mr. Sulu."

"Aye, sir?"

"These orders are for both you and Mr. Chekov. See that you heed them should it become necessary." The two men swung around in their chairs to face Kirk. "I want constant monitoring of the Klingon cruisers. If you detect anything out of the ordinary bring up the shields. You are to give no consideration to the landing party. Your first priority is the protection of the *Enterprise.* Is that clear?"

"Yes, sir," Sulu said quietly. He was echoed by Chekov, who looked frightened. It was apparent that the young Russian was just beginning to understand how close he stood to the command of the *Enterprise,* since Spock, Scotty and Uhura would be members of the landing party.

"Mr. Sulu, you have the bridge." Kirk swung out of his chair, and headed for the turbolift.

"I don't recall including you for the landing party, Captain," Maslin said.

"I'm including myself," Kirk said whimsically. "I won't be there constantly, but I'll be in and out to check on your progress, and I'm going down now to oversee the landing."

"That will put all four of your top officers on the planet's surface, leaving only juniors prepared to take the bridge if there should be an emergency," Maslin said, taking up a blocking position before the doors of the turbolift.

"You've been doing your homework, Mr. Maslin."

"I never do anything by halves. Since you forced me into this incredible organization I decided to understand it—so far as that's possible."

"Very commendable."

"Yes, isn't it? But I want to know why you will be transporting down at all? Surely the team you've assembled is capable of setting up a camp without your direct supervision."

"I always do," Kirk said shortly, beginning to eye the composer with some hostility.

63

"Well, that's stupid." Everyone on the bridge stiffened at the musician's abrasive tone, and hunched their shoulders as if preparing for a storm to break over their heads. Kirk opened his mouth to respond, but Maslin drove on before he had a chance.

"Star Fleet has spent millions training you to be a starship captain. I don't want to see all those tax dollars going to waste if you should get killed, and frankly we would all be better served if you stayed aboard the *Enterprise* where your expertise and training can do us some good, rather than mucking about on some god-forsaken planet. Besides, I don't want some second stringer trying to rescue my ass if we do get into difficulties."

Sulu and Chekov glared at the composer.

"Thank you, Mr. Maslin," Kirk said very quietly, and with great control. "Your objections have been noted. But I can assure you that all of my officers are fully capable of commanding the *Enterprise*." Sulu and Chekov looked mollified. "Now, shall we get started? As I pointed out to Commander Kor, that phenomenon seems unwilling to wait for us to settle our petty differences." And he pushed past the smaller man into the turbolift.

Kor sat staring at the shimmering image of the space warp on the viewer in his private quarters. It was not a thing he could destroy with a good blast of disruptor fire or a well-placed torpedo, nor could he use his own cunning to solve the problem. He had to rely on others to answer this puzzle, and it frightened him.

Suddenly hands slipped over his shoulders to stroke the metallic fabric of his shirt front. Startled, he threw back his head, and looked up into the face of Kali, his wife of five months.

"You're off early," he said while admiring the way her delicate, bifurcated brows accentuated her golden eyes.

"No, you've just lost track of time," she replied as she

moved to the bed, and stripped out of her short tunic and thigh-high boots.

"Um," Kor grunted noncommittally, watching the play of muscles beneath her bronzed skin as she shrugged into a soft robe. "So, how was your day?"

"It could have been better."

His brows rose at her uncharacteristic response. "How so?"

She crossed to him and, slipping an arm around his neck, settled into his lap. Her piquant face, with its high cheekbones and pointed chin, was grave. "Why have you agreed to work with the humans? You're giving Karsul just the opening he needs."

"First Kandi, and now you," Kor grumbled. "I'm not blind to Karsul's ambition, but I am also not blind to the dangers inherent in *that*." A blunt finger jabbed out at the twisting colors of the phenomenon as it played across the small screen.

"But *humans?*" Kali protested.

"In spite of what you may have heard or read in Imperial propaganda, the humans are a highly capable and advanced race. It would be foolish to waste that expertise in a senseless battle that might leave us severely crippled. The humans can always be dealt with later if the need arises."

She pulled out of the circle of his arms, and paced the small, drab room. "It alarms me when you say such things about our Empire." She shook her head, sending her shoulder-length black hair flying about her face. "I don't like it, and if you won't think of yourself, at least think of me."

"Kali, Kali," he sighed, rising and crossing to her. He slipped his arms around her, feeling the tension in her slender body. "I am not disloyal to the Empire, but I have traveled widely in this crazy galaxy of ours, and I have learned to separate truth from doctrine. This phenomenon is too dangerous to ignore while we battle the humans for territory. We will conquer the humans; it's just a matter of picking the most advantageous moment."

"All of this philosophy is all well and good, but what about Karsul?"

"I've been handling puppies like Karsul for years," he said contemptuously.

"Then don't get careless now. You have me to think of."

"As if I could ever do anything else," he murmured, bending to press his lips against the soft skin of her neck.

"I'm serious, Kor," she said as she avoided his embrace. "What will become of me if you fall?"

A small, ironic smile flickered across his dark face, and he seated himself on the bed. "I have no doubt that Karsul would take you. You would maintain your rank."

She was on him instantly, her hand connecting with a ringing slap against his cheek. "How dare you! If rank and position were my only concern there was a fleet admiral who would have been happy to marry me. You can question and doubt everyone around you, but not *me!* However hard you find it to accept, I *do* love you. You are the man I want, and I'll not lose you to a mutiny which you are foolishly courting."

"Vixen," he said lovingly and, capturing her hands, he pulled her down atop him. "You've made the past two years bearable," he murmured against her lips. "And I'll risk you for nothing. We'll solve this problem, and I'll handle Karsul. Who knows," he said, pushing up on one elbow to look down at her, "you may end up married to a fleet admiral after all."

"What nonsense. A commander is enough for me." And she pulled him into her arms. Behind them the phenomenon writhed and twisted, advancing another few kilometers toward the Taygetian sun.

Chapter Five

Getting started took longer than had been anticipated. There was equipment to be gathered, and Spock had to run scans of the planet's surface before the landing party could beam down. After some two hours of sitting on the bridge, and watching others work, Kirk had become bored. He left the bridge in Spock's capable hands, and began to wander agitatedly through the ship looking for company. Finally he decided to settle in rec room C, and wait it out. Apparently others had had that idea too, for when he stepped through the doors Maslin's staccato and rather harsh voice filled the room.

"One *and* two and," he snapped, jabbing at the music with his violin bow. Uhura's smooth brow furrowed with concentration, and she bent in close to study the notes. Maslin leaned in over her shoulder until they were virtually cheek to cheek. In an unconscious gesture the composer rubbed his cheek against hers, but none of that tenderness was evident in his voice.

"*That* is an eighth note. Stop treating it as a quarter note. When you hold it too long you ruin the symmetry of the phrase."

Uhura said something inaudible, and they began again. Her rich, dark voice wove a beautiful harmony against the pure tones of the violin.

Kirk shook his head, and dialed up a coffee. Since they had relaxed from full alert the room was, as usual, filled with listeners. Every day since their selection Maslin had worked with the landing party, and they had always drawn large audiences. The music that was being created was outstanding, but Kirk had the feeling that esthetic appreciation was not the sole reason for the popularity of the rec room. Most of the crew was at least peripherally aware of the growing attachment between Uhura and the composer, and like most small and closed societies, the ship loved a romance and the gossip it engendered.

Kirk had given up worrying about the growing intimacy between Maslin and Uhura. It wasn't the first time Uhura had been interested in a man, and it had never interfered with her efficiency. Kirk made a face at the taste of his now-tepid coffee, and wondered if he was displaying a male bias. After all, he had had his share of romances during his time as captain of the *Enterprise,* and no one had ever questioned *his* efficiency.

The whistle of the intercom cut dissonantly across the music of the Bach duet. A young yeoman rose and punched the wall button. She listened for a moment, then indicated to the captain. Kirk rose, dumped his cup in a disposal, and crossed to the intercom.

"Kirk here."

"Captain."

"Yes, Mr. Spock, what is it?"

"Request permission to take the *Enterprise* out of orbit so I may closer investigate the fourth planet of the system."

"Find something interesting, Spock?"

"I believe so, Captain. I was reviewing the scanner tapes which were made when we first entered the system. I have found some curious anomalies on the fourth planet, and I would like to verify the readings."

"You're the science officer, Mr. Spock. Just be sure to let our Klingon friends know what you're doing so they don't get nervous and trigger-happy."

"Naturally, Captain."

"Keep me posted. Kirk out." He punched off the intercom, dialed a fresh coffee and returned to his seat to enjoy this moment of relaxation. Once the landing party beamed down to Taygeta he wouldn't have time for such moments.

Spock concluded his conversation with Kor, and shook his head over the illogic of the Klingon mind. Once Kor had learned that Spock's investigation of the fourth planet would most likely have nothing to do with the phenomenon, he lost all interest and declined to send a Klingon vessel as backup or watchdog. There was little interest in knowledge for knowledge's sake in the Klingon makeup, an attitude which Spock found inconceivable.

"Mr. Sulu, please take us into orbit around the fourth planet, and the com is yours while I make my observations."

"Aye, aye, Mr. Spock." The helmsman's slender fingers flew over the board. "Course is plotted and locked in, ETA in twelve minutes."

"Thank you, Lieutenant." Spock gravely inclined his head, and surrendered the command chair to Sulu. The Vulcan then took up his position at the science station, and waited patiently to begin his scan.

The seared and barren surface of the planet slid monotonously away beneath the main screen of the *Enterprise*. Sulu shifted in the command chair, and wondered how much longer Spock was going to spend staring at an empty rock.

"Mr. Spock," he said at last. "This place looks as if it's been hit by a missile bombardment. It has the same appearance as planets that were heavily irradiated during the Romulan War."

Spock raised his head from the hood of his viewer. "Quite correct, Lieutenant. Sensors indicate that this system was swept by the frontal wave of a gigantic nova some three thousand years ago. Only rudimentary life now exists on the planet below us."

"Three thousand years?" Sulu echoed. "But, Mr. Spock, if that's the case how are—"

"The Taygetians still present on their world? An interesting question, Mr. Sulu." The Vulcan stepped down from his station and crossed to the command chair. Sulu quickly vacated and returned to the helm. With his eyes still on the barren face of the planet, Spock depressed the com button, signaling the rec room. This time it was Kirk who answered.

"Thought it might be you," the captain said. "What have you got?"

"A fascinating contradiction, Captain. If you could come to the bridge."

"On my way."

Kirk found Spock standing impassively at the science station. Before he could speak, the Vulcan's long fingers were playing over the console.

"These are the results of the scan taken over the past thirty minutes. I will play it on the main screen, magnification eight."

Kirk turned to regard the screen. The seared landscape rolled by, every crack and fissure clearly discernible at this high magnification. Suddenly a highly regular stone structure came into view. Kirk's eyes narrowed, and he tugged thoughtfully at his lower lip. Spock reached over, and froze the tape on the blackened structure.

"Obviously an artifact. Those kinds of angles don't occur in nature. What do you make of it, Spock?"

"At some point this planet was inhabited by a race of

intelligent beings. Given the design and sophistication of the buildings I would estimate them to have been developmentally comparable to your Babylonians at the time of their destruction."

"Destruction?"

"Yes, Captain." The science officer snapped on the screen above his station. "Scanners indicate that this system took the brunt of a frontal wave which issued from a nova occurring here." The screen switched to a geodesic star map, and a red arrow pinpointed an irregular splash of light among the stars. "I have backtraced the wave of radiation, and it is clear that it swept through this system approximately three thousand one hundred and five years ago. A distance scan of the other planets in this system indicates the same radiation destruction. All except Taygeta."

Kirk leaned on the back of Spock's chair. "Is it possible that life managed to take hold on Taygeta faster than on the other planets?"

"The odds of that occurring are infinitesimally small, Captain. On an evolutionary time scale three thousand years is as a second to us. To assume that sea life, and the simple vegetation of Taygeta, evolved in three thousand years is inconceivable. To further assume that a race of intelligent sea dwellers evolved in that same span of time is impossible. No, it is apparent that the Taygetians were here when the nova reached this system."

"And their survival?"

"Is a mystery. I suggest that the answer cannot be found from the *Enterprise*. I think we can only determine how the Taygetians avoided the holocaust that enveloped their system on the surface of their world."

"You sound like a man who's impatient to get his landing party into action."

"Impatient?" Spock echoed, slightly raising one eyebrow. "No, Captain, I should say it is logic rather than impatience that dictates my suggestion that the landing party beam down. We have clearly gone as far as is scientifically possible from the bridge of the *Enterprise.*"

"All right, Mr. Spock. All the supplies have been readied, and if you're finished here we may as well get to it." Kirk crossed to the command chair, and opened an intership frequency. "This is the captain. The Taygetian landing party will report to the transporter room immediately."

"Hadn't we better inform the Klingons that we are ready to beam down?"

"Oh God, yes. They'll want to be right on our heels, or they'll suspect us of double dealing."

"It is very wearying to deal with beings who judge everyone by their own irrational suspicions," Spock said disdainfully.

"Still, I'd rather be dealing with them than shooting at them, Spock. It's not helping my nerves any knowing that there are two of them against one of us."

"Logical, Captain, but I would point out that mere numerical superiority will not always determine the outcome of a military engagement. Tactical expertise must also be considered, and you are well known for your talents in that area."

"Thank you for the vote of confidence, but we don't know what sort of talents Kor might have in that direction. We've only encountered him as a garrison commander on Organia."

"Then we shall hope that events will not require a test of military skills."

"Amen to that, Spock. Shall we go?" Kirk said, indicating the turbolift. "Mr. Sulu, the ship is yours. See to it that our Klingon allies are informed of our landing."

"Yes, sir."

"You were supposed to be in the transporter room five minutes ago," Uhura said mildly while Maslin vibrated about the room like a hysterical pinball. She was dressed in cold-weather fatigues. The grey-and-white pants and knee-high boots covered her long legs, and her elegant figure was masked by the bulky parka.

"God damn it!" he yelled, flinging a handful of loose musical notation pages into the air. "I am not a watchmaker," he continued as he stood in a blizzard of falling papers. "I'm an artist! I will not be hurried!"

"I know you're nervous and frightened, but don't you dare take it out on me," Uhura snapped. "If I had known you weren't ready I would never have agreed to that musical session in the rec room. Now get packed before the captain comes himself instead of just sending me."

His energy and tension evaporated, and he sank down on the edge of his bed. "I don't know what to take," he said quietly.

The communications officer moved to the hidden dresser and pulled out an armful of underwear. She then gathered up his personal toiletries from the bathroom, and dumped the entire load into his arms. Cold-weather fatigues had already been called up from stores, and lay across the foot of his bed.

"Now, I suggest that you get changed. A balmy day on Taygeta is around thirty-five degrees Fahrenheit, and those linen suits of yours just aren't going to cut it. As for musical equipment I think you might be able to handle that yourself," she concluded dryly.

He looked up into her beautiful and impassive face. "You won't let me get away with anything, will you?"

"No. Spoiled brats and temper tantrums don't amuse me. I don't have time to bother with them."

"I thought you loved me," he said, sounding somewhat like a child who has just discovered that mother spanks.

"I sleep with you," Uhura corrected. "Don't confuse the action with the emotion. And even if I did love you it's not license for you to treat me like a doormat." Maslin kept his eyes nervously averted from her, and concentrated instead on folding and placing the clothes in a backpack. "Your medicine," she added abruptly as he started to close the pack.

"Oh yes." He crossed to the dresser and removed the bottle of pills from the top drawer. He tossed it into the pack, seamed it shut, and headed for the door.

"Do you need any of these?" Uhura asked, bending to retrieve one of the notation pages.

"No, I just use them for doodling . . . and as a prop for my tantrums," he added with an apologetic glance toward her.

A smile tugged at her lips. "And I suppose that passes for an apology from you?" she asked.

"Yes," he replied shortly, and stepped into the corridor.

She sighed, and shook her head. "Okay, I suppose one can't settle for everything."

"Ah, but in me you come very close."

She couldn't think of a sufficiently crushing retort so she let it pass, and led him quickly to the transporter room.

Kirk was jigging with impatience when they arrived. He looked at Maslin as if debating whether to speak, then seemed to think better of it. Instead he busied himself with last-minute instructions to Lieutenant Kyle, who stood behind the transporter console. Uhura looked around the transporter room, thinking how strange it seemed to see the landing party without their identifying uniform colors. Only the gold braid on the sleeves of the jackets distinguished one white-suited figure from the other.

"We're ready, sir," Lieutenant Kyle said, finishing some final adjustments to the transporter. "We're going to put you down near a large group of the Taygetian cubs."

"Very well, Mr. Kyle. May as well find out right away if the natives are hostile," Kirk added as he bounded onto the transporter platform. "Signal the freight transporter to send down the equipment after we've had a chance to take a look around, and find a suitable campsite."

"Yes, sir."

Spock, Uhura, Maslin, Scotty and Yeoman Chou, a diminutive Chinese girl who looked like she ought to be wearing a silk kimono rather than toting a phaser, joined Kirk on the platform. Lieutenant Donovan hefted his guitar in its case, and watched as the transporter hummed to life. He and the three security guards would follow the first group to the Taygetian surface.

They became aware of the song even before they had fully materialized. It seemed to reach deep into the soul and set up an answering resonance in the listener. Even to an untrained ear like Kirk's it was apparent that they were hearing only a thin slice of the total melody. Fascinating and beautiful motifs would catch the ear, then whirl away into a range beyond human hearing. Certain harmonies would weave and blend, but there was always a disconcerting feeling that a voice or two was missing. It was almost a sensory overload, and for several moments the humans stood in rapt contemplation of the music.

Spock, as always unmoved by externals, had switched on his tricorder the moment materialization was complete, and was busy monitoring the readings. Maslin, an expression of enchantment on his narrow face, took a step forward, and almost lost his footing in the soft, glittering sand. Uhura instinctively reached out to steady him, and for once he didn't snap at her for her solicitude; he was too intent upon the song.

Overhead the sky was a strange silver gray, but there was no evidence of clouds. Behind them the ice green waves boomed onto the beach and ran hissing and foaming up the sand. Small birdlike creatures, their sparkling blue head feathers fluttering from their speed, retreated, peeping, from the advancing waters. Then, as the waves receded, they would rush back toward the ocean, feeding on something the waters had left behind. The breeze from the sea was clean, tangy and bitterly cold.

"Sweet Jesus," Scotty murmured, covering one ear. "If these beasties keep this up day and night it's a hard time we're going to have sleeping."

"Evidence indicates that to be the case, Mr. Scott," Spock said. "But I expect we will become accustomed to the sound after several hours."

"Look, Captain," Yeoman Chou said, pointing down the beach. "We're arousing some interest."

They all looked quickly in the direction of her gesture. Several hundred yards down the beach thirty or so white-pelted Taygetians gazed at them with wide blue eyes. Many lay tumbled over one another as if the arrival of the humans had interrupted them in the midst of some game. For several seconds the two groups regarded one another, then the cubs set up a veritable cacophony of chirpings, warblings, hums and whistles, all the while glancing fearfully from the humans to the glistening crystal cliffs that rose like ice castles from the diamond-bright sands. It was from the cliffs that the mighty chorus rose, and by narrowing their eyes against the brilliance of the cliffs and sand, the humans could distinguish several adult Taygetians in their crystal grottos.

"It's like they're warning the adults," Uhura said quietly.

"And with absolutely no result," Maslin added, shading his eyes with one slender hand. "They're just continuing the song."

"The behavior of the cubs strongly indicates intelligence, but the adults . . ." Spock shook his head. "Such disregard for potential danger would argue against their being intelligent."

"Not necessarily, Mr. Spock," Kirk said. "Animals will always panic and flee when faced with a potential threat. The major exception I can think of to that rule—animals who are able to put their fears aside and stand in the face of danger—are *very* intelligent ones like humans, and Vulcans, and Andorians. I could go on, but you get the idea."

"Then you are suggesting that the Taygetians are responding to some higher duty, or that we are just not important enough to merit a response, Captain?"

"It does sort of look that way." The distinctive hum of the

transporter rose from behind them, and moments later Donovan and the three security guards coalesced from the shimmering particles.

"Lt. Kyle said to have you signal him when you've located a campsite. He also suggested that you pick a place that's in the shelter of a cliff so that if there should be a storm we'll be protected."

"Thank you, Donovan, and I think Lt. Kyle's suggestions are well merited."

They began walking, and about three hundred yards down the beach the cliffs made a sharp bend, creating a sheltered cove. Kirk liked the defensibility of the location, so it was there that Kyle materialized the substantial amount of equipment required by the landing party. Kirk gave a nod of satisfaction.

"Okay, let's get to it. The sooner the camp is up the sooner you can erect a perimeter, and the better I'll feel."

"You don't think we're in any danger, do you, Captain?" Uhura asked.

"With two Klingon battle cruisers orbiting above us, and a party of Klingons about to land on this planet, not to mention a race of unknown beings inhabiting the cliffs around us? Why no, of course not," he concluded with a twinkle in his hazel eyes. Uhura chuckled, but her face was thoughtful as she joined Maslin.

The cubs watched as the humans began to unpack their equipment. When the landing party approached the base of the cliffs the cubs' cries took on an almost hysterical note, then died into a confused melodic murmuring as the humans continued to erect their camp, paying no attention to the adults who serenely sang above them.

"They think we're going to hurt the adults," Maslin said as he uncrated the synthesizer.

"And we've confused them by not heading up the cliffs to kill the older ones," Uhura added, pulling off the protective wrapping that covered the keyboards of the synthesizer.

"After all, their only experience with humans has been with hunters."

"Well, maybe after they see we're not going to hurt them they'll start to approach us. I want to start mimicking their sounds back at them, and start building up a vocabulary in the synthesizer."

Kirk, who had been perambulating from group to group, lending a hand and overseeing security's defenses, paused at Maslin and Uhura. "We may be able to convince them that *we're* not going to hurt them, but what about our Klingon friends? Let's just hope they don't get trigger-happy, or decide to play soccer with the cubs."

"But they're so cute, how could anybody hurt them?" Maslin objected.

"Cute doesn't mean a lot to a Klingon," Uhura said. "Remember the tribbles," she added to Kirk.

The captain put a hand over his eyes. "Oh God, don't remind me. Let's just hope the Taygetians and the Klingons don't arouse that kind of antipathy in one another."

"Have I missed something?"

"Another story," Uhura said, touching Maslin on the arm. "But one that you should hear. I'll tell you later."

"Well, let's get back to it," Kirk said, glancing up and down the beach. "The Klingons will be here soon, and I want us set up by then."

"You don't anticipate trouble do you, Captain?" Maslin asked.

"I may not anticipate trouble, Mr. Maslin, but I'm always prepared for it," he said over his shoulder as he walked away.

"Somehow that doesn't make me feel very confident," Maslin confided in an undertone to Uhura.

"It should. It's Captain Kirk's preparations that have saved us in a good many encounters."

Kor watched as Kali strapped on her holstered disruptor, and tied it down with the thigh belt. The thin leather strap was a macho affectation that never ceased to amuse him, but it was not all for show. Despite her fragile beauty Kali was an intelligent, well-trained and highly capable female. In fact, she was one of the best sharpshooters in the Imperial fleet. As he watched the way her hair fell forward to caress her cheek he felt his heart squeezed with love for his young bride, and he almost regretted his decision to include her in the landing party.

As if she had read his mind she looked over at him where he lay on the bed and said, "I wish I didn't have to go."

"I too, my love, but I need you there to keep an eye on Quarag and Jennas."

"If there's going to be trouble it's going to start here. I don't like to think of you facing Karsul alone."

"I can handle Karsul, and if I can't your presence isn't going to make any difference."

"At least I would be with you."

"My dear, they aren't going to let us die nobly together. You at least will be spared."

"I know. That's what worries me."

"Come here," he said, gesturing with one hand. She came to his side, and he pulled her down next to him on the bed. He pressed his lips against her silky hair, breathing in the sweet smell of her perfume. "I don't want to send you from my side, but I need you to watch not only our own people but the humans as well. With you there I will know I am getting accurate information."

"Quarag is in command of the landing party. It is he who will make the daily reports."

"True, but you will contact me every evening on a scrambled, closed beam to this cabin."

"Communications will pick up the private transmission."

"Let them. That will keep Karsul guessing, and perhaps a little off-balance."

"Keep them guessing," she repeated, rubbing his black hair. "I think that should be your motto."

"If we live long enough to start a family it shall be the code of our house." He smiled, and she tugged at one end of his trailing moustache.

"You are impossible, but I'll keep you. Am I not to see you again until this mission is over, or will you come to the planet?"

"I expect I'll beam down at least once. I want to take a firsthand look at these Taygetians."

"Do you really think the answer is on the planet?"

"No, but if the humans send down a party I must counter them. Strategy, my dear."

"No, politics, my dear," she mimicked sarcastically. "Now I must go." She pressed a kiss onto his lips, and bounced off the bed. "I will contact you tonight."

He rose with a grunt, and smoothed down the front of his tunic. "I'll walk you to the transporter room. That far at least I can go with you."

The rest of the landing party was milling about in the transporter room when they arrived. Kor crossed to the officer behind the transporter console.

"Are the humans down yet?"

"Yes sir, some twenty minutes ago."

"Excellent. Put the landing party down one-half mile from their camp."

"Yes, sir."

"Kor," Kali said quietly, crossing to his side. "Is that wise? You will be putting a great deal of stress on both parties."

"I want them to be nervous. It wouldn't do to have them too cocky."

She gave him a quizzical look and shook her head. "Keep them guessing?"

"Absolutely." The landing party began to arrange themselves on the transporter platform. Kor took Kali by the shoulders and looked down into her face. "Survive and succeed," he said softly.

"I will. See to it that you do the same," she added in a low voice.

He nodded and released her, stepping back to stand by the console. She seemed a small figure among the tall, heavyset males who surrounded her. There were several flashes, and the landing party was gone. Kor stifled a sigh, and headed for the bridge. He felt very isolated with Kali gone, and he hoped he could maintain the delicate balance he was treading between the Earthers and his own mutinous, ambitious crew.

Still, he thought with a fatalistic shrug, *if I fail I won't be around very long to worry about it. Karsul will see to that.*

For a brief moment he wondered if Kirk were bedeviled with such problems. Somehow he doubted it.

"Company, Captain," Scotty said with a jerk of his head. His face and tone were grim. Kirk and Spock whirled and gazed in the direction of the nod. Down the beach they saw the distinctive flashes of a Klingon transporter. Ragsdale, Brentano and Lindenbaum, the three security guards, drew their phasers and moved swiftly into cover. Scotty dropped the self-erecting tent he had been holding, and fanned out to the left flank while Uhura took out her communicator and flipped it open.

"Klingons, Mr. Kyle," she said crisply. "Lock onto our positions, and be ready to pull us out of here if the situation should turn ugly."

Maslin glanced nervously from the tensely alert security guards; to Kirk and Spock, gazing intently down the beach; to Scott, lovingly fingering his phaser; to Uhura, her beautiful dark face set in grim lines.

"I think I like our other company better," Maslin muttered with a look to the Taygetian cubs who had been progressively flopping forward to investigate the human camp.

"Unfortunately you sometimes can't choose your friends," Uhura responded. "Why don't you take cover."

"What about you?"

"I can take care of myself, and it's my job to be out here."

"Then it's my job to be out here too."

"Oh Guy, why must you be so damn competitive!" she snapped irritably. "I'm trained for this. You're not."

"Why do you always assume that everything I do or say is motivated by ego? Has it ever occurred to you that chivalry and affection might play some part in this?"

Their eyes met, and suddenly the Klingons seemed very remote and unimportant, for she saw in his eyes that which she had not wished to see. Shaken, she dropped her eyes, and for one wild moment wished she could return to earlier, simpler emotions. Flirtation—even their affair—seemed safer than the warmth, affection and, yes, love that she now found in his eyes.

"I'm sorry," she said at last. "I had no right to make assumptions about your motives."

"Gracious lady," he said, touching her lightly on the cheek with one long forefinger. "Now, do I get to stay or do I have to go skulk in a tent?"

She was grateful for the return to the original topic. She had no desire to deal with this shift in their relationship right now. "I suppose you can stay. Since nobody's started shooting yet we may be okay."

"I thought we had a truce with the Klingons?"

"What an innocent. The Klingons' basic law of life is that laws are made to be violated."

"I had no idea," he said slowly as he watched the five dark and saturnine men, and the one delicate, black-haired woman approaching. "I thought it was just propaganda to keep the tax dollars rolling in for Star Fleet."

"Beginning to see a reason for our existence?" Uhura asked with an ironic glance. At a gesture from Kirk she holstered her phaser. The security men followed suit, but somewhat more slowly.

The five Klingons paused, and gazed curiously down at the

Taygetian cubs who ringed the human camp. The cubs stared up at them fearlessly out of pale blue eyes. Uhura didn't like the way several of the Klingon males eyed the glorious silver white pelts of the Taygetians, and she shifted nervously.

"Greetings, Kirk," a tall, slim Klingon called as he stepped over a Taygetian. "I am Lieutenant Commander Quarag, science officer aboard the *Klothos*."

"Welcome to Taygeta, Commander," Kirk said with a faint smile.

"Are you claiming this world already that you so boldly act as if we were your guests?" Quarag smiled also, but it was a wolfish, unpleasant expression.

"Neither your Empire nor the Federation is able to lay claim to this world," Spock interjected. "The planet is inhabited. It will be the decision of the natives to determine which, if any alliance, they desire."

"Natives?"

"All around you," Kirk said.

Quarag glanced about. "These *animals?*"

"Natives," Kirk repeated.

"If this is some Earther trick to take this world—"

"There is no trick," Spock said. "These are intelligent, sentient creatures. They have a complex language. That alone qualifies them for classification as a sentient race."

"My science officer, Mr. Spock, who commands the landing party, believes there is a link between the Taygetians and the phenomenon," Kirk said mildly.

"So we have heard," Kali said softly. "But I fail to see why."

The Earth party eyed her curiously, for women were rare on Klingon vessels. Only once before had they met one, and that had been Kang's wife, Mara. Mara had been tall and angular with beautiful, but almost harsh features. Kirk had been in the habit of thinking of her as the typical Klingon woman, but this was clearly not the case, for the woman who stood before him was small and fragile. There was even a

Dresden-china quality about her in spite of her honey gold skin. She seemed disconcerted by Kirk's scrutiny, and she shifted her topaz-colored eyes away, fixing them at last upon Uhura.

"Is it because of the song?" she suddenly asked, with a quick look toward the cliffs.

"Why would you reach that conclusion?" Maslin asked, taking a step forward, and watching her intently.

"I'm not sure. There is something very compelling about the song. I feel that if I could just turn a corner in my mind I would be able to understand its meaning. It seems to speak of . . . well, of many things," she finished lamely. Maslin wondered what she had really been going to say.

"You're very astute," Kirk said with his best smile and a warm light in his eyes which he always acquired when he was interested in a beautiful woman. "Yes, it is the song. That's why we've brought one of the Federation's best musicians." He indicated the composer. "Mr. Guy Maslin."

Kali nodded politely, and Quarag looked disgruntled. It was apparent that the Klingons were not prepared for a scientific inquiry that took this particular direction.

"Well, I am certain we shall make equal progress using our own methods," Quarag said somewhat huffily.

"Oh, I don't doubt it," Kirk replied. "Where are you planning to camp?"

"There," the Klingon said, indicating a high knoll. From that vantage point the human camp would be in plain view.

"Trusting, aren't they," Ragsdale muttered to Brentano.

"I don't mind them watching," the blond security guard replied. "But I sure as hell wish they'd do it some three or four miles down the beach. I don't like having them so close."

"That'll do," Scotty snapped, catching Kirk's irritated look, and realizing that the Klingons had overheard the security guards' exchange. The two men looked embarrassed, and subsided.

"We will set up our camp and begin work," Quarag stated.

Kirk nodded. "Feel free to use any of our equipment. The closer we work the more likely we are to solve this problem."

"I don't think that will be necessary," one of the heretofore silent Klingons said with a sneer. "I doubt there is anything we could learn from Earthers."

"Don't be a fool, Jennas," Kali said, exasperated. "Our first duty is to determine the cause of the space/time rip and repair it."

"Who's in command of this team? You or I?" Quarag demanded. "I will discipline anyone if it becomes necessary."

"You know my authority," the Klingon woman said cryptically.

"Your position in Kor's bed does not give you power over me, woman!" Jennas said. "Keep to your place."

Kirk exchanged a quick glance with Spock. He then stepped forward and lightly touched Kali on the arm. She shrank back, and he wondered if she, like Mara, had been told stories of Earth torture and death camps.

"Don't be afraid. We won't hurt you."

"My husband said you were different from most humans."

"And I could say the same about him."

"We will set up our camp now," Quarag announced in an overly loud voice as he tried to reassert control, and separate Kirk and Kali.

"Do you need any help?" Kirk asked sweetly, enjoying baiting the Klingon.

"That will not be necessary," Quarag gritted. "Come, Kali." He turned on his heel, and marched off down the beach with his landing team trailing after him. The Taygetian cubs seemed to sense the Klingons' anger, for they skittered nervously out of the way.

"An interesting female," Spock said, as Kirk gazed thoughtfully after the retreating Klingons.

"Yes, very. I just wonder what she *is* doing here."

"You suspect something?"

"I'm not sure. Call it a hunch, but I have a feeling that something's not right among the Klingons."

"Isn't it likely to be a bonus for our side?" Scotty asked, joining the other two officers.

Kirk grimaced, and clucked dubiously. "Hard to say. Sometimes you can get hurt worse on the periphery of a dog fight than if you're right in the middle of it. Well, we'll just have to keep our eyes open."

"Have you got a few minutes or are you still being Madam Star Fleet?"

Uhura looked up from the stationary tricorder she was calibrating, frowned and brushed back a trailing wisp of hair. "I thought I asked you to stop calling me that."

Maslin shrugged. "You looked so officious it just sort of fit."

"I am *busy,* not officious. These tricorders need to be placed at the perimeter of the camp. They'll make a constant record of conditions to a radius of one hundred miles, and the information will be transmitted back to the computers aboard the *Enterprise.*"

"My, my, I'm impressed," he drawled, dropping down to sit on the sand. He scooped up a handful of the micalike grains, and stared moodily at it as it trickled from between his fingers. Uhura sighed, and knelt next to him. She took his hand, dusted the clinging grains of sand from his palm and held it between her slender, dark hands.

"Is there some reason why you're being so cranky or is it just another example of artistic temperament?" Her tone was gentle, softening the harshness of her words.

He flushed, bringing some color to his pale cheeks. "Sorry. You must get tired of me acting like a five-year-old."

"Good heavens," she said, a smile crinkling the corners of her eyes. "You're not cranky, you're sick. A real apology from you?"

He smiled crookedly. "Oh, I occasionally remember how to behave. Just don't get used to it—it won't last."

"I'm sure of that. Now, what is the matter?"

The frown descended again, and he rested his elbows on his knees, and stared out at the ocean. "I'm bored and I feel useless. Everyone is busy setting up equipment, taking readings, standing guard, while I'm just a piece of baggage."

"It's a little late for you to start analyzing the Taygetian song this evening. Besides, once we have the camp set up and running we'll be moving aside for you. If anyone's baggage it's us. What we've done, we've done to help you, but you're the one who has to solve the mystery of the song. We're just here to assist."

He touched her cheek. "You have the most amazing ability to make a person feel important."

She turned her head, and pressed a quick kiss onto the palm of his hand. "Thank you." She rose and brushed the sand from the knees of her pants. "Give me five more minutes, and I'll have this finished."

"And then?"

"And then maybe we can go for a walk."

"Great. I want to get the feel of this place."

"So do I, but go and check with Spock first."

"Do we need permission to go for a walk?"

"There are a party of Klingons camped a half mile down the beach, and this is an uncharted planet."

"Christ! Okay, okay," he said, holding up his hands. "I'll try to act subordinate."

She watched him walk back toward the cluster of metallic shelters, and felt again that rush of joy and excitement that his presence always brought to her. Something was happening here, for it was now obvious that the affection and attraction didn't flow in just one direction. She knew that soon she would have to face the situation and evaluate it, but not just yet. There were too many decisions and potential changes in that evaluation, and she was reluctant to deal with them.

She hoped he would get Spock's permission to do a bit of exploring for she, too, was drawn by the silver-lit beauty of the world, and the pervasive and compelling song that wove its complex harmonies across the silent ocean.

Near the water's edge the covey?—herd?—school? She pondered the proper designation for a group of Taygetian cubs, and finally decided that school was the closest description. The cubs were scooping out hollows in the damp sand, and settling down for the night. This task was accomplished with a great deal of humming, tweeting and horseplay. The pups were flinging sand with their front flippers, and rolling and tumbling about in furry balls as they wrestled.

Guy came trotting back to her, stumbling a bit in the deep sand. "Spock says we can go so long as we're back in thirty minutes," he panted. His breath puffed whitely out in front of him, and Uhura realized that the temperature was dropping with the sun.

"That's not much time."

"True, but I guess he's concerned about having us out at night. The sun's almost down." He pointed out to sea.

She turned, and shaded her eyes against the slanting rays of the Taygetian sun. Overhead the clouds were turning a rich orange and peach, and the ocean shimmered red gold in the dying light. It was the first time since their arrival that there had been any color evident other than the varying shades of silver, white and clear crystal, and Uhura found it a welcome change.

Realizing that she was wasting time, she slung her tricorder over her shoulder. Guy took her arm, and they headed off in a generally northerly direction. They skirted the cubs, not wishing to alarm the youngsters, but the Taygetians now seemed unconcerned with their presence. They watched the humans curiously out of their pale blue eyes, but showed no fear. As Uhura and Maslin moved past several of them chirped and trilled while bobbing their heads up and down.

"They certainly seem intelligent," Maslin remarked. "I mean, that sounded an awful lot like a greeting to me."

"To me too."

"How could the Federation have classified them as animals? When I think about some hunter coming along and giving them a jolt of electricity to the head it makes me want to do the same to some bureaucrat, and see how they like it."

Uhura looked distressed. "How did you find out about this?"

"Ex-girl friend wanted a crystal tear. When I'm contemplating spending that much money I do a little research."

"Did you buy it for her?"

"No, I found the way they were obtained to be disgusting and barbaric."

They rounded an outcropping and discovered what appeared to be a trail heading up into the cliffs. The sand had been smoothed and packed as if by countless large bodies. They exchanged glances.

"Think it's a path up to the adults?" Maslin asked.

"Quite likely. We've still got a few minutes. Let's go a little way and see what we find."

The path wound between crystalline formations and fallen boulders, climbing higher into the tumbled outcroppings at the base of the cliffs. Uhura frowned and took a slow turn, studying the trail and the surrounding area.

"What's wrong?"

"I'm not sure. This trail is well worn, as if it's been here for a long time, but it doesn't seem well used, if you take my meaning."

Maslin copied her slow look, then shrugged. "I don't see anything."

"I'm not sure there is *anything* to see, but I have the impression that this trail is not the scene of constant comings and goings between the adults and the cubs."

"So?"

"It just seems odd that the adults of a race would show so little interest in their young. That doesn't seem to be a very prosurvival trait."

Guy sucked thoughtfully at the insides of his cheeks, then shook his head. "Maybe the adults think there's something they have to do that's more important than watching the kids."

"Spock suggested something like that earlier, but it still seems odd."

They resumed their climb. Suddenly Uhura froze. Maslin, who had been looking back toward the ocean, bumped heavily into her. He opened his mouth, then bit back the words at her sharp, chopping gesture. He then discerned the reason for her abrupt halt. Beyond a curve in the trail someone was holding a low-voiced conversation in a language he didn't understand. Uhura lifted her tricorder, and carefully switched it on. The murmurings continued for several more minutes. Then there was a sharp snick, as if some device had been shut off. Uhura switched off her tricorder and let it fall to her hip. She then darted around the crystal outcropping.

This time Maslin was ready for her because he had seen her tense as she prepared to launch herself around the rock, and he was right behind her as they exploded around the curve in the trail.

The Klingon woman, Kali, knelt in the sand, caught in the act of replacing a communicator on her belt. Terror flared in her golden eyes at the sight of the humans, and her hand jerked for the disruptor at her hip.

"Christ, don't . . ." Guy began, but Uhura was quicker. She crossed the intervening distance in one bound, and her booted foot lashed out, kicking the disruptor from the Klingon's hand. Kali grimaced and gripping her wrist pillowed it in her lap.

"I'm sorry," Uhura said, dropping down next to her. The woman flinched away, then relaxed into hostile alertness when she realized that Uhura wasn't going to hurt her again. "Is it broken?"

"No, only bruised."

Uhura glanced at the disruptor lying in the sand. "We do tend to react without thinking, don't we?" she asked a little ruefully.

Some of the tension leached out of Kali, and she nodded slowly. "Perhaps that is why we lose so many ships and men."

"It's one possibility," Uhura replied cautiously.

"What are you doing out here?" Maslin asked, perching on a nearby boulder.

"Getting a feel for the world."

"But—" Uhura shot him a warning look, and he subsided. "What?"

"Well . . . ah . . . it might be dangerous," he improvised.

Kali laughed, a light, musical sound that blended well with the omnipresent song. "I am not your typical Earthwoman— weak and helpless. I can take care of myself."

"I would say Lieutenant Uhura has done a pretty good job of taking care of herself too," Guy said challengingly.

Maslin and Kali locked eyes, and Uhura stepped in. "Arguing racial superiority has always been a useless exercise, both on my world and in space. The captain is right, we have to work together if we're going to solve this mystery. What do you make of the Taygetians now that you've had a chance to look around?"

"A number of our officers would like to classify them as animals." She glanced at the two humans. "It makes it much easier to colonize an uninhabited planet."

"But what do you think?"

"I think they are unquestionably intelligent, but I still do not understand why you think there is a correlation between the phenomenon and the Taygetians."

"Actually, I don't either," Maslin said, sliding down onto the sand so he could sit between the two women. "That's

Spock's theory, and we can't prove it or disprove it until we can understand what they're singing about."

"If it's a language why not use your universal translator?"

"Spock tried that this afternoon," Uhura said.

"But all he got was gibberish," Guy added excitedly. "When I first listened to a tape of the Taygetian song I could tell that large pieces of it were missing. Apparently the translator picked up on that also, so it couldn't make sense out of what it was recording."

"How could you tell the song wasn't complete?" Kali asked, shifting until she could relax with her back against some rocks.

"Music is audible mathematics. Just as there is a logical progression in math so there is in music." He shrugged. "I have this quirk that enables me to translate music into numbers almost instantly. When I heard the tape it was obvious that it didn't track."

"And now?"

"It's even more apparent now."

"I'm not certain I understand, but it would be interesting to watch you work."

"Then come on down and watch. Tomorrow I'll begin programming the synthesizer to the Taygetian song. With its help I'll be able to build a picture of their musical theory."

"And that will enable you to understand their language?"

"It will certainly help."

She sat in thoughtful silence for several moments, then looked up. "Perhaps I will come to your camp."

"Do," Uhura said, picking up the disruptor, and presenting it butt first. Kali stared in confusion, first at the weapon, then at Uhura. "Go ahead, take it. I think we can agree that neither of us is a killer or a monster."

Kali hurriedly holstered the weapon. "It will be dark soon. I must get back to camp."

"And so must we," Uhura said, rising and dusting off the

seat of her pants. "Spock will kill us if we don't get back before the sun sets."

"Wouldn't that be an illogical reaction?" Maslin asked.

"He would find a logical reason to justify it."

"That must be convenient. Sort of like having a selective conscience or memory." He held out his hand to Uhura, and she helped him to his feet.

"Come to our camp, Kali. We'd like to have you."

"I will try. You are a professional musician?" she asked Guy. He nodded. "Well, perhaps you will play for me. I like music." She turned and started down the trail with Maslin staring incredulously after her. Uhura chuckled.

"Play for her? Like I'm some sort of nightclub musician who'll play for anyone at anytime. Doesn't she have any idea who I am?"

"No. Based on what we know about Klingon society, I'm quite certain that being a musician is not one of the more respected functions. Besides, you played for us."

"I played *with* those of you who were going to be in the landing party, and coached you," he corrected as he took her hand, and they started back toward camp. "I'm used to being paid for what I do, and very well. A lieutenant's pay in Star Fleet doesn't cut it." His jaw set, and his nostrils flared a bit with anger.

"I thought you were beginning to accept your position on this mission, even to enjoy it."

"I'm intrigued by musical puzzles, but I still don't like the way your captain impressed me into service, and I intend to go to Star Fleet when this is over. As for enjoying it . . ." He stopped, and placed his hands on her shoulders. They were at the base of the cliffs now, and the sun was a blazing orange disc that seemed to rest upon the face of the waters. "I enjoy you."

His mouth sought her, and she didn't avoid the embrace. As they stood locked in each other's arms the sun seemed to plunge into the water, and the sky turned a dark blue. The stars gleamed like white gems through ragged openings in the clouds, and below them at the water's edge the cubs pushed up on their front flippers, faced the cliffs and began a soft and haunting song that cut across the music of their elders.

Their heads jerked up, and the two humans stood mesmerized by the melancholy night music. Once more the elder Taygetians paid no heed. They just continued their song in sublime disregard of their young, who sang so mournfully below them. Maslin stood with his hands clenched at his sides, and his eyes glittered greenly with unshed tears. Uhura, too, sensed the longing and deep sadness inherent in the song, and she stepped closer to Guy. His arms went around her.

"Sad, so sad. If only I knew what they were saying."

"You will soon. I only hope we can help them."

The last vestiges of light vanished, and the song ended. The cubs settled back into their nests, and prepared to sleep. Down the beach they could see the lights of their own camp, and beyond that the Klingon camp like a watchful eye on the hill overlooking the humans.

The Taygetian song went endlessly on, and Guy and Uhura began to hurry for the security and warmth of the camp. The immensity of this new world, and the mystery of the song, oppressed and frightened them. Fred Ragsdale's round face seemed a welcome sight as they came through the perimeter of the camp.

Late that night Maslin lay quietly in his tent listening to the song. Uhura's thigh was warm against his, and her soft breaths fluttered the hair on his arm as they lay wrapped in the sleeping bag. He shifted her to a more comfortable position, easing the cramp in his arm. She murmured something, then dropped back to sleep. He brushed his lips across her hair and allowed his head to fall back against the pillow.

The song lulled and beckoned him, yet he feared this place

with an unreasoning dread. The chorus softened, and shifted in key, reminding him of "Die Winterreise." His arms tightened about Uhura, and softly, almost below his breath, he began the song.

> As a stranger I came here,
> a stranger I depart again. . . .
> For my journey I cannot
> choose the time,
> I must find the way for myself
> in this darkness.
> A moon-cast shadow goes
> along as my companion.
>
> I will not disturb you in your dreams—
> it would spoil your rest.
> You shall not hear my footstep—
> softly, softly, close the door!
> As I pass I write
> on your gate: "Good night,"
> so that you may see,
> I thought of you.

Chapter Six

"Has Lieutenant Mendez completed translating the message that Lieutenant Uhura intercepted, Captain?" Spock had taken a folding camp stool and placed it at the mouth of their cove. From this vantage point he could watch both the Klingons in their hillside camp, and the cubs who were gamboling about and plunging in and out of the frigid ocean. Now from a position of relative privacy he had contacted Kirk.

"She certainly has, Mr. Spock," Kirk's voice came back over the communicator. "And it confirms my suspicions that Kor has his hands full."

"How so, Captain?" Hearing the sounds of an altercation, Spock shifted slightly on his camp stool, and glanced back over his shoulder toward the small group clustered about Maslin's CompuSynthesizer. Maslin and Brentano were squared off and shouting into each other's faces. Spock almost interrupted communication so he could break up the fight when he saw Uhura heading out of her tent. He relaxed back onto his stool, knowing that she would handle the situation. He found human emotions confusing at the best of times, and he couldn't fathom the instantaneous dislike that had sprung up between Maslin and the chunky security guard.

"Spock, are you there?"

"Yes, Captain. Something took my attention. You were saying?"

"It seems that the lady is not reporting to her immediate superior on the planet. Rather she's using a tight-beam, scrambled transmission to contact her husband."

"But why communicate secretly with Commander Kor?"

"My question exactly. There's nothing to give us any indication of the problem in the conversation we intercepted, but I would say the very fact the conversation took place supports my theory that Kor is not in full control of his ship."

"You suspect a mutiny?"

"It's not unknown among the Klingons."

"Let us hope, for our sakes then, that Lieutenant Commander Kali keeps her husband well informed, and that he is not replaced by some less conciliatory commander."

"Believe me, I'll be watching for anything out of the ordinary. I haven't forgotten that we are outnumbered, and that the Klingons are vicious fighters. How are things on your end?"

"Everything is progressing on schedule. Mr. Maslin is set up, and he will begin programming the synthesizer today."

"How long is this likely to take, Spock?"

"Uncertain, sir. The fact that the universal translator was unable to fathom the song indicates that there is more at work here than mere language."

"You're not comforting me, Mr. Spock."

"I wasn't aware that I was supposed to, Captain. I assumed you wanted accurate facts, not meaningless reassurances."

"A joke, Mr. Spock."

There was a pause. "I see. Will there be anything more, Captain?"

"Not for the moment. I'll probably be down in the next day or two, but right now I need to get down to engineering. Riley's been reporting some odd fluctuations in the dilithium crystals."

"Do you wish me to assist Mr. Riley? It would be most unfortunate if we had occasion to need power that the crystals were unable to supply."

"I would say that's an understatement, but no, I see no reason for you to return to the ship. If it looks like more than a minor problem I'll recall Scotty."

"Very good, Captain. Spock out."

Spock flipped shut his communicator, and replaced it on the back of his belt. There was a flurry of activity at the Klingon camp, but it didn't seem to be directed toward anything coherent. The Vulcan shook his head, feeling strong disapprobation for the unscientific methods employed by the Klingons. He had little hope that their reluctant partners would contribute anything meaningful to the research, and he suspected that they might become hostile and obstructive if they thought the humans were about to make a major discovery. He decided to warn the security guards to maintain their vigilance, and not to be lulled by the peace and serenity of this world. Rising, he moved off to talk with the three men.

Uhura fitted the receiver onto the large stationary tricorder that would keep a constant record of seismic and climatic conditions, and reached for the sonic connector. Her hand groped futilely across the packing box, and she realized the tool must have rolled into the sand while she worked. Muttering a bit beneath her breath she began to paw through the sand while still trying to keep a grip on the receiver.

There was a sudden and insistent pressure against her left thigh. Startled, she jerked around to look over her shoulder.

The receiver tumbled to the ground, and she found herself eye to eye with one of the Taygetian youngsters. The connector was delicately gripped in its mouth. The picture presented was a fairly ludicrous one: the small, screwdriverlike tool protruding from the cub's smiling mouth, the proud and eager expression in its blue eyes. Uhura chuckled, and sank back on her heels in the sand.

"Why, thank you," she said cordially, removing the connector from the creature's mouth. "Are you trying to help?"

The Taygetian hummed and tweeted, its little, round-skulled head bobbing with enthusiasm.

"You probably have no more idea of what I'm saying than I have about your remarks. I hope we can change that soon."

The cub chirped, then nosed the tricorder.

"Curious about this thing, are you? Well, this is a tricorder," Uhura explained as she recovered the receiver, and attached it to the body of the device. "It's a much larger one than we usually use, but it also has a much greater range. It's going to constantly monitor the environmental conditions of your world so we can get a better idea of how you developed. Now, what do you think of that?"

The cub seemed uninterested in the evolutionary implications of its own development, but very interested in the phaser which rested on Uhura's hip. The creature reached out with its mobile mouth and tried to slip the weapon from her belt.

"Hey, none of that now. You could get hurt playing with this." She shook the phaser under the cub's nose admonishingly.

The Taygetian responded with a long burst of agitated song, and began flopping happily around the woman. Uhura was forcibly reminded of her little sisters, and how they had often tried to entice her into a game of tag on the grass in front of their parents' home.

Laughing, she tapped the Taygetian on the head. Its fur was exceptionally soft and silky beneath her fingers. Then, bounding up, she began to back hastily away from the creature. The Taygetian seemed to grasp the rules of the game almost immediately for it followed after Uhura, and managed to whirl about and lay part of its back flippers across her boot with a resounding thwack. It then raced away with Uhura pursuing. They continued the game for several more minutes, then the Taygetian plunged into the ocean, and lay floating on its back while gazing impudently at Uhura, who stood balked on the shore.

"If I weren't in uniform, and if that water weren't arctic in temperature, I'd come in after you," she called, shaking her fist at the singer who reposed among the whitecaps. She shook her head, gave a laugh and started back toward camp. It was decidedly warmer than when they had arrived, and Uhura opened her parka, allowing the breeze to cool her. Suddenly her friend was back, flopping along at her side with the water sheeting from its silver white pelt.

Hours later the singer was still with her, pressed up against her leg as she tuned Spock's lyrette.

"I'm going to get jealous if your little buddy doesn't make room for me," Guy called. He was smiling, but there was a hint of grayness in his face, and he moved slowly and stiffly. She forced back her immediate impulse to ask if he were all right, knowing it would only aggravate him.

"You don't have to worry, he's just a baby."

"*He,* is it? Earlier *he* was an *it.*"

She stroked along the Taygetian's spine, causing him to shiver with pleasure. "He gives off a very definite male feeling."

"How so?" Maslin asked, dropping to the ground on the other side of her stool.

"Because he's spoiled and demanding, of course," she teased, ruffling his black hair.

"Ah lass, now how can you be so hard on the entire sex just because of this one bad example?" Scotty called, pointing at Maslin as he entered the circle formed by their shelters. He grinned at Maslin, who glared at him in mock anger. "What ye need is a little time with a fine and gentle man who'll treat you with respect."

"Why, Mr. Scott," Uhura crooned. "I never knew you were interested."

"And I never knew if you'd spare me a glance."

"She won't," Guy interjected. "She prefers a man who can speak Basic without hoking it up with an outdated ethnic accent."

"Hoo hoo," Uhura murmured, glancing from one man to the other. "Things are getting rough now."

Maslin grinned up at Scott, whose twinkling eyes belied the frown that creased his forehead. "All right, you Ssasenach, I'll concede this round to you, but I warn you, I won't forget."

"I'm sure of that. You people have the most amazing capacity for nursing a grudge. You've been stealing that damn coronation stone for the past six hundred years."

Scotty gave a modest little cough, and clasped his hands behind his back. "Aye, and the last time was a mere twenty-eight years ago."

"And you were in on it too," Uhura said with a laugh. "Scotty, I'm ashamed of you."

"It was for the honor of Scotland, lass."

"I wasn't aware that the Scots had any," Maslin said *sotto voce*.

"I heard that."

"Now don't get started again," Uhura said at the same moment.

The rest of the landing party began trickling into camp. They were treated to the same spectacular sunset that had painted the sky and struck prismatic colors from the cliffs the day before. Chou and Donovan prepared the evening meal while the remainder of the party sat chatting around a campfire. Spock sat somewhat removed from the humans, dictating into a recorder. The fire was really unnecessary. The party was well supplied with thermal lanterns and a food processor, but it added to the sense of warmth and closeness to have the fire flickering in the center of the camp. Spock had raised an eyebrow at the illogic of this form of heat generation, but he had not demurred when several of the landing party had taken an hour from their duties to gather driftwood. He had learned, after repeated and sometimes not very successful attempts, not to try and impose his rigid notions of duty and logic on the humans.

After dinner the group sat in a drowsy circle staring somnolently at the leaping flames. Maslin lay with his head pillowed in Uhura's lap, and her slender fingers ruffled through his hair, straightening and smoothing the dark strands. The young Singer, with a fine show of fickleness, had transferred his affections to Guy, and now lay draped across the composer's legs.

Guy opened one eye and, reaching up, captured Uhura's hand and brought it gently to his lips. She smiled down at him and, bending forward, pressed a quick kiss onto his forehead. Aboard ship such an open display of emotion would have been unthinkable, but here on the surface of this silver-lit world Uhura felt less inhibited. The other members of the landing party had tacitly accepted the deepening relationship between her and the composer, and she felt less shy about displaying the affection she felt for this small, intense man.

Spock, who had reclaimed his lyrette from Uhura, struck a soft chord that hung vibrating in the air. His long fingers played over the strings, and Uhura lifted her head, recognizing the introduction to "Beyond Antares," the song she had written in a moment of loneliness.

Her voice rose, warm and rich in the darkness, and the other people about the fire stirred and stretched, listening appreciatively.

Spock, with the sensitivity of a natural telepath, became increasingly certain that they were under observation. His fingers continued to move smoothly and swiftly across the strings, but he raised his head, and peered intently out into the darkness. His Vulcan sight enabled him to discern the shadowy figure hovering hesitantly near an outthrust spur of cliff.

Keeping his voice low he said, "Mr. Ragsdale, there is an intruder about thirty yards to our right near the base of the cliff. Maintain a casual attitude, but please apprehend the individual."

"Yes, sir." The heavyset security guard rose, stretched and headed toward one of the shelters, yawning as he went.

Uhura had her back to the intruder so she couldn't turn and look. She felt as if a target had been drawn in the middle of her back, and her shoulders tensed as she sat waiting for the burn of a disruptor. She wondered why the Klingons would send only one person or if there were more lurking in the rocks. As Ragsdale vanished into the darkness she suddenly realized who had to be standing and watching the camp.

"Mr. Spock," she said quietly. "I think it may be the young Klingon woman. When Guy and I discovered her yesterday we invited her to come to our camp. If she becomes frightened it could upset our truce with the Klingons."

Spock glanced in the direction where Ragsdale had disappeared. "I rather fear that it is too late to recall Mr. Ragsdale. We shall have to wait upon developments," he concluded with a wry twist to his mouth.

"I have a better idea," Guy said, pushing himself to a sitting position. "Why don't we just ask her to join us before your gorilla has a chance to jump on her?"

Uhura cocked an eyebrow at Spock. "It is logical."

Spock looked faintly miffed, perhaps that Maslin had found the simpler solution, but he nodded. "Very well, call to her, Lieutenant. She is at least acquainted with you."

Uhura rose, and looked in the direction of Spock's gaze. She could see nothing in the darkness, but if the Vulcan said there was a person standing in the shadows of the cliff it was certain there was someone there."

"Kali?" she called. "Why don't you come and join us?"

For several moments there was no response, then Uhura became aware of the Klingon as she seemed to coalesce like a figure conjured from wizard's smoke.

Kali moved cautiously into the fire's light. She knew she was probably exceeding Kor's instructions, but she had to confess that she was curious about the humans.

They were all staring at her now, their faces white and blank in the darkness. All but Uhura, whose skin was even darker than a Klingon's. They seemed strange and alien in the cold darkness of this new world, and all the stories she had heard of human cruelty and treachery came back to haunt her. Her fingers twitched spasmodically near the butt of her disruptor. If any of the humans had moved she would have used it, but they sat quietly at their ease as she approached. She resented their relaxation, for it pointed up her own tension.

But why shouldn't they be relaxed, she thought resentfully. *I am on their territory, and I am one against many.*

As she stepped fully into the firelight her eyes flicked quickly about the circle of humans. Everyone except their captain, and a security guard, were present. She had assumed Kirk would return to his ship. She wondered at the guard's absence.

A tall, slim man with dark hair and gentle blue eyes leaned forward, and lifted a pot from the edge of the fire. "Would you like a cup of coffee?" He wore the badge of security. His companion, a heavyset blond, frowned at his friend's cordiality.

So, Kali thought, *perhaps they are not all so certain about working with the hateful Klingons.*

"That is a human beverage?"

"Yes," the Vulcan replied. "The humans find it pleasant, but it contains large amounts of caffeine which I find objectionable. We Vulcans have no need of such artificial stimulants."

"So that's why they're such a lot of cold fish," Scotty said, as he delved about in his pack, and withdrew a small flask. "I myself like a bit of stimulant in my stimulant," he added as he deepened his burr, and splashed a liberal dollop of an amber liquid into his cup of coffee.

Puzzled, Kali glanced from one man to the other. Uhura rose, and touched her lightly on the elbow, indicating a vacant stool.

"I don't blame you for being confused. You're listening to another installment of a long and ongoing battle about human versus Vulcan customs. It's usually our ship's doctor who carries the standard for humanity, but in his absence Mr. Scott is standing in. Please, won't you sit down?"

Kali settled gingerly onto the stool. The dark-haired guard handed her a cup of coffee. She sniffed at it suspiciously, took a sip, then nodded. "It's good."

"There, you see, Mr. Spock, another race with some taste and sense," Scotty chortled.

Ragsdale came looming up out of the darkness, shaking his head like a frustrated St. Bernard. "I searched all over those rocks, Mr. Spock," he called as he lumbered into the circle of light, "and I couldn't find a thing."

"The intruder has in fact been located," Spock said.

"And is in fact a guest," Maslin added quickly, and Kali relaxed back onto her stool. Apparently the humans were not contemplating imprisoning her. She took another sip of the coffee to cover her nervousness. All conversation had ceased, and the Earthers stared uneasily into the fire or off into the night sky. Their obvious nervousness helped banish hers, and she turned to Uhura.

"I heard you singing. It was very nice."

"Thank you. It's something I enjoy doing."

"Will you do it again?"

"Yes, if you would like."

"Let me get my violin, and we'll give the lady a real taste of human music," Guy said, and pelted off toward his tent. He was back in a moment, and he quickly tuned to Spock's lyrette. The two humans and the Vulcan conferred briefly, then began a simple but haunting song. It was obvious they were improvising, for no two verses were the same, but it all blended together in a harmonious whole.

Kali wrapped her hands around the mug, enjoying the way it warmed her chilled fingers, and began to relax. The intonations were very different from Klingon music, but she found it pleasant to listen to, and it made her think of that night months ago when she and Kor had gone to a wine garden on Klinzhai, and sung and danced until the three moons had set. Thinking of Kor made her once more aware of her loneliness, and she wondered how things were going aboard ship. Worries about Karsul, the phenomenon, her separation from her husband, began to chase each other through her head, and she lost track of what was happening around her.

"Kali?" someone asked questioningly, and her head snapped up.

"Guess that's a comment on our abilities," Maslin said wryly. "We put our listener to sleep."

"I wasn't sleeping," she said hurriedly. "Only thinking."

"You seem worried," the dark-haired guard who had given her the coffee said. "Is there anything we can do?" Kali eyed him suspiciously but he seemed sincere, and another of her cherished notions about humans went down in ruins.

"I do not mean to pry," Scott said. "But it had occurred to me that your presence here might cause trouble for you. You're not likely to walk into a hornet's nest when you go back to camp, are you?"

She smiled faintly, and adjusted the golden sash of her rank where it cut across the front of her heavy cape. "No, my position as Kor's wife gives me certain advantages."

"I've read that a Klingon woman can only enter the service by marriage." Yeoman Chou asked. "Is that true?"

"Yes, as far as it goes. A woman cannot enter the service

unless she has a male sponsor or protector. He may not necessarily be a husband." Her lips twisted in a wry little smile. "We do not hold the favored position in society that you Earthwomen have."

"We don't have a favored position, just an equal one."

"That, to me, would seem very favorable."

"How do you gain rank then?" Uhura asked.

"By working hard, doing a good job and by attaching yourself to a man whose star is ascending."

"And what happens if his star ever descends?" Donovan asked as he tossed another piece of driftwood onto the fire.

There was an explosion of sparks, and Kali stared bleakly into the blazing inferno. "You fall with him."

"Sounds like a hell of a way to run a fleet," Brentano snorted, and gave her a hostile look.

"I'm sure there are things in your service that could be improved."

"But you don't *know*, do you?" he sneered.

"Watch your mouth, Brentano," Lindenbaum snapped, starting to rise.

"You want to go a round, buddy boy? Well come on." Brentano gestured menacingly.

"That will do, Mr. Brentano!" Spock's voice lashed out, separating the two men, and sending them grumbling back to their places. "I would advise you to remember not only our directive, but the philosophy contained in the IDIC."

"After all, mister," Scotty purred quietly, "it's all that diversity that makes the universe an interesting place."

Kali glanced down the beach toward the lights of the Klingon camp. "I must return now. Thank you for your hospitality."

"Come any time you like," Uhura said.

"I wish I could say the same, but some things are not possible."

"If the Organians were accurate such things will, in due time, become possible," Spock replied.

Kali smiled, and held out her hand to the Vulcan. "Would it be treason if I said I hoped so?"

"I would say rather it would be good sense," Spock replied, lightly touching her hand.

All of the humans, except Brentano, wished her a good night, and Lindenbaum, the blue-eyed, gentle-faced security guard, offered to walk her back to the Klingon camp. She smiled up at him, thinking how young he seemed by comparison to Kor.

"That won't be necessary. It is only a short distance, and there is nothing to threaten me on this world." She paused, and surveyed the star-sprinkled sky and the silver ocean booming onto the sand in a deep counterpoint to the Taygetian song. "In fact," she continued, "I have never been in such a peaceful place before."

"I know. There's something about this world that sort of gets to you. Well, good night."

"Good night, Mr. Lindenbaum." She walked into the darkness, and felt a tug of regret as she left the beguiling warmth of not only the fire, but the people as well.

She felt a surge of anger with herself for succumbing to the blandishments of the humans, but she could not dismiss it as mere playacting. There was something very honest and sincere about the Earthers and she found it a welcome relief after the hostility and hypocrisy that riddled the ship.

She found herself beginning to worry once more, but she pushed it away. For the present there was nothing she could do about the dangers which beset Kor. She decided she could best serve them both by relaxing, enjoying the peace of this new world and preparing for the next battle.

Using the darkness as a cloak she crept up the slope of the hill and, scooping out some sand, she wiggled in beneath one wall of her tent. In this way she avoided the five men who sat talking and drinking about a portable heater in front of the circle of tents. She had no desire to explain her absence to Quarag, nor did she feel comfortable being the only woman in the landing party. She feared that the liquor might arouse both hostile and amorous emotions in her companions, and as a precaution she slipped her disruptor beneath her pillow.

Pulling off her boots she slid, shivering, into her sleeping bag, and then lay listening to the song which wove mysteriously through the night sky. It seemed to speak of peace, and rest and harmony, and for an instant she felt a flicker of resentment at the circumstances which forced her to spend her life constantly armed, and constantly on guard.

She wrapped her arms around her body, and at last fell asleep dreaming that she lay safe within Kor's arms, and that they both lay in some place far removed from the plots and politics of the Imperial fleet.

Chapter Seven

"Mr. Spock! Mr. Spock!" Donovan shouted as he and Chou came running into camp. Spock straightened from where he leaned over Maslin's shoulder at the synthesizer, and the other members of the landing party dropped whatever they were doing and came hurrying to hear the news.

"Trouble, Mr. Donovan?"

"No, sir, I don't think so, sir," the lieutenant panted. "But we just saw the most incredible thing."

"We were exploring a tidal inlet about four miles south of here," Chou said. "Suddenly fish, hundreds of them, started throwing themselves out of the water and onto the beach. It was happening for several miles because we walked down the beach watching."

"And then the cubs arrived," Donovan broke in. "They all gathered around this carpet of fish, and began this strange song. And . . . and then wham!" His arms circled excitedly in the air above his head. "The next thing we knew the fish were gone!"

Spock thoughtfully tapped a forefinger against his lips, and eyed the two young humans. "I trust you made a copy of this song."

"Only a part of it," Chou confessed. "We were so startled that we didn't get the tricorders on right away."

"Let me have it," Maslin ordered, holding out his hand. "I'll run it through the synthesizer. Maybe it'll help make some sense out of this gibberish," he added under his breath.

"Interesting. Is it possible that this was part of some sort of breeding frenzy on the part of the fish?"

"No way, Mr. Spock," Donovan said firmly. "I'm a biologist, and this resembled nothing I've ever seen. It was almost as if those fish were being yanked out of the water."

"Good work, Lieutenant, Yeoman. Dismissed." The members of the landing party drifted back to their various duties, and Spock crossed swiftly to his tent. Entering, he sealed the door flap behind him, and flipped out his communicator.

"Spock to *Enterprise*."

"*Enterprise* here," came T'zeela's raspy voice.

"Get me Dr. McCoy."

"Right away . . . oh, wait, sir. Lieutenant Mendez needs to speak with you."

"Mr. Spock, I've either got a problem with the scanners that defies analysis, or there's something going on on that planet that defies *logic*," the woman said without preamble.

"Explain."

"I was reviewing the scanner tapes taken during our first pass over the planet. I then checked the most recent tapes, and that's were the problems began. Whole sections no longer correlate. Where there was desert I now get a reading for forest, and so on. I've checked and rechecked the scanners—"

"The problem may not be in the scanner, Lieutenant," Spock said, cutting short her aggrieved recitation of the problems she had been enduring. "Two of our members observed a phenomenon which closely resembles what you are describing. Please locate the captain, and Dr. McCoy. I wish to speak with them."

"Yes, sir."

"What is it, Spock?" McCoy's voice came over the communicator. "If it's anything less than your discovery of the lost ship of the Agravean Emperor, I don't want to know. I'm a busy man."

"First, why you would believe in that fable, much less that it would be present on this world is—"

He broke off abruptly as a keening, agonized cry ripped through the air. It cut across the Taygetian song, marring the perfect harmony with its hideous, pain-filled note. Spock jerked open the tent flap, and rushed into the open.

People stood like statues, stunned and horrified with the sound. All except Maslin. He clutched at his head, and toppled from the synthesizer bench.

"What in God's name was *that?*" McCoy yelled.

"Trouble, Doctor. Please get down at once. Mr. Maslin seems to have collapsed." Spock shut the communicator and joined the knot of people who had gathered around the composer.

"I'm all right. I'm all right," Maslin said, pushing away the supporting hands. But he didn't look it. His skin was stretched tautly across the bones of his face, and he was white as a skull.

"What happened, Mr. Maslin?" Spock asked as he caught the smaller man under the arm, and helped him to his feet.

"I tell you I'm all right!" Maslin insisted again.

"I am not interested in the state of your health. I want to know what caused your collapse."

Maslin stood shivering in the center of curious onlookers. "I'm not sure," he said at last. "I was working on the synthesizer, trying to match resonances with the song. Then that. . . ." He paused, groping for words. "That terrible cry came, and I felt as if a part of me had been ripped away."

Spock stared at the musician, and considered what he had heard. What Maslin was describing sounded like a telepathic experience, but the talent was rare among humans.

"Mr. Maslin," Spock began, only to be interrupted by a melancholy, dirgelike descant. The cubs gazed up at the crystal cliffs and sang a song of such pain and despair that several humans turned away, fighting back tears.

"Fit up a reconnaissance team, Mr. Scott. Somehow one or more of the Taygetians has died. We will investigate."

"Aye, sir. It'll be a pleasure to find what ever it was."

"Probably those stinking Klingons," Brentano muttered.

"Conjecture will not supply us with facts. We will rendezvous back here in ten minutes."

There was a hum, and a sparkling of molecules, and McCoy appeared. He quickly surveyed the camp, ascertaining that everyone was safe, then moved to Maslin.

"What are you doing here?" the composer asked rudely.

"I was in the neighborhood so I thought I'd make a house call."

"Well it's not necessary. I'm fine," Maslin said shortly, then swayed, and clutched at Uhura's arm.

"Yeah, fine," McCoy repeated and, taking him by the other arm, he and Uhura propelled Maslin to his tent.

Ten minutes later Scotty, Spock, Ragsdale and Lindenbaum headed out of the camp, moving quickly along the base of the cliffs. Spock lifted his tricorder, took a reading, then frowned.

"What is it, Spock?" Scotty asked as, phaser drawn, he kept a forward watch.

"There is a group of five humans about two miles to our north."

"Humans?" Ragsdale echoed.

"But how did they get here?" Lindenbaum asked.

"Let's find them, and ask them," Scotty said with a smile, but it was not a pleasant expression.

The two groups spotted each other simultaneously. Painstakingly working their way down the rugged cliff face were five heavily loaded men. Backpacks and bedrolls thrust above their shoulders, and shockwands hung at their waists. One of the men on the cliff glanced down, and saw the landing party. He gave a Comanche whoop, and waved vigorously. The men quickened their descent, and soon joined the *Enterprise* party at the base of the cliffs.

"Are we glad to see you," a big, heavyset man called as he shouldered through his companions. His biceps looked like tree trunks, and his head seemed to sprout directly from his beefy shoulders. His small, pig eyes flicked evaluatingly over the men from the *Enterprise*.

"We've been waiting weeks for a pickup, but we never expected Star Fleet."

"You can keep waiting," Scotty growled, having taken an immediate dislike to the man. "We're not here for you. Whoever you are."

"Garyson, Max Garyson."

"Lieutenant Commander Scott of the starship *Enterprise*. But what are you doing here? We had no information of human presence on this world."

"Isn't that just like that turd Ridly. First he maroons us here, and then he doesn't even inform anyone."

Spock turned to Scotty. There was a slight frown of aggravation on his chiseled face. "Forgive me, Mr. Scott. I have been remiss in my duties. The captain and I knew of the presence of the hunters. Commander Li mentioned them during our meeting at Star Base 24, but when we did not find them in evidence I confess that it slipped my mind."

"It's no real problem, Mr. Spock, but meantime what the hell do we do with them?" Scotty asked, jerking a thumb in the direction of the hunters.

"Hey, what's going on here?" Garyson demanded, apparently becoming irritated at being discussed as though he weren't present. He thrust out his chin belligerently, and stared challengingly at the party from the *Enterprise*.

Spock turned coolly to face him. "Captain Ridly was returning to pick you up when, regretfully, both he and his ship were lost in the space/time warp that now exists in this system."

"Tough luck about Ridly," Garyson said with a dismissing shrug. "But at least you're here, and we can get home. God knows we're ready."

"Yeah, and it's gonna be party time when we get back," hooted one of Garyson's companions.

"Say, what brought you fellows out this way if you didn't know we were here?" a small dirty man with long stringy hair asked.

"We were investigating a death cry. We believe that one of the Taygetians has been killed."

"That's right, and we did it," Garyson said, jabbing at his barrel chest with a forefinger. "Great big male, but the take was worth it. Thirteen tears."

"*You* killed that creature?" Lindenbaum demanded, his normally gentle expression replaced by one of loathing.

"Sure, that's what we come here for."

"Mr. Garyson, have you been continuing your hunt?" Spock asked.

"Yeah, but about fifty miles from here. We'd picked over this group pretty well, so we went north to another large herd up there."

"That would explain why we were unaware of your presence until today." Spock paused, and considered how best to approach his next topic. "Mr. Garyson, you and your men are naturally welcome to remain at our camp, or aboard the *Enterprise* until our mission is complete, but I must tell you that all further hunting must cease."

There was a confused and hostile babble from the hunters. Garyson cut it off with a slash of his spadelike hand. "What the hell are you talking about?"

"The Taygetians are not animals as first believed. They are an intelligent life form, and this destruction must cease."

"You got proof of that, Vulcan? 'Cause I got a piece of paper here that says these critters are animals, and I've got a license to hunt them. Unless you can show me where the law has changed I've got my rights. And my rights included harvesting crystal tears." Garyson spat neatly to the right of Spock's boot.

Ragsdale gave a growl of fury, and lunged forward. Spock's arm caught him across the chest. It was like running into a steel bar, and the security chief quit moving. "I do not have the documentation you request for it is our research which has established the sentience of the Taygetians. But I can assure you that the law will be changed once we return to the Federation."

"You hear that boys?" Garyson, yelled, turning to face his companions. "He says our little gravy train is about to be derailed." He turned slowly back to face Spock. "Well, if that's the case I guess we're going to have to move fast, and get what we can while we can." His broad face twisted in an expression of disgust. "Before you government types interfere again with an honest man's right to make a living."

"You do not have the right to make a living at the expense of another creature's right to live."

"Until the law says they've got rights." Garyson's arm thrust up at the Singers. "I don't have to respect them."

"Then you refuse to stop your killing?"

"Read my lips." He leaned in close to the Vulcan, and Spock drew back, his nostrils narrowing fastidiously at the sour odor of the man. "I refuse."

"I will report your refusal to Captain Kirk."

"Go ahead, and by the way, I think we'll pass on your," he paused and grinned, "hospitality."

Spock turned on his heel, and headed back for camp. His spine was stiff with outrage, but he did not know what other choice he had. Garyson and his group were legally within their rights to continue hunting, and until a determination to the contrary could be obtained from the Federation there was little, short of violence, he could do to stop it.

McCoy snapped off his tricorder, and stared grimly at Maslin, who lay stretched out on his cot. "What the hell have you been doing? These readings are horrible. Your pulse is doing a cha cha, respiration and heart beat are up, white cell count—"

"Spare me a recitation of my physical failings, Doctor," Maslin said, swinging his feet to the ground. "I'm well aware of them."

"If that were the truth then you wouldn't be pushing it. I let you out of my sight for three days, and I find this." He shook the tricorder in the composer's face. "If these readings don't improve I'm going to yank you back to the *Enterprise,* and place you in sick bay."

"No, Doctor, please don't." The sophisticated mask slipped, and Maslin looked genuinely distressed. "I'll try to relax, but I can't go back now. I'm just beginning to get a feel for the Taygetian song."

McCoy sighed. "All right, but prove to me your good intentions by lying down now, and resting for a while."

"Okay." Maslin pulled off his boots, opened his sleeping bag and crawled in. McCoy started to prepare a hypo, then glanced back over at Maslin, and realized it wasn't necessary. The composer's eyelids had fluttered closed almost as soon as his head hit the pillow. He would be sleeping for hours. McCoy left the tent, and went in search of Uhura.

He found her at the edge of the sea with one of the Taygetian cubs draped across her lap and gazing adoringly up at her while she scratched at the base of its skull. He dropped down next to her on the sand, and stared out at the swelling ocean.

"How is he?"

"Not too good. It looks like he's entering a flare."

"I take it you mean the disease is flaring up."

"Yes."

"What can be done?"

"Rest will help. Just getting him to slow down will probably quiet the disease."

"He won't. Not voluntarily anyway."

"Then make him."

"Why cast me as the heavy? You make him."

"I don't have your influence with him."

She dropped her head, and concentrated on the way her fingers ruffled through the thick white pelt of the Taygetian. "I'll try." They sat in silence. "He shouldn't be here!" The words exploded from her, and she looked embarrassed at her outburst.

"I think he's glad to be here now."

"Oh yes, of course. He's got a musical puzzle to solve. A minor matter like his health won't make him let go of that." Her tone was bitter.

"I've never seen you like this before. Are you sure you can handle it?"

"Don't fish, Doctor. I prefer to keep my private life private."

"I'm not trying to pry, Uhura, really. I care, and if you ever need it, I'd like to help."

She held out her hand to McCoy. "I'm sorry. I suppose I'm not handling this very well."

His hand closed warmly over hers. "It's a difficult emotion. We all fumble along the best way we can when we're beset by the condition."

"I thought it was supposed to be wonderful to be in love," she said quietly.

"It is. It makes the pain of life endurable."

"Even when it causes pain?"

"That's what makes us human. Our ability to feel and experience."

She gazed into his kindly blue eyes, considering what he

had said, then leaned over and pressed a kiss onto his cheek. "Thank you, Doctor. You're good medicine."

"We aim to please."

Uhura slid the cub off her lap. It tweeted in protest, then gave a shake, and flopped off to rejoin its fellows.

"You sure have a way with those critters."

"Anybody could have a way with them. They're the friendliest creatures I've ever encountered."

"Sure would make it easy for the Klingons to move in. The little guys seem utterly defenseless," McCoy said as they walked back toward the tents.

"I'm afraid they are, and I don't even like to think about what the Klingons would do to this planet. I hope the Federation makes it a protectorate."

"They never take that action unless there's something particularly vital to preserve on the planet."

"How about the Taygetians? Aren't they particularly vital?" Uhura said as they stopped in front of Maslin's tent.

"To you and me maybe, but probably not to some bureaucrat back on Earth. They tend to think only in terms of tangibles."

"And music isn't much of a tangible," Uhura said as she unsealed the flap. "See you later, Doctor," she added as she ducked into the tent.

McCoy stared at the silver surface of the tent, and wondered what she was going to do in there. Probably just watch him sleep, he concluded. He frowned and turned away, wondering what the outcome of this attachment was going to be.

He saw Spock and his party on the outskirts of the camp, and he went to meet them. Spock's lips were pressed into a thin line, and he strode along at a great rate, leaving the smaller humans behind.

"You look grim," McCoy said, falling into step with him. "What's the trouble?"

"Hunters, Doctor. I must report to the captain at once."

He flipped out his communicator, and within moments had vanished. McCoy stood irresolutely in the middle of the camp, and wondered if he too ought to return to the *Enterprise*. Before he could make up his mind there was the hum of a transporter, and Riley sparkled into view.

"Grand Central Station," McCoy muttered under his breath.

"Hi, doc. Where's Mr. Scott?"

"He was here a minute ago. There's so much comin' and goin' in this place that a man can hardly—"

"Thanks," Riley said, ignoring the rest of McCoy's remarks, and chugging off in search of the chief engineer.

McCoy, who had a fine sense of knowing when things were happening, trailed after him. They found Scotty hunkered down in front of one of the smallest cubs, honking at the Singer with his bagpipes, and then recording the creature's responses.

"Come on, wee beasty, can't you make the same sound twice running?" Scotty said, staring at the readings on his tricorder. "How are we going to learn your language if you keep using only new words?"

"Mr. Scott."

"Aye, Riley, what is it?" he asked, straightening up with a grunt.

"I know you put me in charge, sir, and I hate to run to you the first time I have a problem, but this one is frankly beyond me. Even the captain hasn't been able to help."

"Well spit it out, lad. What seems to be the trouble?"

"It's the dilithium crystals, sir."

"Dilithium crystals," he repeated ominously.

"Yes, sir. They're decaying, sir."

"Decaying!" Scotty yelped. "What the hell have ye been doin' up there?"

"Nothing, sir. That's what's so frustrating. There's just been this slow but steady drain on the power. We've checked and rechecked every circuit, and it shouldn't be happening."

"Have you at least got a theory, boy?" Scotty demanded over his shoulder as he gathered up his equipment, and marched for his tent.

"Yes, sir. I think it has something to do with that phenomenon."

The engineer stopped, and stared at Riley. "Why couldn't you have come up with something *simpler,* lad?"

"Sorry, sir, but I call 'em like I see 'em."

"Donovan!" Scotty bawled.

The young biologist came charging out of his tent. "Sir!"

"See to it that my things get beamed back aboard the *Enterprise.*"

"Yes, sir."

"And tell . . . no, never mind. I'd best tell him myself." He crossed to Maslin's tent, and stepped inside.

Uhura rose quickly from the stool where she had been sitting. "Scotty, what is it?"

"Trouble, lass. I've got to get back aboard the *Enterprise.*"

"Klingons?"

"No, engineering problem. I just stopped in to tell Mr. Maslin."

"Don't wake him, I'll tell him later."

"Tell me what later?" Guy said, pushing up on one elbow, and regarding Scotty out of one bleary eye.

"I've got to go back to the *Enterprise.*"

"Isn't this a little sudden?"

"There's a problem with our power source. I've got to get it fixed."

"I had understood that solving the puzzle of the Taygetian song was first priority for this mission, Mr. Scott. It just becomes that much harder if I lose people."

"No, Mr. Maslin. Keeping the ship running is first priority."

"Is it as serious as all that?"

"If the dilithium crystals decay far we won't be able to fight or run if the Klingons decide to get ugly."

Maslin sat up fully in bed. "Then by all means go, Mr. Scott, and with my blessings."

"I thought you'd see it my way."

"Artistic temperament notwithstanding, I'm a man of extraordinarily good sense. You take care of our defense. We'll handle things on this end." Scotty turned and headed out of the tent. "I've got to get to work. With Scott leaving we've got to pick up the slack," he heard Maslin say.

"Dr. McCoy wanted you to rest. A few more hours isn't going to make that much difference," Uhura remonstrated with him. The falling tent flap cut off Maslin's reply.

Another anguished cry wailed down from the crystal cliffs, and Kali covered her ears with her hands. As the last echo died, and the cubs began their mournful dirge, Kali marched to her tent, and emerged moments later, strapping on her disruptor.

Quarag looked up from a set of readings he had taken. "What are you doing?" he demanded.

"Going to put a stop to this. If the Earthers are too cowardly, I am most certainly not!"

"They're just stupid animals. What do you care?"

"They are not animals, and they are not stupid, and I will not allow them to be slaughtered," she yelled over her shoulder as she headed out of camp.

"You come back here! I have not given you permission to leave the camp!"

"So report me."

"I will! I am in command here!"

"If you say so," Kali said wearily, and loped down the hill with her black hair streaming behind her.

"I can't *stand* it!" Quarag howled, and flung his readouts onto the ground, where they were immediately whirled away by the brisk wind that was blowing in off the ocean. "Report her, you better believe I'll report her," he muttered to Jennas. "There must be *someone* who can control her."

"If you think it's her husband, think again," Jennas snorted. "The old man's lost his touch. He's soft on Earthers, and scared of a fight."

"Maybe, maybe not," Quarag said cautiously, remembering all the times that Kor had resisted threats to his command. "Anyway, I'm tired of dealing with her. Let him come down, and try to make her behave."

"Soft, soft on women too," Jennas mumbled into his cup of quavas, the hot, spicy Klingon brew.

"Oh shut up! He's probably not too soft to use the agonizer on you if he hears you carrying on." Quarag pulled out his communicator and signaled the ship.

Kali strode briskly down the beach and wondered why men were such fools. For a solid day the men of her race and the humans had dithered and debated while the slaughter went on. She and Uhura had encountered one another on the beach, and in a brief and hurried conversation had agreed that murder was too good for the hunters—castration seemed a more attractive prospect. Unfortunately neither of them was in command so the talk went on, and the Taygetians died and the cubs sang their mournful dirge until she had decided she could no longer stand it.

She was passing by the opening into the humans' sheltered cove, and she momentarily considered stopping to see if Uhura wanted to join her. She hesitated, nervously twining a lock of hair between her fingers, then decided against it. She liked the woman, it was true, but she was still an Earther, and it was probably not wise to put too much reliance on her. Having an armed human at her back was not something she could view with equanimity no matter how pleasant she might seem to be. She tossed her hair over her shoulder, and continued her march to the hunters' camp.

The camp was deserted when she arrived. She glanced about, evaluating the positions of the tents, rocks, and noting possible approaches to the campsite. She then took up a position against a tall boulder which afforded her a clear view and angle of fire into the entire camp, and had the added benefit of protecting her back. She settled down to wait.

She smelled them almost as soon as she heard them. There was always a subtly different scent about the humans, but the people from the *Enterprise* seemed to make a habit of bathing and the odor was bearable. The men who came stomping and shouting into the camp obviously did not share this habit, and the rank and alien odor of them washed over her almost like a physical wave. Her nostrils pinched fastidiously together, and she hefted her disruptor, testing the balance. For a moment the hunters didn't notice her, and she had ample time to study them. What she saw made her begin to wish that she had not come alone to confront them, for they were large, brutish men with a look about them that she could only describe as threatening. She reminded herself that she was a Klingon and an officer, and she stepped into a defensive firing position.

One of the men, who had a lean, whippetlike body, dropped his pack. As he straightened he found himself staring down the barrel of Kali's disruptor. He placed his hands on his hips, and rocked back on his heels giving an appreciative whistle.

"Well, well," he drawled. "Look what's come to visit." His three companions whirled, and moved in to form a loose semicircle around the woman.

"She's a Klingon," one of them muttered out of the corner of his mouth.

"Why so she is," the biggest man said, leaning forward to peer at her. "I've never seen a Klingon woman before." He grinned. It was a feral, ugly expression. "Course, if they're all as pretty as you are, little lady, I can see why your men keep you hidden away."

These were humans as she had been taught to expect them, and she felt her mouth go dry. She forced herself to swallow, and took a firmer grip on the weapon. "I will not waste time with you," she called. "You will stop the hunting or I will kill you."

"Oooh, she's a dangerous as well as a pretty little filly," the big man cooed, looking about at his companions. They laughed, and Kali felt the blood rise in her cheeks. She fired, sending a spray of sand into the air directly in front of the leader. The laughter cut off as abruptly as if they'd been throttled.

"Now that I have your attention again," she said smoothly, "we will discuss my *proposal.*" Excitement and a sense of power coursed through her, and she began to enjoy the situation.

Suddenly a rock grazed past her head, cutting open her ear, and exploding in a burst of crystal fragments on the boulder behind her. She cried out and flinched away, and in that instant the men were on her. A heavy weight slammed into her and the disruptor was wrenched from her hand.

"Looks like the tables are turned, pretty lady," the big man crooned into her face. She twisted her head, trying to avoid the fetid breath. He laughed, and caught her by the back of the head in a viselike grip, forcing her to stare up into his face. "Now let's see what little Klingon girls are made of."

Her words of protest became a cry of pain as his hand impacted on her cheek with the sound of an axe striking deep into wood. A gray curtain seemed to draw across her eyes, and her knees went weak. She slumped in the man's arms and he laughed deep in his throat. His hand gripped the back of her neck.

Kali forced back the panic that was threatening to overwhelm her, and began to evaluate her situation. If she could just shift slightly to the left she would be in a position to slam her knee into his testicles. She pretended to relax in his arms, and was rewarded by a loosening of the hand that gripped the back of her neck.

Her knee was just coming up when there was the distinctive whine of disruptor fire, and her captor fell back with a bellow of agony. His sudden move ruined her aim, but she was gratified to hear him yelp yet again as her knee scraped across his groin. It wasn't a direct hit, but it probably didn't feel *good,* she thought with some satisfaction.

The disruptor sizzled the air twice more, then it was over. The *five* men, the four she had confronted and the fifth who had arrived late and flung the rock, lay face down on the sand. One cradled a hand against his shoulder, and her attacker was moaning and nursing a blackened hole in his upper thigh.

Kor stood nonchalantly over the hunters, his disruptor dangling slackly in one hand. Kali gave a cry of joy, and flung herself across the intervening space. He caught her with his free arm and held her close, but he never took his eyes off the humans, or allowed her to block his line of fire.

"Kor, oh Kor, I'm so glad! How did you find me? Oh, I'm sorry, I was so stupid."

He cocked an amused and indulgent eye at her, and kissed the top of her head. "My darling, if you must be a heroine can't you at least bring enough troops to make it successful?"

She looked embarrassed and hung her head, but after a moment she threw back her head and gave him a militant look. "I would have if you had provided me with a landing party made up of something other than dithering fools."

"Oh ho, and when did it become *your* landing party?"

"When that idiot Quarag stood by and let these animals," she gestured contemptuously at the cowering hunters, "kill the Singers."

"Do the humans know of this?"

"Of course, but they also do nothing."

"So you decided to act. Couldn't you have at least told me?" he asked plaintively.

"I didn't want to give you something else to worry about."

"My dear one, you are amazing." He brushed the back of his hand down her cheek, then looked back at the prisoners. "I'm going to spare you this time, but I warn you I won't be so lenient when next we meet. Don't any of you move a muscle for ten minutes." He fired a warning shot between one of the men's legs and, taking Kali's hand, they hurried out of the camp.

"Why didn't you kill them?" she asked as they jogged down the beach.

"Because they are humans, and Kirk probably wouldn't like it if I started killing Federation citizens."

"But they are killing the Taygetians!" Kali protested.

"I know that, and I will meet with Kirk and see what, if anything, should be done." They slowed to a walk, and he gave her a curious look. "Why does it matter so much? If the Empire claims this planet the Taygetians may be an inconvenient presence that will have to be removed anyway."

"No!" She stopped, and placed both hands against his chest. "You don't understand, Kor, you haven't been here with them, listened to them, worked with them. The Singers are beautiful, special. We must not harm them."

He looked down into her beautiful, distressed face, and took her hands in his. "I've never seen you feel this strongly about anything before. What is it about this world, these creatures?"

"I don't know. It is as if the beauty and harmony of the song has the power to wind itself into your consciousness." She groped for the words, then gave a defeated gesture. "I can't explain."

"Perhaps I ought to spend some time on the planet and see how these Singers affect me."

"Please do, Kor, then you will see why we have to protect them."

"All right. But first we must see Kirk and decide what to do about our aggressive friends back there. They aren't going to stop killing on our say so, and after our little altercation they may decide to add Klingons to the hunt."

Chapter Eight

"I brought you some lunch," Uhura said to Maslin's hunched back. He didn't respond. Instead his long, slender fingers continued to play across the synthesizer's double keyboard. She moved to his side and tried again. "Guy, I said—"

"I heard you the first time," he said, not looking at her. His eyes were locked on the long, narrow screen where two lines of indecipherable dots and dashes marched monotonously past.

"You have to eat. Otherwise you're going to end up in the sick bay, and be of no use to any of us."

"Never mind all that. I'm finally on to something."

"What?" she asked. She set aside the plate, both food and her concern over Maslin forgotten in the excitement that they might at last be on the verge of a breakthrough.

"Come on." He slid off the bench and, grabbing her hand, began pelting down the beach. "If I'm right," he panted as they slogged through the deep sand, "an entire group of

Singers up there," he gestured at a section of the cliff face, "will drop out of the song, and I want to be there when they do."

"Why?"

"Because it finally started making sense."

"I'm glad it does for someone," she said with some acerbity.

"I'm sorry, I'm being cryptic. Remember when Chou and Donovan reported the strange fish behavior?"

"Yes."

"Well, I went back and checked the recordings the synthesizer had made at that time. I keep a recorder on at all times because I keep hoping that the more passages the machine hears and compares the easier it will be to decipher the language. Anyway, at approximately the time that Donovan and Chou observed the fish the cubs began a very rigid and coherent song. It's totally unlike their usual random hoots and tweets. Moments later a group of voices in the adult song dropped out. Since then I've been watching for it, and it happens with clockwork regularity every twelve hours."

"So what do you think it means?"

"I've got a theory, but I'd like to see if I can find any evidence to support it before I go out on a limb." He paused and stared up the cliff face. "This ought to be just about the place. Feel like a climb?"

"I do, but how do you feel?" Uhura asked, studying his drawn face.

"I can make it. Just knowing I may finally be on to something is enough to totally rejuvenate me."

She questioned that statement, but prudently kept her doubts to herself. She didn't want to fight with Guy, and since she had begun to nag him about rest and food, fighting seemed to have become their major form of communication. She began searching the base of the cliff for a way up to the grottos, and found a place where the rock had slipped and shifted, forming a series of natural steps and handholds. It wasn't going to be an easy climb, but they wouldn't need special equipment.

She went first, carefully testing each foot- and handhold for stability. She was glad Guy was small and light for there were several points where she doubted that the rock would have held under a man of Spock's or Kirk's weight. After fifteen minutes of steady climbing she reached the first grotto. She gripped the lip of the ledge, and pulled herself up.

And found herself face-to-face with a Taygetian adult who lay placidly feeding in the midst of a mound of fish. The blue green scales still gleamed wetly, and sea water puddled about the bodies of the quivering fish. She had become so accustomed to being ignored by the adults that she was startled, and almost lost her grip on the ledge when the creature stopped chewing and lifted its head to regard her out of deep blue eyes.

"Uhura, could you go up or come down, but please don't just stay there. My arms are about to break."

She quickly boosted herself onto the ledge and, rolling over, reached back for Guy. He accepted her hand, and she could feel his arm shivering with strain as she helped him onto the ledge. His face was bone white except for two hectic spots of color that burned high on his thin cheeks, and a spasm of coughing seized him as he collapsed face down in the grotto. After a few moments the spasm passed, and his breathing eased. The Taygetian continued to watch them until Guy pushed up into a sitting position, then it went placidly back to its meal.

"Is this what you expected to find?" Uhura asked with a gesture to the fish.

"Yes."

She sat back on her heels, and wrapped her arms around her knees, thoughtfully watching the Taygetian. "Donovan's been going nuts trying to figure out how the adults maintained themselves when they never left their grottos."

"And he really isn't going to be happy when he hears about this."

"You must have some idea how this happens. After all, you made the connection between the cubs' song and the fish."

"I have ideas, but none of them makes any sense. If only the great song weren't so ragged. It's like trying to learn a language when only half the words and none of the grammar are available." He stared silently out at the ocean for several minutes, then nodded. "But this is going to help. At least now I have a direct action that flows out of a song. I'll just start cross checking to see if any of the phrases and passages in this song reoccur in others."

"Do you want to start back down?"

Maslin peered over the ledge and shivered. "We climbed *that?*" he said, pointing down the cliff.

"'Fraid so. It did look easier coming up, didn't it?"

"Do you suppose if we sit here long enough the action of wind and weather will lower this cliff by two or three hundred feet?"

Uhura chuckled and reached out for his hand. "We could always call the ship and have them beam us back to camp."

"Maybe that's how the Taygetians get the fish up here, they have transporters hidden beneath the crust of the planet."

"You've been reading too much fantasy. Our sensors would have picked up that kind of activity."

"Must you always be so literal," he complained, sliding over to her, and lying back with his head in her lap.

"It's in my job description," she said, softly running her fingers through his heavy hair.

"What would it take to give you a new job description?"

"I don't know. How much clout do you have with Star Fleet?"

"Not near enough, I'm sure." He paused, and picked up her free hand, twining her fingers through his. "So maybe we ought to find you a new position outside of Star Fleet."

An aching lump seemed to settle into the pit of her

stomach, and she cast wildly about for some way out of this situation. She wasn't ready for this conversation. She had no idea what she felt or really wanted, and she didn't want to be forced to make a choice. They had never spoken of love, and her commitment to Star Fleet was so strong that it would take a very powerful and driving need to pull her away from her chosen career.

She wanted a ship and a command of her own, and she thought she had a good chance of getting them—but it was going to cost. The price of a starship was ceaseless devotion to work and career. She had seen it with Captain Kirk. However much he might yearn there was only one lady in his life and her name was *Enterprise*.

But do I want to become a lesbian? she thought rebelliously. *Devoting my life to a mass of circuits and metal that by some ironic quirk of phraseology has been designated a she?*

Or did she want the comfort of home, husband and children? And was it possible she could have both? Or was that a foolish dream placed forever beyond the reach of a woman in Star Fleet?

She looked down into Guy's face and found him intently watching her. She touched his lips with the tips of her fingers, and he pressed a soft kiss against the sensitive skin. She realized she was probably reading too much into his statement. Guy was a man who could have—did have—any number of women on a dozen different worlds. He couldn't possibly be offering her anything more than a casual affair. She had been foolish to immediately begin thinking of long-term commitments and agonizing over career decisions.

She smiled, and leaned over to kiss him. He reached back to clasp his hands behind her neck and pull her into a far deeper embrace than she had planned. She closed her eyes, savoring the taste and touch of him. Finally he released her.

"Frankly, my darling, I wouldn't trust you to find me a new position," she teased.

"And why not?"

"You won't even take care of yourself. How can I be sure you'd do any better looking out for me?"

"I don't need to take care of myself. I have more than enough people nagging me at any given moment," he grumbled, his face thunderous. He sat up and scooped up a handful of loose crystal flakes, and allowed them to trickle through his fingers.

"And I'm going to start nagging just as soon as we get back to camp," she replied placidly. "Dr. McCoy wanted you to rest," she continued, pulling out her communicator. "I'm sure climbing cliffs was not what he had in mind."

"What are you doing?"

"Calling the ship so they can transport us back to camp."

"I am perfectly capable of walking back to camp," he said stiffly.

"I'm sure you are, but *I* don't want to go back down that cliff."

"Why didn't you have the ship transport us up here in the first place?" he asked suspiciously.

"Because we had no coordinates. Now they can pick us up on their scanners, and send us back to camp. Those coordinates they have."

"Then you're really not doing this just to baby me?"

She sighed and shut her communicator before it could signal the ship. She then rested her hands on his shoulders and looked seriously into his face. "Of course I am. You're not well, Guy, that's a fact." She hesitated. "I care for you, that's another fact. Anything I can do to protect and care for you I'm going to do." She dropped her hands, and turned away. "Now go ahead and jump down my throat."

"Ah, Madam Star Fleet." He sighed as he wrapped his arms around her body and rested his cheek against her back. "You constantly force me to rise above my own naturally unpleasant nature. Call the ship. And I promise I'll go to bed like the very best of boys when we get back to camp." He glanced over his shoulder at the Taygetian who was just

133

finishing its meal. "Are the females of your race as difficult to handle as ours are?" The creature eyed him serenely and, drawing in a great breath, resumed the song. "Clearly they are," he said to Uhura. "He is forced to take refuge in art."

She flipped open her communicator and gave him a disgusted look. "I'm sure if I compared notes with Kali, and ever managed to communicate with a Taygetian female, we would all agree that it's the males of *any* species who cause the problems."

Kirk, if he could have heard her, would have totally agreed. After Spock's report on the hunters Kirk had immediately signaled the Federation requesting that the Taygetians be reclassified as an intelligent life form. He then settled back to wait while the message made its way to Earth and a reply was returned.

Spock remained on the *Enterprise,* checking the scanners for malfunctions. He finally had to concur that Lieutenant Mendez was correct. The bizarre readings were the result of some phenomenon on Taygeta, and not mechanical failure. Perplexed, he joined Kirk in the rec room for a game of chess.

Kirk leaned back in his chair and watched Spock's slender fingers lift a piece, momentarily caress the figure, then swiftly place it in its new location. He realized, as he listened to Spock's report, that he had missed his first officer. It wasn't often that their duties separated them, and he had found the absence of that tall, quiet figure strangely disconcerting. He remembered Edith Keeler's description of their relationship when Spock had asked her where she thought he belonged. She had replied, *at his side, like you've always been there and always will be.*

Yes, Kirk thought. *That pretty comprehensively covers it.* He realized that Spock had concluded his report, and was quietly waiting for some response. He cleared his throat, and straightened somewhat in his chair.

"So we're no closer to breaking the Taygetians' language than we were when we started?"

"I must regretfully agree with your estimation of the situation. We have learned a great deal about the creatures physiologically, but we are no closer to understanding the reasons behind their strange social structure or the reason for this great song."

"Then maybe bringing Maslin was a useless gesture."

"No, I cannot agree. I still believe that the music is the key, and Maslin is the person best suited to discover its meaning." Spock momentarily frowned. "In fact, there was an odd occurrence when the first Taygetian died. Everyone was naturally shocked by the terrible death cry, but Maslin was physically and mentally shaken. Almost as if the music had pulled him into some sort of rapport with the Taygetians. His reaction was very similar to what I've seen when a telepath is violently pulled out of contact."

"Esper powers aren't common among my people."

"I am aware of this, but Maslin may be one of those rare cases. My primary reason for mentioning this occurrence is that it might indicate the presence of esper powers on the part of the Taygetians. If such is the case perhaps I should try the Vulcan mind meld."

"I know such melds are difficult for you, Spock, and I always hate for you to try it on an unknown race. You never know what's going to happen. Let's continue the more traditional forms of research until it becomes certain they're not going to work."

"As you wish, Captain."

The wall communicator whistled. "Captain Kirk, there's a message for you from Federation Central."

"I'll take it in my quarters. Coming, Mr. Spock?"

"I'm very sorry, Captain, but under article 5, section 301 of the Code a race cannot be reclassified without a full investigation by a xenological team. The *Enterprise* does not carry such a complement, and your request is therefore denied."

The fat-faced man on the screen nodded placidly and the screen went dark.

"And that's it? After ten hours of waiting that's all we get?" Kirk said incredulously. "I told them in my message that there had never been an adequate study made of the planet. Why then do we have to have a full investigation to rectify an earlier mistake? How can the man be so stupid?" he demanded, bringing his hand down with a slap on the top of the communicator.

"Then our hands are tied?"

"You know me better than that, Spock. Perhaps a little conversation with Mr. Garyson—"

"Captain," T'zeela's voice interrupted him. "A call for you from Commander Kor."

"Put it through, Lieutenant."

"Kirk, you have some extremely unpleasant members of your race squatting on that planet," Kor said without preamble.

"Yes, I know, Commander. Mr. Spock and I were just discussing what to do about them."

"Well, while you've been talking my wife went off to try and do something. Fortunately my men called me, and I was able to extract her from what could have been a very unpleasant situation. Kali is very upset by the killing of the Taygetians, and she feels it could be dangerous to all of us."

"Does she have some evidence to support this theory?"

Kor looked rueful. "I've tried to pin her down, but she just keeps saying it's a *feeling*."

"Where are you now?"

"On the planet. I thought it was time I had a firsthand look at these troublesome creatures."

"Mr. Spock and I are coming right down. Meet us at our camp, and let's see what, if anything, we've got."

"We'll be there."

Maslin was seated at the synthesizer, surrounded by every member of the landing party. There was an agitated hum of conversation, and periodically someone would give a shout of delight and point at something on the synthesizer's screen.

"I think we missed something, Spock," Kirk said as the transporter materialization ceased.

"Yes," Spock said shortly.

"What's all the fuss?" Kirk called as he jogged over to join the group.

"Mr. Maslin's done it!" Yeoman Chou replied, her china-doll face pink with excitement.

"Well, not by a long stretch," Maslin said, swinging around on the bench and holding up a hand to forestall the question he could see forming on Kirk's lips. "All I've done is start to see how this musical language fits together. I'm still not able to speak it or understand what's said to me."

"I'm not certain I understand," Spock said. "If you have ascertained the grammar surely meaning must follow?"

"Ordinarily I'd agree with you, but there are still these troublesome gaps in the song."

"I thought you'd adjusted the machine to take into the account the problem of the sonics?" Kirk asked. He noticed Kor and Kali hovering at the outskirts of the group, listening with interest.

"I did, and the problem isn't the sonics. These gaps are totally unnatural. It's as if I simply cut out sections from a symphony orchestra. You know there's a bassoon solo that's supposed to come in at this point, but instead you get nothing because there's no bassoon to play the passage."

"What are you saying?" Kor asked, pushing through the humans.

"That the problem is the hunters. It's like somebody went

through one of my orchestras with phaser fire, taking out a flute here, two violins, a trumpet. The result is a sound that seems pretty coherent until you start listening closely."

"Then I was right," Kali said, giving Kor a challenging look. "The hunters should have been stopped."

"Yes, you were right in theory but wrong in the execution. You do not go hunting for Cxentares cats with a slingshot." He smiled to lessen the sting of his reprimand, and brushed his thumb along the line of her jaw.

She was mollified, but only slightly. She threw back her head, and gave her husband a challenging look. "The women have known all along that the hunters were dangerous, and now that we have finally convinced you men, what are you going to do about it? If you are going to continue to dither and hesitate, and discuss the legality of this and the properness of that, then we women will act. Right, Uhura?"

"Right," the Bantu woman said with an amused glance at Kirk and Spock.

Kirk grinned, and said in an undertone to Kor, "I don't envy you."

"I enjoy a challenge," the Klingon responded blandly. Kali glared at him, and his smile broadened at her tiger-cub expression.

"Well, Commander, since we are clearly about to lose all respect and therefore our ability to command unless we take action—shall we take action?"

"An excellent suggestion, Captain."

"Mr. Ragsdale, you and Mr. Lindenbaum will accompany me to secure the hunters."

"Yes, sir."

"Would you care to join us, Commander?"

"Yes, but I would feel somewhat less outnumbered, and it would seem more of a bipartisan effort, if I could have one of my men join us."

"Fine." Kor stepped aside, and opened his communicator. "How about you, Mr. Spock?"

"I would prefer to stay here, and study Mr. Maslin's work. I am fascinated to see how he made this breakthrough."

"Intuitive leap," Maslin said wickedly, knowing it would irritate Spock.

A few moments later there were the soundless flashes of a Klingon transporter, and an extraordinarily handsome Klingon, but one unknown to the humans, appeared in the camp.

"Kandi, captain of the *Emperor's Pride,*" Kor said briefly. He then introduced the humans. Kandi nodded to the men, and gave the women a devilish grin. He lifted Uhura's hand, and bestowed a light kiss onto the wrist.

"I had no notion that human women could be so beautiful."

"And I had no notion that Klingon men knew how to flirt," she said, twisting her hand free and retreating to Maslin's side. The Klingon pursued her, and leaned nonchalantly on the synthesizer, to Maslin's immense irritation.

"Tell me," he said conversationally, "you don't happen to have any recent Earth fiction tapes that you would be willing to part with?"

"Kandi," Kor said significantly, "we would like to settle this sometime before next week. You can importune people for trashy novels some other time."

The younger man sighed. "Perhaps later," he said to Uhura, and jogged after the other four men who had already started down the beach.

"This is pleasant," Maslin said, slipping an arm around Uhura and Chou's waists, and pulling them down on the bench with him. He then reached out and took Kali's hand. "Let the he-men go off and duke it out with the badasses. I'll stay here and entertain the ladies."

"My hero," Uhura murmured with ironic affection, and brushed back his forelock.

Ragsdale led the way to the hunters' camp. He chugged along like a human tank, his heavy legs pumping up and down in his eagerness to reach the hunters and settle a few scores with Garyson. Kirk, too, was eager to reach the camp, but for different reasons. The long hours of patient scientific research aboard the *Enterprise* had been not at all to his liking. His nature craved involvement and action, but on this mission he felt as if he could have gotten lost and nobody would have noticed. This problem with the hunters was something he could handle, and he was grateful for the opportunity.

He looked back over his shoulder, and noticed that Kor and Kandi were holding back somewhat from the humans, and that they were deep in a low-voiced conversation. Not for the first time he wished he could speak Klingonese. The younger Klingon was speaking urgently to Kor who, although he looked thoughtful, kept shaking his head. Kirk now regretted Spock's absence. With the Vulcan's tricorder they could have recorded the conversation, and perhaps gained an insight into what was going on aboard the Klingon vessels. Kirk was still convinced that Kor was in some sort of difficulty with his own crew.

He was given no more time to ponder the problem, for Ragsdale stopped, and indicated an outcropping of rock. "The hunters set up camp just past that formation. I've scouted around the area a few times, and they didn't have much of an eye for a defensive position. They ought to be easy to take."

"Mr. Ragsdale, this isn't a commando raid. Mr. Garyson may be open to persuasion," Kirk said, but the security guard spotted the twinkle in the captain's hazel eyes, and grinned in response.

"If you believe that, sir, I have a sweet piece of land for sale on Tumbolt V, the pleasure spot of the galaxy."

"Thank you, mister, I'll pass on that offer." Kirk turned and looked at Kor. "Well, shall we go find out how unpleasant Mr. Garyson and his crew intend to be?"

"I will be right behind you, Kirk. They gave insult to my wife, and for that they must pay. I did not punish them earlier for I thought you might object to such treatment of Federation citizens. Now that I know you don't mind it will be a pleasure to teach them manners."

"Don't get too carried away," Kirk warned as they resumed their progress. "I don't want anyone hurt if it's at all possible, so all weapons are to be placed on stun."

They were lucky enough to find all five of the gem hunters present in camp. The men were gathered around a heating unit drinking coffee, and tossing crystal tears to one another for inspection. They looked up as the party from the *Enterprise* appeared on the outskirts of the camp. Kirk gave a signal, and everyone quickly fanned out. An ugly frown creased Garyson's face when he recognized Kor.

"What the hell is this?" he demanded, rising to his feet.

Kirk thought he had never seen such an unprepossessing group of people in his entire life. Everyone looked as if he hadn't changed clothes in several years, and one man had dirty blond hair that hung in greasy, ropy strands about his face. "Just a friendly visit to try and convince you that the hunting has to stop," Kirk said agreeably. He stepped forward to face the burly leader of the hunters.

"And who the hell are you?"

"Captain James T. Kirk of the starship *Enterprise.*"

Garyson rocked back on his heels, and stared contemptuously down his nose at the captain. "So, another little government toady. Well, I'll tell you what I told your pointy-eared first officer: Until you produce a directive from the Federation stating that these creatures are intelligent I'm gonna keep on doin' just what I've been doin', because I've got a piece of paper that says I can." He glanced about at his companions, who murmured agreement and looked approving.

Kirk lost his genial smile, and stared coldly up at the other man. "And I've got the firepower of a starship, and the people aboard her, that say you can't. Care to up that ante?"

"You've got no legal right, Kirk."

"Maybe not, but representatives of Star Fleet have a right to make on-the-spot decisions regarding the treatment of alien creatures even if such decision is contrary to a Federation ruling. You are free to enter a complaint, but it won't be settled until we return either to Earth or a star base, and in the meantime—what I say goes."

"Now, that sort of depends, doesn't it, Kirk?" Garyson drawled, stepping back a few feet. "On whether we decide to listen. Mehmet!" he suddenly shouted, and several things happened simultaneously. The four other hunters bolted in all directions, and Lindenbaum gave a moan and collapsed to the ground clutching at a knife that protruded from his upper thigh.

The lean, swarthy man who had thrown the knife went crashing to the ground near the edge of the camp as Kor's stun blast from his disruptor caught him neatly between the shoulderblades. Ragsdale let out a bellow of rage, and went charging like a maddened bull after the man with the dirty dreadlocks.

Kirk knelt next to Lindenbaum, and checked the leg. "I'm okay, sir," the security guard forced from between white lips. "It's minor. Go on and catch the others."

Kirk looked around, and saw Garyson just vanishing behind a large rock. He leaped up and started in pursuit, only to be arrested by a flash of purest blue among the crystal grains of sand. Unable to stop himself, he knelt, and lifted the tear. It shone like living blue fire in his hand, its many facets seeming to capture and throw back a shifting view of eternity. He felt lost in the mystery of the stone. Closing his hand over the gem, he placed it carefully in a pocket.

Leaping to his feet he again set off in pursuit of Garyson. He was furious with himself for the foolish delay over the stone, but he had been unable to resist the lure of its sapphire beauty. He only hoped that the two Klingons could handle the remaining hunters while he captured their leader. He needn't have worried. As he raced along the base of the cliff he passed Kandi, circling one of the downed hunters and taunting him to get up. When the man did, the Klingon neatly knocked him to the ground again. This happened twice more before they were lost to sight behind the rocks.

Kirk trotted steadily along the cliff, following the deep, irregular footprints left by Garyson as he ran through the sand. Suddenly the footprints vanished. Kirk stopped and made a slow circuit of the surrounding area, looking for any place where the man might have branched off in a new direction. There was no indication that Garyson had tried to double back, or headed down toward the water's edge, so only one option remained. Kirk turned to face the cliff just as a large, jagged piece of crystalline rock went rushing past his head.

He jerked back, but the missile still managed to hit his shoulder with a glancing blow, numbing the left arm from his shoulder to his fingertips. Before he could recover, Garyson was upon him. The larger man slammed feet first into his chest and sent him crashing to the ground. The breath was driven from his body in a massive whoosh, and Kirk had a feeling that if he removed his shirt he would have three-inch-deep footprints on his sternum. Fortunately he was wearing a heavy parka which absorbed some of the blow or he might have had his chest crushed.

Garyson reached out and gripped him by the throat, and Kirk realized that he didn't have any more time for recovery or inane thoughts. If he were going to survive he would have to start reacting. His body seemed to howl in protest, but he managed to bring up his knees and feet, and with a hard thrust sent Garyson flying over his head.

Kirk staggered to his feet, and walked right into a pile-driver blow that sent him reeling backward. He cautiously worked his jaw. Nothing seemed to be broken, but several teeth were decidedly loose, and there was the sharp, coppery taste of blood on his tongue. He was disgusted with his poor performance thus far, and decided it was time to get serious.

He was hampered by the loss of his left arm, but that didn't affect his kick. Tensing, he launched himself into the air, and gave Garyson a violent kick to the jaw. He heard bone snap, and as he tucked and rolled he congratulated himself, assuming that the fight was over.

He was wrong. A lesser man would have been rendered unconscious by such a blow, but Garyson seemed only dazed. He shook his head, and then plowed back in, fists pumping like a piston.

Rather like a dinosaur, the captain thought sourly as he danced out of reach of the hunter's bearlike arms. *Their brains are so small that they don't even know when they're unconscious—or ought to be,* he added, feeling a rush of wind past his face as he ducked another swing from Garyson.

His last wild punch had left the hunter off-balance, and Kirk moved in. Using his still-awkward left arm for defense he began to lay a series of punishing right jabs into Garyson's face. His knuckles were beginning to hurt from the damage he was inflicting on the other man, but it was nothing compared to what Garyson had to be feeling. Both eyes were beginning to swell shut, and blood was trickling from his slack mouth. He continued to fight back, if somewhat feebly, and he did manage to land one punch on Kirk's already sore mouth. One of his loose teeth let go, and Kirk paused to spit it into the sand.

That brief moment of inattention was enough. Garyson moved in and enveloped Kirk in a powerful bear hug, trapping his arms against his sides. With a grunt the hunter tightened his grip, and began to bend Kirk inexorably backward over his heavy thigh, trying to snap the captain's spine.

Kirk felt sweat popping out on his forehead from the strain, and his mouth opened in a soundless scream. His mind seemed to run in frenzied circles as he sought some way out of the trap he was in. Out of the corner of his eye he could see Garyson's massive torso, and below . . . he gave a mighty effort, and twisted slightly in the man's grip. The action tore at his already overstressed back, and he thought he would pass out from the pain, but it had accomplished what he needed. His knee was now in position, and with one final exertion he slammed his knee into Garyson's groin.

The man released him with a gagging groan, and clutched at his crotch. Kirk struggled to his feet and, drawing back his booted foot, gave Garyson one final kick to the head. The big hunter collapsed in an inert heap at Kirk's feet.

"I like the way you reasoned with him." Kor's voice came floating from behind him, and Kirk turned painfully to face the Klingon. "After all, it wouldn't do to have anyone hurt."

"How long have you been here?"

"I arrived just as you gave Mr. Garyson the coup de grace, as I believe you Earthmen call it." He took the captain's face in one hand, and turned it this way and that as he inspected the damage. Kirk winced at the touch and pulled away. "I do think that he took the worst of it, if it is any comfort to you."

"Not much. Did you get the rest of them?"

"They are all sitting very quiet and subdued at their camp, waiting for your pleasure."

"My pleasure is that we get them back to the *Enterprise*, and lock them in the brig before my more vengeful nature takes over and I kill them."

"Let us handle it for you. We're not so squeamish as you humans."

"That's all right." Garyson groaned, and began to regain consciousness. "How's Lindenbaum?" Kirk asked as they jerked Garyson to his feet and started slowly back toward the camp, supporting the semiconscious hunter.

"Fine, but I think he will be glad to get to sick bay."

"That's understandable. Hell, *I'll* be glad to get to sick bay."

By the time they reached the transporter room Garyson had recovered enough to attempt another lunge for Kirk. Ragsdale grabbed him by the back of his collar, and pulled him away from the captain. Scotty eyed the four glowering prisoners who accompanied the security guard and the captain, and prudently sent for more security.

As soon as the first group had left the platform the engineer beamed up the remaining prisoner together with the two Klingons and the injured Lindenbaum. McCoy, who had been waiting with a medical team, stopped his running monologue of complaints and, stepping forward, helped the young man onto an antigrav stretcher.

"You better come too," he said, pausing before Kirk and eyeing his battered face.

"Once I see these people safely in the brig."

"Have it your way, but God knows I think you have enough muscle in this room," he glanced about at the eight security guards who ringed the hunters, "to handle these characters without your help."

Kor and Kandi continued to stand on the transporter platform. As Kirk started to leave Kor called to him. "Captain?"

"Yes, Commander?"

"If you would prefer not to have, shall we say, semihostile aliens aboard your ship you can send my officer and myself directly to our ships."

Kirk paused at the door and grinned over his shoulder. "As strange as it sounds, Commander, I'm beginning to trust you. Why don't you come along while we see our 'guests' safely locked away, and then I think McCoy can be persuaded to break out the Saurian brandy while I have my face repaired."

Kor exchanged a quick glance with Kandi, who looked hopeful. "Very well, the offer of Saurian brandy is too good to pass up. We accept your hospitality."

Garyson had listened to this exchange with what was obviously a growing sense of outrage. His heavily jowled face took on a deep, brick red color, and he stared murderously at Kirk. One of the security guards gave him a quick push on the shoulder, propelling him into motion, and the entire group left the transporter room.

They received more than a few curious and startled glances as the motley crowd of fourteen humans and two Klingons went marching through the corridors of the *Enterprise*. Kor noticed that they were taking what seemed to be an inordinately circuitous route to the confinement area, and he assumed Kirk was bypassing any sensitive areas. He didn't blame the Earth captain; he would have done the same.

The hunters were deposited in the brig, and the force field brought up. Garyson approached the door, and stared hostilely after Kirk as he walked down the corridor with the two Klingons.

"You're a traitor, Kirk. A traitor! Working with Klingons, allowing them to attack Federation citizens. I'm gonna see you *fried*, Kirk, when we get back."

The captain stopped, and half turned to look back at the burly hunter. There was an amused and ironic twist to his lips. "That's fine, Mr. Garyson, but I'm afraid you're going to have to take a number and stand in line. Someone else has first claim on taking a piece out of my hide."

Chapter Nine

Kali stormed off the transporter platform, heading for the door. The transporter operator started to speak to her, then thought better of it when he saw the angry frown that pulled her delicate bifurcated brows into a straight black line over the bridge of her nose. The commander's new wife was well known for her quick temper, and he didn't want to attract her attention when she was so obviously on a tear.

She continued to seethe as she marched through the corridors heading for the bridge. She couldn't believe that Kor would return straight to the *Klothos* after dealing with the hunters. Surely he would have wanted to spend time with her since they had been separated for several days now. Unfortunately that didn't seem to be the case, for she had waited for over two hours in the human camp without Kor returning. Kirk had checked in with his first officer, informing the Vulcan of the successful capture of the hunters, but he made no mention of her husband so she could only assume he was back aboard the ship.

She rode the power lift to the bridge. Before the door opened she stiffened her back, and set her jaw in a tight line of outrage. She was determined that he would have no doubt of her anger. The doors opened and she strode onto the bridge, only to have her outrage evaporate when she realized that Kor was not at his usual position in the command chair. Instead she recognized the back of Karsul's shaved neck. He always wore his hair cut close to the scalp, like a common jevul fighter, a low-class affectation that she found silly and irritating. She decided that she really didn't want to talk with the first officer, and she began to retreat back onto the power lift.

Before she could make her escape Karsul spun about in the command chair, and pierced her with his dark gaze. There was always something so intense and brooding about the man's look which made her feel like some small insect held beneath the merciless gaze of a microscope.

"Looking for your husband?" he asked. He drew out the last word, making it seem almost an epithet.

"Yes, but as he's clearly not here I shall go to our quarters."

"You won't find him there either."

"Then where is he?" she demanded, becoming tired of Karsul's baiting tone, and the knowing look in his eyes.

"Still aboard the Earther ship."

"Nothing is wrong, is it?" she asked, stepping toward him in her agitation.

"No, nothing's wrong. I suppose he just enjoys spending his time with Earthers." The bridge had grown very quiet, but there was a quick titter from one of the crew at his sardonic tone. The sound was abruptly cut off as Kali stared hostiley about the bridge, seeking the source of the laugh.

She stood with her hands tightly clenched at her sides, and tried to think of something to say. To bring up the temporary truce in the face of such obvious hostility seemed foolish. Nor could she admit that she had been spending a good deal of time with the humans and actually enjoying it, and suspected that Kor felt the same. That would be more than foolish—it would be suicidal.

"So," she muttered, dropping her head. "I suppose I will wait for him in our quarters."

"I will escort you."

"No!" she said sharply, taking a step back. Karsul's face darkened with anger, and she backpedaled frantically, trying to regain the ground she had lost with her rude outburst. "I mean, I thank you for the offer, but that won't be necessary. Besides, it is probably best that you remain on the bridge in case of emergency."

"What could possibly happen? After all, our noble commander is no doubt keeping a watchful eye on the humans to make sure that they don't attack us." There was again a ripple of laughter across the bridge.

Kali stiffened, and drew herself up proudly. "The Earthers are not our only worry," she said coldly. "Do not forget *that!*" she said, thrusting out her arm toward the screen where the phenomenon billowed and writhed. "It is a foolish man who barricades and guards the door while leaving the windows open behind him."

"Why, thank you for telling me. It is always enlightening to study tactics at the feet of such a master of strategy as yourself."

"Don't crow too soon," she gritted from between clenched teeth. "I'll have your job someday." And turning on her heel she reentered the power lift. To her dismay Karsul crowded in after her, backing her into a corner of the small elevator.

"I know a way for you to have the job much sooner than you expect."

"How? By killing you?" she snapped.

He laughed deep in his throat, an ugly, predatory sound that sent a shiver of fear through her body. He then reached out and captured her chin between his fingers. She jerked her head aside, trying to escape his touch, but he tightened his grip until his fingers dug painfully into the sides of her jaw.

"Little wild cat. No, that wasn't what I had in mind. Rather, you should be very nice to me. Then when your husband is gone, and I have become captain, I might make you my first officer . . . among other things," he added significantly.

The elevator hissed to a stop, and the doors opened. Kali brought the side of her hand down on his wrist in a numbing blow. Karsul let out a yelp and released her. She leaped past him out of the door and beyond his reach. She froze in the corridor in a defensive half crouch, glaring at him and panting a little with hatred and fright.

"Be nice to you? The very thought of it nauseates me! And as for being your first officer and *other things*—I would rather be a galley cook on board a garbage scow!"

Karsul cradled his injured wrist with his other hand, and gazed at her with a combination of anger and lust. "If that's what you want, I'll see to it that you get it, but only after I teach you the proper respect for men. Your husband is too weak to keep you in line, but I'm not! Under my tutelage you'll learn the proper position for a woman—at the feet of her man!"

Kali gave him a scornful smile and threw back her hair with an impudent toss of her head. "Any Klingon woman is happy to take that position, but only if there's a *man* available. I confess I don't see one right now."

Karsul let out a roar of rage, and leaped at her. Whirling, she fled down the corridor, and nipped into her and Kor's quarters. She slammed her hand against the lock panel just as Karsul's heavy footfalls reached the door. She began to shiver with reaction and, resting her back against the door, she slid to the floor where she sat hugging her knees to her chest.

"Kor," she whispered aloud, her voice catching a little on a half sob. "Why aren't you here? Why aren't you doing something to protect me?" She knew she was being unreasonable and, disgusted by her own weakness, she pushed herself to her feet. Unable to relax, she flitted agitatedly about the room, dusting the already spotless dresser, straightening Kor's collection of antique weapons that hung on one wall, smoothing the coverlet on the bed.

As she gazed down at the bed that she shared with her husband she found that her mindless activity had not managed to banish her fears and worry. She had only been back aboard *Klothos* for a scant thirty minutes, and already she had the temper of the officers and crew. It wasn't good. Mutiny hung like a miasma in the air and drifted through the halls, carried by the mutterings of disgruntled men.

Instead of being here, aboard his ship where he belonged, Kor was lingering among the humans, doing what the gods alone knew. *Adding fuel to the already prevalent attitude that he is a lover of Earthers,* she concluded sourly, staring down at the bed.

Working with the humans had made sense to her when they had first been faced with the phenomenon, but now she wondered if Kor wasn't carrying things a bit too far. In the beginning he had intimated that they would deal with the *Enterprise* once the space/time rip was successfully resolved, but she had begun to have doubts about his sincerity in that direction. She had known Kor for two years before she had finally convinced him to marry her, and during that time she had heard a great deal about Captain James Kirk of the starship *Enterprise*. He had a great deal of admiration for the man, and had always regretted that the Organians had interfered before they could test their strength against one another.

She wished she had not thought of the debacle on Organia, for it raised a fear that she had not even discussed with Kor. After the Organians had dispersed the Klingon and Federation fleets without allowing a battle, and forced a treaty upon the two warring powers, the Empire began to search for a scapegoat to bear the blame. It didn't have to look very far, and the full fury of the thwarted ruling party fell upon Kor. He had been severely punished, and indeed had lost everything he had fought to gain in a long and distinguished military career. In fact, when she had met him he had been a mere lieutenant teaching tactics at the military academy outside of the capital, stripped of all rank and honors, and more importantly, mourning the loss of his beloved ship.

She had stood beside him, falling ever more deeply in love with this brilliant, ironic man, while he struggled to regain his position. Finally a shift in the political climate had returned him to his ship and his command. When he once again felt he had something to offer her he had proposed, and she had gladly accepted. Now it seemed he was ready to throw away everything they had fought so hard to regain.

She sank slowly down onto the bed, and forced herself to face the fear that had been torturing her for months. *Was Kor still loyal to the Empire?* And if not, what should she do? Duty dictated that if she suspected such disloyalty she should immediately report her suspicions to Imperial Command. But Kor was her husband, the mate she had chosen for life, and yes, as trite as it sounded, the love of her life. What was duty when compared to the love that she felt for this man?

She was appalled at her own thoughts, and she rose and took a quick turn about the room. She was a Klingon. Surely the Empire that had raised her, educated her, given her a career, deserved her service and her loyalty. She thought of the unwarranted and unfair treatment Kor had received at the hands of the Empire, and her lips tightened into a rebellious line. They had had no right to treat Kor like that. No commander could have done more against the awesome might of the Organians.

And they've lied, she thought suddenly, beginning to warm to the logical construct that she was beginning to form. *They said that the humans were cruel and barbaric. That their only response to a Klingon was death or the camps.*

"And it's not true," she said aloud. During the time she had spent with the humans on the surface of Taygeta she could see that they were all, humans and Klingons, very much alike. Oh granted, the humans were weak and overly sentimental, but they were by no means despicable. One could begin to like them with some exposure.

She turned and stared at the door, her jaw tightening into a militant line as she considered Karsul, and her probable fate if he led a successful mutiny against her husband. By Klingon law she was booty, spoils to the victor. If Karsul succeeded in his bid for power she would be expected to go meekly to his bed. Her hand reached out and snagged a bottle of perfume from the dresser. She sent the glass vial crashing against the door.

"Never," she whispered hoarsely, watching the amber liquid flow down the door and fill the room with the sweet scent of deenaela blossoms. "I will never submit myself to that man!" If this was what Klinzhai expected from its women then she refused! She would stand by Kor whatever action he might take.

"What is it with you?" Guy asked softly as he hunkered down in the sand to pet his Taygetian shadow.

There was a dull ache that seemed to have settled behind his eyes, and he felt faintly sick, but he was unwilling to return to camp to face Spock's impatient and questioning glances, and what he felt was mute reproach from the other members of the landing party. He had felt so cocky a few days ago. The answer seemed just around the corner, but that corner had been followed by another and still another until he felt as if he was in some bizarre musical maze. And out in space the phenomenon grew and advanced, devouring yet another segment of Taygetian space, and drawing ever closer to the system's sun.

The Taygetian trilled gently and nudged his hand with its muzzle. "Why don't you respond to me?" Maslin continued.

"It's so important that I understand you, yet nothing I do seems to reach you. I know I'm not that stupid. My machine and I have pretty well figured out the rudiments of your language. We've removed the hunters that were hurting your parents. So why won't you respond?"

The Taygetian youngster seemed to sense his mood, and it hooted mournfully up at him. "I'm not trying to make you feel bad since you've been such a good and constant friend to me. In fact, you're not even the worst. Your parents are the really impossible ones. You at least have the courtesy to listen while the synthesizer and I hoot, and tweet, and hum and trill at you. But your elders . . ." The composer made a hopeless gesture in the air. "They don't even know I exist. What can possibly be so important that they don't even acknowledge the presence of alien invaders on their world?" he added almost to himself. He had stopped his steady stroking, and the cub sang a fretful and complaining little passage, then took the human's hand in his mouth, and gave it a gentle shake.

Guy resumed his steady stroking through the silken fur, and the cub gave a sigh of contentment and closed its eyes. Guy smiled with wry amusement at the blissful youngster.

"Little hedonist. Don't you realize you're in dreadful danger?" The cub opened one eye and peered up at him, then dropped back into its semisomnolent state. "Apparently not, and apparently you don't give a damn either. Just so long as there's someone around to pet and pamper you the rest of the universe can go to hell. Actually, you sound a lot like me," Guy said, and the thought struck him as so amusing that he gave a short bark of laughter. Short, because the laugh triggered a violent coughing spasm that left him weak and breathless.

He lay back on the sand, trying to catch his breath, while the cub pushed itself up on its front flippers, and stared worriedly down into his white face. Maslin started to rise, then fell back exhausted onto the beach. His arms seemed to have lost all strength. The Taygetian had begun to chirp, and flop in agitated circles about the prone human. Suddenly it broke into a complicated song, and began haring up the beach.

"Hey!" Maslin shouted, struggling up onto one elbow. "Where are you going? Don't leave me," he cried after the rapidly retreating cub, but the creature paid no attention. He fell back on the sand, and fear gripped him. Never in all the years of living with the disease had he felt this horrible. Pain gnawed at his chest and stomach, and seemed to send burning tendrils coiling along the nerve endings into his legs and arms.

He reached into a pocket, searching for his pills, and realized that he had left them back in the tent. He thought with longing of the camp. Suddenly it seemed far more comfortable and attractive than any resort planet he had ever visited, and just as distant. He had walked for miles trying to outrun his depression and frustration, and no one knew where he was. He closed his eyes, and tried to ignore the pain.

"Uhura," he whispered softly. "Oh God, I need you." After a time he slipped into a fevered sleep in which he seemed to be dancing on a tide of golden music. Uhura was in his arms, and they went spinning and whirling like chips in a stream. A golden light was all around them, and they were one with the music. It swept them past stars and planets and great glowing dust clouds, where life was beginning. He reached out and captured some of the precious substance. It spilled from his hand like diamond dust, and he quickly raised his hand so it fell gently onto Uhura's black hair. The particles sparkled and flared like miniature stars against the veil of her hair, and she seemed crowned by an incandescent aura.

"Quick," he said to her. *"Do the same for me. This is the stuff of life. We can live forever."*

But faceless, uniformed figures suddenly appeared and, taking her by the arms, pulled her slowly, inexorably away into the blackness of space. He cried out to her, and tried to follow, but the music swelled and crashed about him, and swept him away.

"No!" He jerked upright, his head throbbing with pain, and reached out, trying to capture her and bring her back. His flailing hands were caught and held immobile while he stared uncomprehendingly into her concerned and beautiful face.

"It's all right, Guy. I'm here. You're safe."

"You went away!" he cried accusingly. "Went away and left me alone. You never even gave me a chance," he said, his voice catching on a half sob.

Uhura caught him to her, and held him while he struggled feebly against her. His cheek where it pressed against hers was burning hot. She drew back and studied him, noting the hectic flush on his high cheekbones, and the erratic pulse that was fluttering in the base of his throat. Still keeping a grip on him she dug out her communicator and called the ship.

"Enterprise."

"T'zeela! Two to beam up, and this is an emergency. Have Dr. McCoy meet us in the transporter room."

"Aye, aye, sir!"

Seconds later she felt the familiar disorientation as her molecules were separated and reassembled aboard the *Enterprise*. Kyle goggled at her, and she realized what an odd picture she must present, huddled on the transporter platform with Guy in her arms. The door hissed open, and McCoy came pelting into the room. He took in the situation at a glance, and before she could speak had bounded onto the platform and begun running his medical tricorder over Guy's limp form.

"It's the disease," he said tensely. He checked the readings and looked grim. "It's running rampant through his body. Good God, Uhura," he tossed over his shoulder as he hurried down to the transporter control panel, "didn't you notice this coming on?"

Stung by what she considered an unfair attack, she deposited Guy gently on the platform and leaped to her feet glaring at McCoy. "Perhaps if I had some medical training *and* knew how this disease manifested itself, I might have been able to diagnose his condition," she said sarcastically. "Also, I'd like *you* to have done any better when Guy hides how he's feeling, and refuses to admit when he's ill."

"I'm sorry, Uhura," he said, turning back. "I'm not so much angry with you as I am with myself. It's my responsibility to care for the people on this ship, and I hate it when I fumble a situation. I should have been down on the planet checking him over every day."

"And he would have hated it," she said, her tone softening at McCoy's obvious distress.

"That's still no excuse." He punched open a communication line and, calling the sick bay, ordered a stretcher to the transporter room.

"Aren't you going to tell the captain?"

"After I see how bad things are. Besides, he's down in the gym working out, and I'd rather let him know that I screwed up *after* he's released some tension and frustration."

"You didn't screw up," she said, sinking back down on the platform. "At least no more than the rest of us. He should never have been forced to come here," she concluded softly, drawing her hand through Guy's silky black hair.

Kirk came hurrying into sick bay just as McCoy concluded his examination of the unconscious musician. He was dressed in a pair of tight-fitting sweat pants, and a towel was draped over his neck. A fine sheen of sweat still dampened his bare chest.

"What's going on here? And why in hell wasn't I informed by you, Doctor, that we had a casualty?"

"Because I didn't want you cluttering up my sick bay until I'd had a look, and had something to report. Having Uhura hovering over me was bad enough," he daid grumpily, with a glance to the communications officer where she stood at the side of the bed, holding Maslin's hand.

"So what's the problem?" Kirk asked, approaching the bed, and looking down at Maslin. "Exhaustion?"

"I only wish it were that simple. Oh, it's exhaustion all right, but it's triggered a dangerous flare of the syndrome, and if I can't get it back under control—and quickly—it'll kill him."

"Kill him?" Kirk echoed.

"Yes, kill him. I warned you this was a risk we were running by bringing him along on this mission."

"So what are you going to do?"

"Try massive doses of cordrazine. That sometimes throws this disease into an arrest."

"All right. Let me know how it goes. I'll be in my quarters if you need me." He started for the door, then turned back as a new thought struck him. "Has Spock been informed? We don't want him running all over the planet because he thinks two of his landing party have vanished."

"I'm sorry, sir. I forgot," Uhura said quietly.

"Well get on it," he began, then stopped when he noticed the way Uhura was clinging to the composer's limp hand. He gave an inward sigh. "Never mind. I'll handle it." Uhura threw him a grateful look, and returned her attention to Maslin.

"Spock . . ."

"Captain, forgive me for interrupting," the Vulcan broke in, his voice carrying an underlying tenseness. "But we have a problem down here."

"No, you don't," Kirk said as he wiped the sweat from his chest, and tossed the towel onto the bed.

"I beg your pardon?"

"Lieutenant Uhura and Mr. Maslin are aboard the Enterprise."

Spock looked peeved, and pressed his lips together. "May I ask why I was not informed of this decision?"

"It was a rather spur-of-the-moment kind of thing. Maslin became ill; Uhura found him, and brought him to the ship."

"I see. Is it serious?"

"Hard to tell. Dr. McCoy is being somewhat closemouthed about the prospects."

"Undoubtedly because he does not know," Spock said with some acerbity. "I shall return to the ship," he suddenly announced. "If Mr. Maslin is unable to continue his work we will have to make alternative plans."

"Do we have any, Spock?" Kirk asked wearily. "We've been working on this for days, and are no closer to a solution than when we started."

"We have made some progress."

"But none of it relates to the phenomenon, and that beast isn't likely to give us the luxury of a second chance."

"We will discuss this further when I return to the ship. Perhaps I was mistaken in assuming that the phenomenon and the Taygetians were somehow linked."

"I hope not, Mr. Spock, because that would leave us without *any* theory to work from."

Kirk lay back on his bed and stared up at the ceiling while he waited for Spock to arrive. The phenomenon had begun to take on a mocking, almost human persona for Kirk, and he didn't like it one bit. Here he was, James Tiberius Kirk, captain of the starship *Enterprise,* the finest ship in the fleet. He, together with his crew, had quickly and efficiently solved every assignment that had come their way. Until now. This time they were up against something that defied some of the best minds in the Federation. Kirk wondered if he ought to call Star Fleet, and yell for help.

That thought was so abhorrent that he swung off the bed and began agitatedly to pace his quarters. He had never had to ask for help, and he couldn't stand the thought of it now. Also, on a less personal and egotistical level, there was the very real chance that the phenomenon wouldn't give them time for reinforcements to arrive. Each day brought it closer and closer to the Taygetian sun, and if it destroyed that life-sustaining star all those happy, frolicking cubs and their mysterious elders would be swept into oblivion.

This was one of those times when the mantle of command lay heavy on his shoulders. He wished he could cast it aside, and stop being responsible for his crew, the Federation, the galaxy; but he knew he never would. He was a starship captain, and having tasted that power he would never willingly give it up.

Kor understood. They had touched on the subtle opiate of command that day after the capture of the hunters when they had shared a bottle of Saurian brandy and reminiscences culled from years of galaxy-spanning explorations.

Kirk had enjoyed that afternoon. It wasn't often that a captain could confide in anyone, and even rarer was an opportunity to talk to a person in a similar position. There was no doubt that command was lonely. For an instant Kirk envied Kor his bride, and wondered if such a partnership setup could work in Star Fleet. He then shook his head, and dismissed the notion. He wasn't ready for any sort of commitment, no matter how lovely and talented the lady. The *Enterprise* was all the lady he wanted, and he couldn't picture her sharing him with a mere human woman.

The page chimed, and Spock stepped into the room. "I stopped by sick bay before joining you, and Dr. McCoy said that early indications look good. Maslin seems to be responding to the cordrazine."

"Good, but I'd like it better if we can find some way to continue without him," Kirk said over his shoulder as he pulled a fresh uniform out of the dresser, and began to dress. "I did pull the man out here against his will. I'd prefer not to bring him back in a box."

"I have been considering the possibility of transmatrix scans—"

The Vulcan was interrupted by the whistle of the communicator. Kirk crossed to the table and switched on the com. Sulu's face looked seriously out at him.

"Captain, the phenomenon has reached the innermost planet of the solar system. I thought you might like to observe its effect on a relatively large body."

"Thank you, Mr. Sulu, I would. Mr. Spock and I will join you momentarily."

The bridge was very quiet when they arrived. Scotty had wandered up from engineering, and everyone had abandoned his panel to watch the sight on the main screen. Spock moved quickly to his science station, and Lieutenant Mendez scrambled to get out of his way. Taking his seat, he began a running commentary on the planetary readings.

"Mean distance from the sun—60.3 kilometers; equatorial diameter—5023 kilometers; mass—0.069."

The gaudy colors of the phenomenon writhed forward, its outermost tendrils just brushing the pockmarked, cindery surface of the inner planet. The planet seemed to waver, becoming almost transparent, and then it vanished from view as the space/time rip enveloped it.

Spock swung about in his chair and looked at Kirk. "All readings have ceased. Scanners show only the meaningless readings associated with the phenomenon. For all intents and purposes the planet no longer exists."

"But where has it gone, Mr. Spock?" Scotty murmured.

"Into wherever *that*," he pointed at the aurora that danced and sparkled across the screen, "leads."

There was a whistle from the communications station, and T'zeela immediately answered the summons. Kor's face replaced the disquieting phenomenon on the main screen.

"Did you see that, Kirk?"

"I saw it."

"Well, what are we going to do about it?"

"Commander, I'm open to any suggestions at this point."

"Sorry, I'm out of suggestions."

Kirk looked over at Spock and gave a miserable shrug. "Then I guess we just keep doing what we've been doing—only harder."

McCoy stood with his back to Kirk and Spock, staring stiffly at the glass cabinet in his office. The captain had finished speaking several moments ago, and silence hung like a pall in the room. McCoy suddenly whirled to face them, and his normally kindly blue eyes were hard and flat. He shook his head, his mouth twisting with disgust.

"I can't believe what I'm hearing. Well, I'm going to call Uhura, maybe she'll be able to reach you. You sure as hell haven't listened to a thing *I've* said."

"No! Don't do that," Kirk said, catching McCoy by the wrist before he could touch the com.

"What's the matter? Are you ashamed of what you're doing? Don't want to face Uhura? Well, I'd be ashamed too if I had made such a callous suggestion."

"The captain is not being callous, he is merely being logical. We are weighing one man's life against the possible destruction of millions. There can be no hesitation."

"Excuse me, Mr. Spock, but I've never been much of an advocate of Jeremy Bentham. It's damn easy to say that a few ought to suffer for the good of the many when you're not among those few."

"I would not be swayed by such considerations, Doctor. I would always do my duty."

"You would *choose* to do your duty," McCoy said, thrusting a finger at Spock. "That's a completely different situation from this one. Mr. Maslin is not making a free choice, he is being coerced."

"Then you think I was wrong to bring him, Bones? At the time we made the decision you seemed to approve."

"That was then—this is now. The man is now my patient, and he's ill. I'll not willingly have him sent back to that planet."

"None of us wants to do it, but we just don't have any choice," Kirk said.

"You haven't listened to a word I've said!" McCoy shouted furiously, and flipped open the com.

"Communications." Uhura's voice came softly over the com.

"Uhura, this is McCoy. Get down to my office right away."

"Guy?" she said, and her voice was breathless with fear.

"No, no, he's fine. At least for now," he added with a look to the captain and first officer.

"On my way."

The door slid shut behind her, and she looked questioningly at the three grim-faced men. McCoy put an arm around her waist, and guided her to a chair. He then looked challengingly at Kirk. "Okay, tell her."

"Tell me what?"

"Uhura, we need Maslin, need his expertise. Dr. McCoy says he is doing better, and I want both of you to return to the surface of the planet."

"You can't approve of this," she said to McCoy.

"I don't. That's why I brought you down here. I want you to talk some sense into them."

She looked pointedly from her lieutenant's braid to the multiple lines of braid that adorned the sleeves of the men. McCoy gave his head an impatient shake. "Just forget rank, and speak out."

"Have I your permission, sir?" she asked Kirk. He nodded. She drew in a quick breath, and began. "You can't do this, sir. The man cannot survive another flare of the disease."

"And the galaxy can't survive the space/time warp," Kirk said gently. "It's growing, Lieutenant, and destroying everything in its path."

"But Guy's tried, and he hasn't been able to break the Taygetian language! Sending him back down there to try again can only result in his death, and for what?"

"Uhura," Kirk said, moving in and taking her hand in his. "He's our only hope."

"And he's my only hope too!" she cried, leaping out of her chair, and pulling her hand away from him. She then turned away, and covered her face with one hand. She was appalled at what she had said—appalled at the truth in it. Dreams of a captaincy, fame, glory, rank, all shriveled and vanished before her love for Maslin. Somehow, by not expressing it, she had managed to hold the emotion at bay, but now that feeble defense was gone.

She turned slowly back to face the men. "Captain, I am tendering my resignation. I will not return to Taygeta, nor will I permit Mr. Maslin to return. Now, if you will excuse me I shall be in my quarters."

The door whispered shut behind her, and Kirk looked glumly up into McCoy's startled face. "Congratulations, Doctor. Is that what you had in mind? Now I have neither resident expert nor communications officer."

McCoy's face took on an expression of mulish obstinacy. "I think it's about time we stopped being so God-damned selfish aboard this ship, and realized that people have a right to a life of their own. Uhura loves this man, and I think we ought to be giving her our support and our congratulations—not making her feel bad for choosing something beyond Star Fleet."

"A touching and emotional outburst, Doctor," Spock said dryly. "But it is highly likely that none of us will have a future if we do not find a way to remove that space/time rip. I suggest you think on that," the Vulcan concluded as he walked through the doors of the sick bay.

Kirk gave McCoy an inquiring glance, but the doctor had nothing more to say.

Chapter Ten

He was out of bed, and standing half-dressed at the table feverishly scrolling pages across the reader's screen.

"What do you think you're doing?" Uhura asked from the doorway.

"I just had an idea, and I was checking out the theory. If I'm right I ought to be able to—"

"No," she said bluntly and, striding across the room, snapped off the reader. "It's over. You're finished . . . I'm finished."

"What the hell are you talking about?"

"They were ready to send you back down to the planet—"

"Well, of course I'm going back to the planet. How else can I complete my work?"

"*Your* work? Why all this sudden identification with the military-industrial complex? I thought you were here under protest."

He grinned sheepishly at her. "Okay, so I've changed my

mind. Maybe you've convinced me that there are some things that are worth a little self-sacrifice."

"We're not talking about a *little* sacrifice, we're talking about the possible loss of your life! And while we're on the subject of change, let's consider this one—I just resigned. How's that for a little change?"

He sank down onto a chair, and stared incredulously up at her. "You did what?"

"You heard me."

"But why?"

"Oh no," she said with an ironic laugh and a shake of her head. "You're not going to get me on that one. If you can't figure it out then I'll leave it to your imagination, but I'll be damned if I'm going to pander to your ego by explaining what ought to be self-evident. I may not have enough pride to stay away from you, but I do have enough to keep from crawling to you." She turned away, and stood hunched over the dresser, her hands balled into tight fists on the hard metal surface.

He crossed to her and, taking her hands in his, gently loosened her clenched fingers. "Come here," he said, leading her to the bed, and pulling her down to sit next to him. "We have to talk."

"This sounds bad. Are you about to give me my walking papers?"

"No, hardly. I'm overwhelmed and honored that you want to be with me, especially since you've seen me in all of my possible moods, most of which aren't pleasant. If you can put up with me you're a stronger woman than I thought, and certainly more than I deserve. But that's for the future," he said with a dismissing gesture. "And we can't get there without living through the present. Uhura, I *have* to go back to Taygeta, and not just because your captain wants me to. Unless we solve this puzzle the Taygetians are going to die, and I won't willingly see that music pass from the galaxy.

They deserve a life just as much as we do, and I couldn't be happy," he paused to touch her cheek, "even with you at my side, if I knew I hadn't made every effort to save them."

"But you might die," she said in a voice so low that he had to strain to hear her.

"I might, but I don't think I will. I'm feeling much better, and I think we're right on the verge of a breakthrough. Please, stick with me on this one, Uhura," he pleaded.

She sighed and shook her head. "How could I not? One way or the other I'm committed to you—even when you're stupid."

"That's my lady. Now go tell the captain that you overreacted, and let's get back to work."

"I'm going to look like an idiot; and worse, I've wasted one of the great exit lines of all time. I'll never be able to use the threat of resignation again with Kirk."

"You didn't really want to do it anyway," Maslin said as he continued dressing. "You only did it because you were trying to keep my puny body from the ravages of overwork."

"Yes, and look how well I succeeded," she said from the door. She started to leave, then paused and looked back. "It doesn't bother you anymore that I'm in the service?"

"I suppose a man can get used to anything," he teased, and blew her a kiss. She made a face at him, and left. She was certain that Kirk would be delighted with the news of her and Maslin's return. As for herself, she couldn't shake a strong sense of foreboding, and somehow that didn't seem right on what should have been one of the happiest days of her life.

"It looks bad for the home team, Scotty," Kirk murmured as he and his chief engineer peered through a chevron mirror arrangement into the guts of the *Enterprise*'s matter/antimatter chamber.

No human could look directly into the hellish glare created by the mixing of matter and antimatter, so a series of angled mirrors filtered out the worst of the light, and gave them visual access to the implosion chamber. There was a steady, quiet glow from the engines, but that was not what was concerning Kirk. What alarmed him, and was beginning to tighten a band of pain around his temples, were the obvious cracks and buckles in the dilithium crystals.

"Aye," Scotty agreed, then glanced over at the captain, and there was a suppressed excitement in his brown eyes. "But . . . I think I have the answer."

"Well, dear God, why didn't you say so in the first place?"

"Because I wanted ye to see just how far the crystals had deteriorated so ye won't fight me when I tell ye what we have to do to preserve them."

"I take it I'm not going to like this."

"You're not going to like it," Scotty verified, and led him back into the main engineering room. "You see, I couldn't think of any explanation for the deterioration. I then remembered how a soprano can shatter a glass by producing certain sonic vibrations that are echoes within the fabric of the glass. There seemed to be a resemblance between that phenomenon, and what was happening to the crystals. I had Mendez start a scan on all frequencies, and this is what she found."

He sat the captain before the main control panel, and switched on a speaker. A strange, deep-throated harmonic began to pulse through the room. Kirk felt as if his bones were beginning to vibrate in sympathetic resonance, and his mind was filled with almost hallucinatory visions of galaxies spinning away into the vastness of space, great suns shuddering in death as huge novas sent the stuff of the stars back out into the universe to coalesce once more into the dust clouds that would be the birthplace of stars and planets. Scott switched off the speaker, and Kirk staggered a bit as the onslaught of sound vanished.

"What in hell was that?"

"It's a harmonic that's vibrating through subspace. It sets

up a sympathetic reaction in the dilithium crystals, and causes them to crack." Scott shrugged. "You felt what it can do to living flesh—imagine what happens to fragile crystal."

"So what's causing the harmonic?"

"That I don't know. In fact, I can't even pinpoint where it's coming from."

"The Klingons?" Kirk suggested.

Scotty shook his head, a quick, negating little gesture. "No, I don't think so. Mendez has been monitoring their ships, and she's noticed that they've been cutting back on power just like we have. Whatever is causing this, it's affecting them too. It occurred to me it might have something to do with the Taygetians." He shrugged. "But I have no proof."

"Have you told Spock about this latest development?"

"Not yet."

"Then do so, and let's get him on it right away."

"Aye, sir. Oh, Captain," the engineer called, stopping Kirk before he could reach the door. "We still have to discuss how to preserve the crystals."

"Oh, right. Well, what is your suggestion, Mr. Scott?"

"Pull back, sir. I think all of this is linked to that phenomenon. The farther we are from it the less deterioration to the crystals."

"How far is far?"

"Out beyond the limits of the solar system."

Kirk shook his head. "Out of the question. It would leave the landing party without support, and Maslin separated from the facilities of sick bay. I just got him back down there; I can't risk losing him. Also there are those two Klingon battle cruisers to think of."

"We could always inform the Klingons of our suspicions, and urge them to pull back too."

"And just how likely do you think that will be?"

"Not very," Scotty admitted.

"I agree, so we stay."

"Sir, we're running dangerously low on power. If we have to fight or run I can't guarantee the consequences."

Kirk gave him a careless grin. "So maybe the Klingons will stay friendly."

"And just how likely do you think that will be?" Scotty mimicked, throwing Kirk's words back at him.

"Well, we can hope. After all, we're in this together. Nothing is going to get solved unless we continue to trust each other."

"I'd sooner trust an Elasian fire devil," Scott muttered to himself as Kirk strode out of engineering.

"We may have something for you, Mr. Spock," Kirk said, after T'zeela contacted the landing party.

"Anything would be welcome, Captain," Spock's voice came over the speaker. "Mr. Maslin's earlier breakthrough has led us once more to an impasse. We have tried every logical line of inquiry, and even some highly questionable methods, and all to no effect. I must confess that we are very nearly as far from a solution as when we first landed." The Vulcan's voice held a wealth of irritation, disgust and even a touch of defeat. For the first time Kirk began to doubt their ability to solve the riddle of the Taygetians and the threat of the phenomenon, and that bothered him. Always before, the *Enterprise* had handled every problem with a speed and ease that confounded other starship captains, and Star Fleet itself. This time they seemed to be up against a blank wall.

"Well try this, and see if it's any help," he said, forcing a confidence back into his voice that he really didn't feel. "Mr. Scott discovered it when he was trying to locate the cause of the dilithium deterioration."

Kirk nodded to Mendez, who switched on a recording of the subspace harmonic. Spock listened in silence for several seconds, then said, with growing excitement in his normally level voice, "One moment while I summon Mr. Maslin. This sounds very much like it fits with the Taygetian song, but I would like to have him verify my conclusion."

There was a babble of voices over the speaker, then Maslin came on. "All right, Captain, I'm ready." Kirk signaled Mendez, who once more played the recording. Kirk heard the composer muttering and humming to himself. Then Maslin gave a loud, inarticulate shout of joy. "That's it! That's it!" There were low murmurings as Maslin turned aside to speak to the other members of the landing party. Then suddenly the murmurs became shouts and whistles, and there were thumping sounds that strongly indicated that an impromptu dance had begun in the camp.

"What? It's what?" Kirk demanded, beginning to wish he were on the planet's surface instead of stuck fifty thousand miles away, and unable to take control of the chaos that seemed to be occurring on Taygeta.

"You see," he heard Maslin's voice rising above the others. "It's like an incredibly complex canon with a secondary theme—"

"Spock!" Kirk bellowed.

"Here, Captain."

"What is going on?"

"I think we at last have the breakthrough we needed, Captain. Mr. Maslin," Kirk heard Spock call. "If you could contain your enthusiasm for several more minutes I would like to learn where Mr. Scott discovered this harmonic. If you would listen now it would save me the bother of having to repeat it."

"Oh, of course. I'm here, Captain, go ahead," Maslin panted.

"Scott had been measuring the cracks that were forming in the crystals, and he said it reminded him of the effect a soprano has on a glass. He then started scanning, searching for a harmonic that would resonate on the same frequencies as the crystals and cause the deterioration. He found this strange sound vibrating through subspace, but on a frequency that is never used by any race known to Star Fleet, so our scanners had overlooked it until now."

"Captain, please tell Lieutenant Mendez to maintain a constant monitor on the harmonic, and arrange to have the information transmitted directly to Mr. Maslin's synthesizer."

"Thank you, Mr. Spock, I hadn't thought of that." Kirk heard Maslin's voice in the background. "But that will be a help."

"So when will you have some answers for me?"

"Unknown, Captain. We will need time to evaluate this latest information. We will get back to you as soon as possible. Oh yes, would you please send Dr. McCoy down to the camp. I think it might be prudent to have him available."

"Good idea, and I think I'll come down with him just to see how you're coming."

"I would advise against it, Captain."

"Oh? Why? Afraid I'll get in the way?"

"I would not have put it quite so crudely, but, essentially—yes. You lack the training to be effective in this particular investigation, Captain. Be assured, however, that we will keep you informed of any progress. Spock out."

"Right," Kirk muttered, feeling once again useless. He sat in silence for several moments, then realized that he'd better call McCoy, and get him down to the Taygetian surface. After all, he thought, pulling a wry face, even errand boys had to be efficient.

Spock ran the long ribbon of printout through his fingers, and studied the information contained there. They had gathered in Maslin and Uhura's tent, and even Kali was present. Spock had sent for her earlier in the day, feeling it was only right that they kept their allies informed of any progress.

Guy's head was a heavy weight on Uhura's shoulder, and while Spock continued to cogitate she whispered to him, "Why don't you lie down?" He stubbornly shook his head, and with a sigh she went back to her contemplation of the three moons of Taygeta through the open tent flap.

At last Spock lifted his head and spoke. "Congratulations, Mr. Maslin. We appear to have the beginnings of a formula."

Maslin, who was still leaning wearily against Uhura, straightened and shook his head. "No, what we've got is a fragment that still doesn't make any sense."

"But a fragment that nonetheless gives some hint of the mathematical progression of the song, which in turn indicates to us how the Taygetian mind works. I would say that is a distinct improvement over our earlier situation."

"It's like trying to put together a jigsaw puzzle with about half of the pieces missing," Maslin muttered, scrubbing his face with both hands like a child who has been kept up too late.

"So where do we find the other pieces?" Kali asked from where she sat near the tent opening.

"I'm open to any suggestions," Maslin replied.

"Before we begin throwing out ideas which may or may not have any basis in logic, let us first reexamine the facts as we know them." Spock lifted one forefinger, like a professor admonishing a group of students. "First, we know that the Taygetians are involved in an undertaking that requires the total energy of the adult population. Second, we know that this undertaking is in the form of a song, but we do not know what it signifies. Third, we know that the Taygetians appear to have the power to teleport objects, as in the case of the fish. And fourth, we know that this song encompasses all frequencies from the audible to the inaudible."

"And that still leaves us with no idea of what the Singers are doing," Maslin interrupted irritably.

"Very well then, let us examine that question. Mr. Maslin, what is your opinion?" The composer pulled his chin down into the collar of his parka and shook his head. "Lieutenant?"

Uhura sighed. "I don't know, Mr. Spock. I've analyzed it so many times that I no longer know what to think."

"Lieutenant Commander?" he asked, turning to face Kali. The Klingon woman sat entranced, with her eyes half-closed as she listened in rapt contemplation to the chorus that swelled and ebbed in the night around them.

"Wh . . . what?" she stammered, pulling herself free from the spell of the Taygetian song.

"I asked for your analysis of the Taygetian song."

"It's magic," she said seriously, looking up at him out of cloudy topaz eyes.

"Yes, quite," Spock said dismissively, then stopped as a new thought occurred to him. "Magic," he repeated to himself in an undertone.

Uhura cocked her head, and gave him a sharp look. "What is it, Mr. Spock? Are you on to something?"

"Possibly," he said slowly, then with greater energy demanded, "Mr. Maslin, would you please describe for me your exact feelings at the moment the first Taygetian died."

"Well sure, I'll try, but it's all rather fuzzy." He closed his eyes, and drew a quick breath. "I was trying to improvise on a theme from the song so I was very deeply involved in the music. Then suddenly I felt as if a part of me had been . . ." He hesitated and looked puzzled.

"Removed?" Spock suggested.

"Yes! That's it. I felt as if a part of me had been torn away, and . . . it's funny, but it almost hurt."

"You did in fact pass out for several seconds," Spock reminded him.

"Yeah, but what's all this got to do with the Taygetians?"

The Vulcan rose, and began to pace the small confines of the tent. "We are all agreed that the Taygetian song extends through the audible ranges and even into ultra- and subsonics. We have now found the song vibrating in subspace, so is it not possible that this music extends through the *entire* spectrum? Even perhaps into warp space and beyond, say, into the realm of the psychic?"

"That's a pretty amazing theory, Spock," Uhura said guardedly. "What do you have for evidence?"

"First, Mr. Maslin's reaction to the death of a Singer." He looked at the composer. "I wondered at the time if you might not be a latent telepath."

"I've always tested high on those psi tests they give you when you enter school, but I never followed up on it."

"Hardly your fault. The Earth people tend not to encourage or train for this gift. However, if you are a telepath it can be easily tested by use of the Vulcan mind meld. We might find it useful to try at some point."

"Assuming all of this to be true, how do we empirically prove it? My husband isn't going to accept wild guesses and what he will call mumbo-jumbo," Kali stated.

"Nor will my captain," Spock countered. "Therefore we must produce the proof."

"But *how?*" Kali repeated.

"By using the scanners of the *Enterprise* to determine if the song is present in warp space. If so it will give us yet another piece of the Taygetian song, and enable us, using the computers, to extrapolate how the song functions on the psychic plane."

"Why not just mind meld with one of the Taygetians?" Uhura asked. "Rather than risking an error of deduction?"

"I hesitate to interfere with the adults, Lieutenant, and I think that a joining with one of the cubs would only produce interesting, but not very relevant, information about the cubs alone. As you know they are not involved in the song, and it is the song that must concern us. Let us try this method first. We can always resort to the meld if it should become necessary."

"So when do we begin?" Kali asked.

"Immediately. It would help matters if you would duplicate my efforts using your own computers. The differences in programming between machines might give us the edge we need."

"All right. I'm sure Kor will agree."

"Uh, Spock," Uhura said, catching him by the elbow, and pulling him aside. "It's very late, and you know what Dr. McCoy said. Wouldn't it be prudent to start this in the morning? Or at least let Guy rest while you do the preliminaries?"

"Time is not something we have in abundance, Lieutenant, and this is the time when I have most need of Mr. Maslin's skills. You must set aside your emotionalism, and allow us to get on with our investigation."

"I am not acting on emotion alone," Uhura began, her voice low, but filled with a deep anger. "I am referring to your God almighty: logic—"

"Uhura," Guy said softly, slipping an arm around her waist, and turning her to face him. "It's all right. You agreed to let me finish my work here. The sooner we make this last push, the sooner it will be over, and we can be together." His eyes gazed intently into hers, pleading, reassuring, cajoling; and at last she reluctantly nodded. "Good lass," he said softly and, catching her chin in his hand, tipped her head, and kissed her.

Kali planted her hands firmly in the center of Spock's back, and pushed him firmly out of the tent. "Come along, Mr. Spock, we can begin the setup in your tent."

"But . . ." he began with a glance back at the two humans, locked in a deep embrace.

"They will be along," she reassured him, as she hustled him across the sand to his own tent. "Trust to my greater experience in these matters. This is one time when logic must take a back seat to sensitivity."

Kirk struggled up through layers of sleep, summoned by the insistent whistle of his desk communicator. Staggering out of bed, he stumbled to the table, and pushed the hair out of his eyes.

"Kirk here," he murmured blearily.

"Spock here, Captain. We need an immediate meeting—"

"Mr. Spock, are you aware," he squinted over at the chronometer that rested on the shelf behind his bed, "that it is four in the morning?"

"Yes, Captain, but I had news which I felt you would not wish to wait before hearing."

"You've broken the Taygetian language," Kirk breathed, all muzziness vanishing before the excitement of the moment.

"Correct, Captain."

"Well?" Kirk demanded after several seconds passed without further elaboration from Spock.

"Lieutenant Commander Kali has requested that a three-way conference be established so we may present our findings to both you and Commander Kor simultaneously. She feels that will prevent the Federation from receiving an unfair advantage by being the first to receive this information."

"Is it bad?" Kirk asked, feeling a cold knot settle into the pit of his stomach.

"Let us say rather that it would grant to the possessor of this information an awesome amount of power."

Kirk stood silent for several moments, digesting Spock's cryptic remark. "Very well," he said at last, and gave a quick nod. "I agree. Have you gotten in touch with Kor?"

"Kali is contacting him now. Is fifteen minutes sufficient to have everything prepared?"

"We'll be ready. Kirk out."

Kirk contacted the bridge, and ordered that a three-way link be established. He then flung on a uniform, and raced for the bridge. His blood was hammering in his ears, and all he could think was: *We did it. We did it!* Suddenly he sobered, and slowed from his half run to a walk.

Kali had insisted that both the Klingons and the *Enterprise* learn the secret of Taygeta at the same time, and Spock had indicated that it was a secret that carried the potential to be a double-edged sword. All of this implied that the Singers possessed some possibly useful or dangerous power. Perhaps both. If so, what would the Klingons do? As a race, they weren't known for honoring treaties and commitments when there was something to be gained.

As he rode the turbolift to the bridge, Kirk considered the two Klingon cruisers that orbited only a few hundred kilometers from the *Enterprise*. Granted, everyone's power was down due to the harmonic that had affected their dilithium crystals, but it was still two to one, and Kirk didn't much like those odds.

Can Kor be trusted? He had thought so that day they had shared a bottle of Saurian brandy. Now the stakes had gone up, and he was no longer so sure.

The main screen flickered to life, revealing Spock, Uhura, Maslin—who was seated at the synthesizer—and Kali. Behind them a portable display board had been erected. Its smooth white surface was covered with a series of complicated mathematical formulae. Maslin looked ghastly, with large dark circles like bruises about his eyes, but he seemed animated by a feverish excitement. Occasionally he would play a quick passage on the synthesizer, then leap up and hurry to the board where he would make some minute change in one of the numbers.

"All right, Mr. Spock, we're ready."

"Same here," Kor's voice came over one of the speakers.

"Everyone has observed the formulae?" Spock asked.

"Yes," the two captains said in chorus.

"Very good. We have put these up for the benefit of the science teams of all three ships. We will not, however, take the time to work through them. A simple summary should suffice."

"Thank you, Spock," Kirk murmured gratefully under his breath.

"I will have Mr. Maslin begin, as it was his observations that gave us our first clue."

Maslin straddled the bench, his hands tensely gripping its edges. "You all know about my report on the fish that suddenly appeared in the grottos when a particular passage was sung by the cubs. I had assumed this to be an example of simple telekinesis. Interesting, certainly, but hardly an unusual talent among the races of the galaxy.

"Then Mr. Scott discovered the subspace harmonic, and things began to come together. We postulated the theory that the Taygetian song extended through the entire spectrum from the audible into the psychic. Using the *Enterprise*'s scanners Mr. Spock discovered the song also vibrating in warp space. This gave strong support to our theory, and using all the available data the computers were able to extrapolate the musical progression of the song in the psychic realm. This," he waved his hand at the tangle of numbers on the board, "is the result of our night's work. We now know that what the Taygetians are practicing is far from simple telekinesis. They are, in a nutshell, able to manipulate their physical environment."

"Forests where only deserts had been before," Mendez muttered softly from her position at the science station.

"Precisely, Lieutenant," Spock said. "There was nothing wrong with the instruments. They were in fact presenting us with accurate readings which we foolishly chose to ignore. If we had been less incredulous we might have had our answer a good deal earlier."

"Let's see if I've got this straight, Spock," Kirk broke in. "The Taygetians are able to adjust their environment to suit themselves?"

"Yes, Captain. Using the power of their song they can literally make the deserts bloom."

"And make marginal planets inhabitable?" Kirk suggested softly.

"Yes."

"Incredible."

"But we're not finished yet, Kirk," Maslin said with a cocky smile. "We've solved the space/time warp problem."

"What!"

"Well, perhaps not solved it, Captain," Spock hurriedly corrected. "But we do understand the mechanics of its creation. The phenomenon was caused by a disruption of the harmonics in warp space brought about by the loss of voices due to the hunters."

"So how do we get rid of it?"

Spock looked hesitant, then shook his head. "Uncertain, Captain. We have several theories which we continue to pursue. I am confident, however, that we will be able to resolve the problem in a relatively short space of time."

"It better be, Spock, because time is the one thing we're running out of. Right, Kor?" Silence answered him. "Kor?"

"Captain," T'zeela said. "We've lost contact with the Klingon flagship."

"Shields up," Kirk snapped at Sulu. "And keep a close watch on those cruisers," he added. "Have they responded in any way to the raising of our shields?"

"Negative, Captain. No increase in engine power, nothing to indicate they're about to move. They're just holding position."

"Damn it, Kali, what's going on? Why did Kor break contact?"

She hesitated for a long moment, obviously troubled by his request, and wondering if it put her in the position of possibly betraying her people. At last she answered. "I expect he had decided it had become too dangerous to allow the crews of our ships to hear any more."

"Why? And dangerous to whom?"

"We are not a wealthy race, Kirk, you know that. Many of the planets of the Empire are barren, rocky, producing little." She hesitated again, her eyes filled with worry. "Surely you can appreciate our dilemma."

"Meaning that the Klingons might try to . . ." He paused, searching for a more tactful word then *enslave*. "To . . . to appropriate the Taygetians for their own purposes?"

"Not Kor," Kali said quickly. "Never Kor, but there are

others . . . less patient and more hotheaded than he, who might decide to act."

"Thank you for your honesty, Kali. I know it wasn't easy for you, but it was essential if we're going to keep this situation under control."

"Captain, do you wish me to return to the ship?" Spock asked.

"No, stay where you are, and find a way to repair that rip. *I'll* worry about the Klingons."

Everyone looked abnormally grim-faced as he broke contact, and he knew his expression wasn't much happier. They were in a devil of a position, with power down and two Klingon battle cruisers off their flank . . . and their only hope to avoid a battle rested with a man who, Kirk was convinced, stood in imminent danger of losing his command.

Chapter Eleven

They were all ranged about the conference room gazing at him with feral, expectant expressions that filled him with a sense of dread. All these officers, these young wolves of the Empire, had been held in check by his authority, and the lack of a clear reason to fight. But all that had changed now. The stakes had just become frighteningly high.

"What is it, Kor? What have the Earthers discovered?" Kandi asked from where he straddled a chair, his arms folded on the back. His cruiser had not been a party to the earlier discussion.

Kor hesitated, and Karsul, his eyes glittering with malice, said, "Yes, Commander, tell them what the Earthers have discovered."

Too late Kandi realized that he had walked Kor into a vise. He threw his friend an apologetic glance, to which Kor replied with a small shake of the head. He then drew in a quick breath and, gripping the edge of the table, began.

"The human, Maslin, together with the Vulcan, has succeeded in translating the Taygetian song. To put it plainly, the creatures have the power to alter and create environments."

Kandi gave a low whistle, and dropped his chin onto his folded arms. "A most useful skill for people beset with less-than-perfect worlds. Not to sound disloyal, but even our home world is no blossoming paradise."

"If we use the mind-sifter will we be able to learn the secret of the Taygetians' power?" the chief medical officer of *Klothos* asked.

"There is no need to use the sifter," Kor replied. "The Taygetians use the power of their song coupled with an extremely high psychic ability to manipulate their environment. Learning their methods will do us little good, for as a race we show only the most rudimentary psychic ability, and the talent is very rare." The door to the conference room slid open, and Kali entered. Kor had ordered her back to the ship immediately upon the conclusion of Spock and Maslin's briefing. He wasn't precisely certain why he had called her back; maybe to provide a firsthand report of the breakthrough, maybe only to provide him with the support he so desperately needed. Her eyes met his, and he found himself soothed by her golden gaze. He gave her a slight nod, and she slid into a chair at the back of the room.

"What is all this talk of *learning* the Taygetian ability?" Tamboli, a young lieutenant who was an admirer and adherent of Karsul's, demanded as he flung himself out of his chair and began to pace the room. "Are we old women that we must negotiate and parley, and beg for crumbs from the Earthers? We are Klingons! We take what we want! Let us take these Taygetians. They will soon learn to bend to our bidding."

"Stupid fool," Kali said, rising from her chair. "And how will you 'bend' the Taygetians to your bidding?" she asked scornfully. "I have been on the planet, studied the creatures. Nothing we can do would affect them. They are totally oblivious to everything but their song. You will kill them all trying to make them obey, and all we will be left with is an empty world, and a mountain of rotting corpses."

"The Lieutenant Commander's point is well made, I think," Kor said softly.

Tamboli began to bluster, then Karsul rose smoothly from his chair, and placed a restraining hand on the younger man's shoulder. "Peace, friend, and it seems you were right, at least partially. Most of us may not have degenerated into women, but it seems we are led by them. Keep to your place, girl," he said with an arrogant look to Kali. "We will tell you when your services are required—and for what."

Kandi threw a nervous glance at Kor, fearful of how his commander would react to this slur against his bride, but Kor remained quiet and impassive.

Karsul rose from his chair and, swaggering forward, seated himself on the edge of the table. In this way he blocked Kor from the view of most of the room, and effectively usurped his position.

"All this talk of reforming worlds is well enough, but it is untimely. The real value of this gift that has been thrown into our laps is its power as a weapon. Time enough to make the deserts bloom when we have swept the humans and their allies from the galaxy. We have the power to devastate a world, but it requires ships and men and bombs. How much simpler to have the Taygetians sweep a world clean of all life. A few such demonstrations of our power, and the Federation would be begging for mercy."

"You haven't been listening," Kali said, obviously undeterred by his earlier rebuke. "We can't even communicate with the Taygetians, much less control them."

"But the humans have a man who will ultimately be able to communicate with the creatures," Karsul replied with a thin smile. "We must attack the *Enterprise*, destroy her, and take this Maslin. After a little 'persuasion' I am certain he will be more than willing to help us enslave the Taygetians."

"No!" Kali cried, advancing into the center of the room.

"They must not be harmed. They are magic, they are beauty. To use them would be wrong, it would be a blot on the honor of our race that could never be expunged." She looked beseechingly around the circle of stunned and angry faces. "Why? Why must we always kill? Is there no other way for us?"

"Traitor!" Karsul shouted, advancing on her with an upraised hand. "You're no Klingon, you're a puling Earther. You shame the uniform you wear."

She faced him defiantly, but her eyes were filled with fear as she watched his hand descending toward her upturned face. It never connected. Kor caught Karsul by the forearm, and threw him over his shoulder into a corner of the room. Spitting blood and teeth from his injured mouth, the young officer tried to rise. Kor moved languidly to him and, placing his boot in the middle of Karsul's chest, held him in place.

"So you want to attack and destroy the *Enterprise,* do you? You young fool, this is *Kirk* we're talking about. Not some useless desk pilot who just happens to have a ship. This man is a legend in his own time. He and his crew have faced and conquered dangers that have defeated even Imperial cruisers. And you *puppies,"* he spat out the word as if it tasted bad, "you puppies think you can take this man? I'm afraid you have much to learn of command," he stated quietly. No one contradicted him as he glanced quickly about the assembled officers. "Therefore, when and how we take on the *Enterprise* will be decided by *me."* Once more he slowly surveyed the room, watching his officers' eyes slide nervously away from his. A humorless smile curved his lips. "I'm so glad we all agree," he said dryly, and held out his hand to Kali. There wasn't a sound as he led her from the room.

"For once in your life would you please not argue with me!" Kor shouted down into his bride's face. She stayed stubbornly on the steps of the shuttle, clinging to the edges of the door with both hands.

"I am going with you to the *Enterprise*. I will not stay here alone."

"I don't want you to stay here. I want you to go back to Taygeta."

"No. That is no better. I have been away from you enough in the past few days. I am going to stay with you now."

"Gods give me patience," he moaned, lifting clenched fists into the air. "Kali, why do you think I am flying a shuttle to the *Enterprise* rather than using the transporter or taking a pilot?"

"You think they are going to make their move," she said, her throat suddenly very dry.

"Yes, and it would be far too easy to scatter my molecules across the galaxy and claim an accident, or place an assassin in the pilot's seat to kill me between here and the *Enterprise*. Now do you see why I need you on Taygeta to keep an eye on Quarag and the others? The last thing I need is to give Karsul a chance to seize the advantage by taking Maslin."

"Oh, Kor," she cried, her voice breaking a little on the words. "What if they kill you and I am far away? I cannot bear it! I cannot bear it," she repeated and, throwing her arms around his neck, clung to him with a desperation that almost snapped his own control.

He held her slender body tight against him, and rubbed his cheek against the top of her head, breathing in the fragrance of her hair. "If things should go badly, go to Kirk. He will protect you."

"Leave my people?" she asked, aghast.

"It will surely be better than life with Karsul, don't you think?" he asked, lifting her chin so he could look into her eyes.

"What are you, Kor? You're clearly not a Klingon anymore."

With a sigh he sat down on the steps of the shuttle and pulled her down next to him. "Yes I am," he said gently. "It's just that I'm an *older* Klingon now, and I've seen too many things to blindly accept Imperial dogma anymore. I say it now: Kirk is an honorable man and a fine soldier. I would welcome a chance to test my skill against his—but not here, not now. He has shown his integrity by maintaining the truce and sharing all the discoveries made by the landing party. I would not willingly prove myself false in the face of his probity. Besides," he said, pressing a soft kiss onto her cheek, "you said it well only a few minutes ago. Why *must* we always kill? Is there no other way for us? And if there is, is this perhaps not the time to try it?"

She ran her hand down his cheek, and sighed. "I will go back to Taygeta, but please let me transport down from the *Enterprise*. Grant me a little more time to be with you."

"I can think of nothing that would please me as much as having you with me." That crooked little smile that she so loved twisted his lips, and he leaned in to whisper in her ear. "And as for time to be with me . . . you, woman, will never escape from me. You will have to guide my tottering feet as I enter my dotage, and everyone will envy this old man with the beautiful young wife."

"Just see to it you stay alive to enjoy it," she retorted as she stood and stepped into the shuttle.

"Drink?" Kirk asked from where he stood near the beverage dispenser on the wall of the conference room.

"Just tea. If I start on anything stronger I might not stop," Kor said.

"Problems?" Kirk asked casually as he dialed up a tea and a coffee.

"Oh Kirk, you are a sly one," the Klingon said as he leaned back in his chair, and regarded the human with amusement. "You would just love to learn my weaknesses, wouldn't you?"

"I can probably guess some of them. Why else would you come alone in a shuttle, and send your wife back to the planet from the *Enterprise* rather than from your own ship?"

Kor waved a dismissing hand. "None of that matters right now. What concerns me more are the findings of the landing party. I must know your mind, Kirk. Otherwise, I may be forced to destroy you."

"You're welcome to try, but my crew and I will have something to say about that."

"Don't you think I know it? You are a legend, Kirk. To fight you and win would bring me great honor. To fight you and lose is not something I wish to contemplate."

"How about not fighting me at all?" the captain asked, leaning back to place his boots on the table, and regarding Kor over the rim of his coffee cup.

"That is the issue, isn't it? To fight or not to fight? To use the power of the Taygetians for good or for destruction? And if I leave the Taygetians to you what will your Federation do with them?"

A frown wrinkled Kirk's forehead. "Do with them? What do you mean do with them? We'll set up diplomatic contact, we'll send scientists to study them, and have them study us, and ultimately we'll offer them membership in the Federation which they can take or leave as they choose."

"You are either very naïve, Kirk, or you bluff very well." He rose from the chair, and began to pace the room. "But what about the other option, Captain? My young officers have seen it. Why not use the Taygetian power to destroy worlds?"

"It could be done, but it's not our style."

"Well, it's not my style either," Kor said harshly, as he whirled to face Kirk. "A clean fight—ship against ship, man against man, that I can accept; but as for the rest . . ." He ran a hand wearily across his face and sank once more into a chair. He sat silent for several moments, then gave Kirk an ironic glance. "I guess I'm getting old, but I seem to have lost my taste for wholesale slaughter on a planetary scale."

"If that's the result of aging, I could almost wish we could spread a dose of that radiation poisoning I ran into on

Gamma Hydra IV around the galaxy. Then, once we had all decided that peace was better than war, we could reverse the process."

"You're a dreamer, Kirk," Kor said with a humorless smile, and took a sip of tea. "War is the natural condition of all races. We'll no doubt stop fighting when the last living creature is gone, or the universe dies."

"I think you're too pessimistic. Peace is possible. Take the Vulcans or the Organians."

Kor made a face. "Thank you, I would rather not. In some ways the Organians are responsible for the problems I currently find myself beset with."

Kirk laced his hands behind his head, and regarded the Klingon for a long moment. He then swung his feet off the table, and leaned in on Kor. "Okay, enough of this discussion of philosophy. You obviously didn't come over here to debate the relative merits of war and peace, nor did you come solely to confess your own inner doubts. So what is it you want?"

"You are a man without subtlety or diplomacy, Kirk."

"As a Klingon you ought to find that refreshingly familiar."

Kor gave a short bark of laughter, and held up one hand. "A hit, indeed I concede the hit." He sobered quickly and, setting aside his tea mug, leaned in on Kirk until they were almost eye to eye. "All right, we will dispense with all this fencing. I am frightened." Kirk raised an eyebrow. "Yes, it is the truth. We are orbiting a planet whose inhabitants hold a terrifying power, and I don't know where my duty lies. If I leave Taygeta to the Federation will you use this weapon against my own people? And if I take Taygeta I will have to fight you, and . . ." He paused and, rising from his chair, turned his back on Kirk. He sucked in a deep breath as if steeling himself for some unpleasant confession, and said, "And frankly, I do not trust my own government not to misuse this power that I will give into their hands if I deliver the Singers. Then that leaves me with the third option, which is to destroy the Taygetians, and deny their secret to both sides."

"There's a fourth option that you've overlooked."

"Oh, what?" Kor demanded somewhat truculently as he rounded on Kirk.

"How about a situation in which the Taygetians, as a free and independent species, provide their talent to various races in exchange for goods and services?"

"Barter? Become merchants?"

"Sure, why not? You say many of your planets are poor and hostile, so let the Singers improve them for you, and you pay them for the service."

"You would allow this?"

"The Federation doesn't own the Taygetians. They'll be free to make any arrangements they wish."

"I don't know," Kor said so quietly that Kirk had to strain to hear him. "I don't know if I can trust you."

"There has to someday be a time for trust, Kor, and I think we've gone a long way toward proving that this just may be that time." Kirk rose, and moved around the table to the burly Klingon. They stood face-to-face for a moment, then Kirk said, "I pledge my honor that the Taygetians will not become a weapon in the hands of the Federation," and he held out his hand.

Kor slowly, hesitantly placed his dark hand in the human's fair one. "That is a pledge worthy of great respect. Very well, Kirk, I will leave Taygeta for the Taygetians."

Chapter Twelve

Kirk was escorting Kor back to his shuttle when Chekov's voice, agitation deepening his accent, came resounding over the open ship intercom.

"Captain! Captain Kirk, please report to the bridge at once!"

The two commanders exchanged glances, and Kirk leaped to a wall com, and thumbed it on. "Yes, Mr. Chekov, what seems to be the problem?"

"We're not quite certain, sir, but the Klingons seem to be doing something odd."

"On my way, Kirk out." He flipped off the com, and gave Kor an inquiring look.

The Klingon held out his hands helplessly, and shook his head. "I am as confused as you are, and perhaps it would be best if I did not set out in a small shuttle until I know precisely what is going on. May I accompany you to the bridge?"

"That might not be a bad idea, and frankly, Commander, I'd like to have you where I can keep an eye on you."

"A wise precaution, Captain," Kor said, falling into step

with the human. "Even though I can assure you I'm not going to sabotage your phasers."

They entered the bridge on the run, and indeed something odd was happening with the Klingon ships. They had pulled abruptly out of parking orbit, and were peeling off to either side of the *Enterprise*. Kirk leaped to the navigation console, and leaned in over Sulu's shoulder.

"Obviously trying to outflank us, and get us trapped against the planet. Take us out of here, Mr. Sulu."

"Aye, aye, sir. Which heading?"

"Straight up. I want maneuvering room."

They began to drift upward, and Kirk cursed the decaying dilithium crystals. He had forgotten how low they were on power, so instead of springing out of the trap that was closing around them they were crawling like an aged tortoise. Fortunately the two Klingon cruisers weren't in much better shape.

"If this was by your order, Kor, your timing was lousy," the captain called over his shoulder. "You should have given yourself more time to get off the *Enterprise*."

"Fortunately or unfortunately, this was not by my design. I would not have handled matters so crudely." He paused to clear his throat. "You see, I regret to inform you, but I think I am no longer in command of my ships."

"Well, we still have a few tricks up our sleeve. Who are we up against?"

"On *Klothos,* no doubt Karsul, my exec. On the other ship I don't know. I'm certain Kandi would not have betrayed me, but I don't know who they would have replaced him with. Karsul is behind this, however."

"What can you tell me about this Karsul?"

"Young, bright, but he is also hotheaded and inexperienced."

"A plus for our side," Kirk said, swinging back up to the command chair and seating himself.

"You seem awfully eager to spill your guts," Scotty suddenly rumbled from his position at the engineering consol. "How do we know we can trust *you?* Why would you want us to win over your own people?"

"He does have a point," Kirk said, cocking an eye up at the Klingon.

"Mr. Scott, believe me, I am fervently hoping that you will succeed because if you don't I'm either going to die with this ship or be executed by my former first officer, and in either case he will then take my wife. None of these prospects fills me with much joy."

"I'd say those are pretty compelling reasons for trusting you," Kirk said. "Mr. Sulu," he said, turning his attention to the navigator. "Bring up the shields and have phasers at the ready. As soon as we clear the planet I want to turn and get a shot at those two ships."

"Aye, sir."

Tense seconds passed as they waited to clear the planet. Kirk felt the hair on the back of his neck rising, and he hunched his shoulders as if expecting a blast of disruptor fire from behind them. They cleared the planet, and he began to release the breath he hadn't even been aware he was holding, when suddenly a new sight drove all the air from his lungs. Directly before them, some three hundred kilometers distant, a Klingon cruiser winked out of warp space. It raced down on them like some avenging bird of prey, and it was apparent it wasn't suffering from the power drain that afflicted the *Enterprise* and the two other cruisers.

"Captain!"

"Oh my God!"

"What do we do?"

"Captain, look!"

The bridge exploded into a discordant babble of frightened voices. Kirk ignored them all, as did Sulu, who kept his eyes riveted on the captain's face. "Down! Take us back where we came from."

"Karsul must have summoned them in secret, and they have been holding beyond the range of the harmonic effect. I should have killed that young man months ago," Kor murmured almost to himself.

"I hope you won't think me gauche for saying so, but I wish you had too," Kirk said ironically while Sulu's deft fingers played over the console, and the Enterprise struggled to respond. A blast of disruptor fire hit the upper edge of their shield as the ship dropped back behind the protective bulk of the planet. The great ship shuddered under the impact of the blast, and people struggled to remain in their seats. Kor gripped the back of Kirk's chair, and in a low voice said, "We are going right back into the line of fire from two other ships."

"I know, but at least we know they don't have the firepower of our friend overhead."

"Unfortunately he will soon come to join the party."

"And then we very well may be damned, but we'll deal with that when it happens." Kirk glanced down at a computer graphic of the tactical situation, and a small smile curved his lips. "Mr. Sulu, take us up to warp speed, and then bring us out at coordinates zero, two, seven."

"Captain, you're burnin' up what little power we have left!" Scotty objected, taking a few steps toward the command chair.

"I have no choice, Mr. Scott. We can sit here while they batter down our shields, or we can use what power we've got offensively."

Kor, who had been staring at the schematic, suddenly smiled and nodded. "I see what you are up to, and yes, Karsul will fall for it."

Seconds ticked past, and the third Klingon cruiser came plunging into warp space after the fleeing *Enterprise*.

"Captain," Chekov said, and there was a nervous catch in his voice.

"I see him, Ensign, but you keep your attention on those other ships. Ready phasers."

"Phasers ready, sir."

They hit the coordinates, and Sulu brought them out down from warp speed directly between the two Klingon vessels.

"Fire!" Chekov hit the firing button, and twin beams of energy lanced out at the ship before them. "Now! Take us out of here Mr. Sulu! Now!"

The *Enterprise* drifted down between the two Klingon ships as they each discharged their disruptors, and caught each other in a vicious crossfire. There was a loud cheer from the bridge crew.

"Very nice, Captain, but what do you do for an encore?" Kor asked as he watched the third, fully powered, cruiser come haring after them.

"Ask me again in a minute. I might be able to tell you by then," Kirk replied as he knuckled at his chin with one hand.

"Holy shit!" Ragsdale yelled as a burst of disruptor fire sizzled the air next to his left ear. He went one way, and the tray of food he had been carrying went the other as he dived frantically for cover.

Maslin, who had been staring with maniacal fascination at the keyboard of the synthesizer while a group of nearly one hundred cubs sat clustered about the instrument waiting patiently for his next musical passage, went diving behind the synthesizer. He realized that he would only draw the fire toward his precious machine so, keeping low, he made a mad dash for one of the tents. Behind him he heard one of the cubs scream in agony as a blast of disruptor fire hit its unprotected flesh, and he almost raced back to help it. Sanity reasserted itself before he had done more than turn, and he continued his dash for cover.

His breath was rasping in his throat, and there was a burning in his lungs by the time he covered the thirty yards that separated him from the tent, so he simply lay on the ground behind the flimsy cover, and tried to calm the frantic hammering of his heart. Around him he could hear cubs singing in discordant terror, and occasionally one or two of them would come flopping past. The tiny cub who had a patch of golden hair on one flank, and who was a particular favorite of the composer's, went howling past the tent. Maslin reached out and, wrapping his arms around the round, furry body, pulled it into cover with him. It seemed the least he could do since the creature had saved him that day on the beach when he had been overcome by his illness. The creature moaned in a minor key, and buried its face in the human's shoulder. They huddled together while energy bolts ripped through the camp.

Across the camp McCoy maintained a steady monologue about the perfidy and duplicity of Klingons while Spock, phaser out, scanned the cliff walls searching for their attackers.

"Damn Klingons! I knew we were making a big mistake trusting them. Why Jim felt he had to rely on—"

"Doctor," Spock interrupted, "since you do not have a phaser could you perhaps try to make yourself useful by contacting the *Enterprise,* and apprising the captain of our situation?"

"I was going to do that," McCoy replied in an aggrieved tone.

"You surprise me," Spock said dryly as he squeezed off a shot at an unwary head which had appeared over the top of a boulder some three-quarters of the way up the right cliff.

McCoy ignored him, having finally managed to reach the ship. T'zeela's voice came faintly through the communicator, overlayed and punctuated with heavy static.

"Doct . . . one moment, the captain will . . . soon . . ."

"Jim!" McCoy shouted into the communicator. "What's going on up there?"

"Klingons, we're . . . ." The rest of his words were lost in a long burst of static.

"What? Repeat please, you're not coming through."

There was a momentary clearing, and Kirk's voice came through clearly. "We're under heavy attack up here so I'm afraid you're on your own. Take care of them as best you can. Kirk out."

"Captain? Captain? Jim!" McCoy demanded, shaking the communicator and twisting the tuning dial, but there was no answer.

"Don't try to reopen communication, Doctor. It is apparent the captain is fully occupied, and should not be distracted by us."

"So what do you suggest we do?"

"Fight, and hope for the best."

"I can think of other people I would prefer to have in command of a battle situation," McCoy muttered as he thought back on that time when Spock had taken command after the Galileo 7 shuttle craft had been drawn off course and forced to land on Taurus II. A bolt of deadly energy buried itself in the sand next to his leg, and McCoy flinched back behind the tent.

"I am aware of your doubts about my command abilities in a combat situation, Doctor, but believe me." He paused and fired, and a small figure jerked and tumbled down the cliff face. "I am capable of fighting when I am forced to it."

"I'm glad to hear it, Mr. Spock," McCoy concluded and, hunkering down next to the tent, he stared at his own quarters some fifty feet away, and bitterly regretted leaving his phaser among his belongings in the tent.

Maslin too was feeling useless, and more frightened than he had ever felt in his life as he lay huddled behind the tent with the Taygetian clutched in his arms. He hoped that no errant shot would find his hiding place, and each time there was a whine from a weapon being fired he could feel his body pull in on itself as if anticipating the burning pain that would precede death from disruptor fire.

He heard the thud of running feet, and he looked up to see

Donovan racing across the open center of the camp heading for new cover. There was a streak of red-tinged energy from somewhere up the cliff, and Donovan tumbled to the ground. His forward momentum had carried him to within feet of Maslin's hiding place. The composer crawled out and, grabbing the officer by the shoulder, he tried to pull him back behind the tent. Donovan rolled ponderously onto his back, his hand flopping uselessly in the sand, and Maslin stared into the burned and bloody mass that had been a face. Turning aside, he vomited into the sand and, wrapping his arms around himself, he sat back on his heels and shook. The Taygetian gave a whine of despair, and began to dig out a hole beneath the edge of the tent. This accomplished, it huddled in the hole with just its eyes peering out between the bottom of the tent and the sand.

A whine of fire brought Maslin back to his surroundings, and he scurried back behind the tent. He then peered out, noticing the phaser that lay where it had fallen from Donovan's hand. It was a scant three feet away, and he decided to risk it. Dropping down onto his belly he crawled on knees and elbows out to the phaser and, grabbing it, went hauling back into cover.

As he inspected the weapon, familiarizing himself with its operation, he wondered where in all this madness Uhura had gotten to? He pictured her killed, like Donovan, and his chest was squeezed with a pain so sharp that for a moment he thought he was suffering from a heart attack.

In his youth he had done some hunting at his family's cabin in the Adirondacks, and he found that the old reflexes still held. Lying prone on the ground, he steadied the phaser on his left forearm, and waited patiently. He saw a flicker of movement at the base of one cliff, and sighting carefully he pulled off a shot. There was a wail, and the running figure dropped. Smiling viciously he thought, *That's for Donovan, and for the cub you killed. Wish Uhura could have seen that,* he ruminated as he waited for another target to present itself.

That would have shut her up about how I lack the training to look out for myself.

Back in the Klingon camp Kali struggled in her bonds where she sat tied to the center pole of her tent. She felt the rope rasp harshly across the skin of her wrists, but it didn't give in the least. An hour ago ten more men had transported down to the camp, and she had overheard Karsul order the now-augmented landing party to attack and destroy the humans. She had been terrified that he would order her back to the ship and, not wanting that to happen, and also wishing to warn the humans, she had tried to slip out of camp. Quarag had caught her before she had reached the bottom of the hill, and he had tied her in her tent.

Now, off in the distance, she could hear the whine of weapons being fired, and she redoubled her efforts to work free. Five minutes later she was exhausted and no closer to freedom, and all she could feel was the warm trickle of blood over her abused hands. She looked desperately about the tent, and spotted her pack. She had a blade stored in there, if she could only manage to reach it.

Sucking in a deep breath she quieted her mind, steadied her nerves and then gave a quick heave. The pole swayed, but held. Three tries later she managed to bring it down, and with it the entire tent. She lay under the suffocating folds of material and tried to get her bearings, then propelled herself across the floor by means of small pushes with her bound feet.

Ten minutes later she was free, and came climbing out from under the fallen tent. Quarag had taken her disruptor, and a quick search failed to produce an extra. Grumbling, she tore a long piece of fine wire out of one of the geocorders, and jerked it experimentally several times between her hands. Since she had failed to find a weapon here she would simply have to make one, she thought with a predatory little smile, and she slipped off toward the sound of the fighting.

She ran swiftly toward the human camp without bothering

to use cover. She assumed that Karsul's men would have all their attention centered on the humans, and never suspect an assault from the rear. She reached the left outcropping of rock that formed one arm of the sheltering cove in which the humans were camped, and here she became a good deal more covert. She didn't want to go stumbling blindly into one of the men she had come to hunt.

Taking cover she listened, trying to pinpoint the location of one of the attackers from the sound of his disruptor fire. There seemed to be someone a scant thirty yards from her sheltering rock. Holding her breath she peered over the top of the boulder, and spotted the head and burly shoulders of one of the new arrivals. Pulling back down she slipped wraithlike from rock to rock until she was directly behind her quarry.

From this proximity she could hear his heavy breathing, and an occasional muttered curse as a bolt of phaser fire came uncomfortably close. She tested the wire between her hands, and was suddenly assailed by doubt. She was about to kill one of her own kind, a comrade in arms. And why? To save a group of Earthers who were her traditional enemies. She hugged her arms about her body, back pressed against the rough surface of the rocks, and tried to decide what to do. She wished Kor were here to advise her.

The thought of her husband steadied her, and she remembered how days ago she had decided if it were a choice between Kor and the Empire she would take Kor. It seemed now that that choice had come upon her. It was apparent that Kor was no longer in command of his ships, and if he were taken he would be killed. As for herself . . . her fate was far less enviable. She would end up as chattel to the man who had murdered her husband.

Her jaw tightened with determination and, keeping her back against the rocks, she slipped up behind her prey. The soft sand muffled any sound from her footfalls, and the man was dead before he knew he had been attacked. Kali calmly removed her garrot from the man's throat and, picking up his fallen disruptor, brushed the clinging sand from its barrel. She then settled down to look for targets.

There was a flash of black and silver from the rocks to her right, and she quietly aimed and blew away his head. Two more fell to her merciless fire before the remaining Klingons realized that they were under attack from the rear.

Down in the camp Spock also realized that something had changed. There was still the whine of disruptor fire from the cliffs, but none of it was being directed *into* the camp. Instead the Klingons seemed to be battling with some unknown assailant.

"What the hell's going on?" McCoy asked as he cautiously lifted his head from the protection of his arms.

"I'm not certain, Doctor, but the Klingons appear to be under attack."

"Well of course they're under attack, Spock," McCoy said in exasperation. "What do you think we've been doing for the past fifteen minutes?"

Spock's lips narrowed into a thin line. "Try not to be more obtuse than usual, Doctor. The Klingons are firing *behind* them."

"But who could it be? Taygetians?"

"Highly unlikely. If the Singers won't protect themselves why should they protect us?"

"Good point."

"At any rate we have no more time to debate the issue. This would seem an opportune time for an assault," the Vulcan said, pulling out his communicator. "Mr. Ragsdale."

"Aye, sir," the security chief's voice came back over the communicator.

"What is your situation?"

"I'm down in good cover. Yeoman Chou is with me."

"Excellent. What of Mr. Brentano?"

"I saw him go down several minutes ago."

Spock nodded and, switching frequency, signaled Uhura. "Lieutenant?"

"Here, sir."

"Is Mr. Maslin with you?"

"No, and I don't know where he is." Her voice was ragged with worry.

"Is any one else with you?"

"No, sir, I'm alone."

"Well ready yourself, we're going to charge the cliffs."

"Yes, sir."

"And what about me, Spock?" McCoy asked.

"You have no weapon, and I would prefer that you waited here. Also, I would like to have your services available to tend any of us who might be hit."

"First time you've ever expressed any confidence in my abilities."

"You are, one is forced to admit, Doctor, better than nothing."

"Thanks, what a vote of confidence. I hope you do get shot so I can make you eat those words," McCoy muttered, but his blue eyes were dark with worry.

Spock tried unsuccessfully to raise Donovan, and finally decided with regret that the young man had been hit. He knew Maslin carried no communicator so he put the composer out of his mind for the moment. Cautiously lifting his head, he eyed the cliffs, and settled upon a plan of attack. In a few quick words he informed everyone of their targets, and then dropped back to wait until there was a particularly vicious barrage of fire, none of which came into the camp.

"Now!" he ordered, and they all exploded from their places of cover heading for the cliffs.

Spock saw Maslin come charging out from behind a tent, a phaser clutched in his hand. "Back!" he shouted. "Go back!" but Maslin kept running.

Uhura suddenly glanced back, and saw the composer.

Spock wondered bitterly if she were going to break discipline and go back after her lover, but she once more lived up to his high estimation of her abilities. She paused, made a quick adjustment to her phaser, and fired a quick stunning burst at Maslin. He went down like a rag doll, and Spock nodded in satisfaction and continued his sprint for the cliff.

They were beginning to take a little fire as the Klingons realized their danger, but with that withering fire from their backs they were unable to make a concentrated effort to stop the humans. Spock saw four more of the Klingons fall as his people opened fire, and that seemed to break their morale. There was a concentrated rush for the beach as the five remaining Klingons tried to escape the deadly crossfire. One more fell, victim to the humans' unknown benefactor, and Yeoman Chou went down clutching her leg as a last random shot from the Klingons managed to hit.

Lieutenant Uhura hurried to the other woman, and Spock saw a small figure rise out of the rocks. Shading his eyes against the glare of the sun on the crystal cliffs Spock recognized Kali. He waved, and she came leaping like a goat down the rock wall to join him.

"Thank you for your timely help," he said formally. "It would have gone badly for us if you hadn't intervened."

"My pleasure."

The Vulcan frowned, and glanced about. "How many did we kill?"

"Ten, I think."

"But there were only five—"

"In our landing party," she interrupted. "Yes, that's right, but some reinforcements arrived a few hours ago."

"And the *Enterprise* is currently under attack," Spock murmured as he began to assemble the entire picture.

"I think we can safely assume that my husband is no longer in command, and that the truce is off."

"Unfortunately I must concur."

Brentano and Ragsdale gathered Chou up in a fireman's

carry, and they headed back to camp. McCoy was bent over Maslin, running his tricorder over the composer's limp body.

"Is he all right?" Uhura demanded, rushing over to his side.

"Yeah, the stun didn't do him any real harm, but I'm not happy with these other readings."

"The disease?"

"Yes, it's on the rise again. Spock, help me get him into his tent."

After Maslin was safely ensconced in bed, Spock moved to the large computer that had been tied into the synthesizer, and began making adjustments.

"What are you doing, Mr. Spock?" Uhura asked, having been shooed away by McCoy.

"This computer was acting as a link between the *Enterprise*'s computer and the synthesizer. It may be possible to reactivate the link with the *Enterprise,* and determine how the battle is going. I could use the communicators," he said, answering her unspoken question. "But it would distract the captain, and that I will not do."

Kali drifted over to join them, and soon Ragsdale and Brentano had gathered about Spock, waiting tensely while he worked. There was a flicker of color, and then the display screen of the synthesizer lit up with a strange elongated view of the main screen of the *Enterprise.* They watched in silence for several moments, trying to make sense out of what they were seeing. Then Kali exclaimed, "There are *three* cruisers present. Where did the third one come from?"

Spock's face tightened into even grimmer lines, and he began to punch a request for data into the computer. There was a whir and a chatter, and then the cold, impersonal female voice of the computer began to speak.

"Screens down fifty-two percent. Phasers operating at one-third normal power, maneuverability reduced by sixty-one percent due to—"

"Stop!" Spock ordered. "Calculate maximum operating time remaining for affected systems."

"Working."

Tension was turning his head and neck into a mass of pain, and he bitterly regretted the series of circumstances which had left him trapped helplessly here on the planet's surface while far overhead, in the frigid darkness of space, his captain battled for his life. Mendez was very young and inexperienced and might be unable to provide Kirk with the sort of split-second information he would require if the *Enterprise* was to survive this encounter.

Suddenly he balled up one fist, and drove it into the protective crate that had held the synthesizer on its journey to the planet. The metal crumpled beneath the power of his Vulcan assault, and the other people around him jumped nervously. It had been an action beyond his own volition, and after he made it he immediately regretted the emotional display. He arranged his face into its usual expression of bland impassivity, and returned his attention to the display screen, watching as the picture from the *Enterprise* buckled and wavered under the pounding the ship was enduring.

McCoy, accompanied by a shaky Maslin, joined the rest of the landing party. Maslin slowly walked to Uhura, and stood gazing thoughtfully at her.

"I didn't appreciate what you did," he said at last.

"I didn't think you would."

"Then why did you do it?"

"To protect you."

"But they killed Donovan and the cub," he said miserably. "And I wanted to do something."

He had that little-boy-lost look again, and Uhura felt her heart go out to him. No doubt this was the first time he had ever seen death, and she could still remember her own shock and confusion when, after a pitched battle against rebels on Wynet V, she had found herself staring down at the twisted body of the captain of the small cruiser that had been her first assignment out of the academy. She reached out to him and, folding her arms around his thin form, pulled him tight against her body.

"I've made Yeoman Chou as comfortable as possible, but she really needs to be in sick bay," McCoy announced to Spock, pulling the Vulcan's attention away from the compuscreen on the synthesizer.

"Regretfully, Doctor, that is not an option that is at present open to us."

"Why? What's going on?" Maslin asked, lifting his head from Uhura's shoulder.

"How do you feel about becoming a lost human colony?" Ragsdale grunted before Spock had a chance to reply.

"Why? What is it?" the composer demanded again.

"The *Enterprise* is under heavy attack," Kali said quietly, "and it seems unlikely she can survive. Your brilliant captain notwithstanding," she quickly added, to soothe the humans who were already starting to bristle at her unconscious slur of Kirk.

"I don't think your visions of a pastoral existence are likely, Mr. Ragsdale," Spock said dryly. "If the *Enterprise* is destroyed we will then be captured or killed by the remaining Klingons."

Everyone stood clumped in miserable silence, and watched the events unfolding on the screen. Suddenly the computer stopped its steady chattering and announced, "Time to full systems failure—nineteen minutes, seven seconds."

There was a stir from the assembled people, but no one spoke. There really wasn't anything to say.

Kirk, like his first officer, was also aware of the steady loss of essential systems. He kept one eye on the tiny readout on the arm of his chair, and one eye on the screen, trying to keep one jump ahead of their attackers.

The *Enterprise* shuddered and bucked under another blast of deadly disruptor fire, and people went sprawling in all directions. Kor grabbed the arm of Kirk's chair, and pulled himself to his feet.

"Perhaps you ought to consider heading in another direction," he said softly into Kirk's ear. "The captains of those other ships are beginning to hit more often because they know where you are heading."

"I too know where I'm heading, and I have no intention of wasting power in useless maneuverings."

"You mean you have a *plan?*"

Kirk winced a bit, and even managed a smile at the unconscious and incredulous emphasis. "Yes, Commander, I actually have a plan." And he turned his attention back to the screen.

He was grateful when Kor stepped silently back to his position behind the command chair, for he didn't want to elaborate upon his plan—he didn't much like it himself, but he could see no alternative. Never, in all his years of narrow escapes and tight spots, had he viewed suicide as the only option, but now he had reached that decision. He knew that the Klingons could not be permitted to take and enslave the Taygetians, and use their awesome power against the Federation. He also knew that the Klingons would be unable to mount another expedition to Taygeta before the phenomenon consumed the Singers' sun, and they went down into a cold, dark and silent death. It seemed a cruel solution, but at least the people of hundreds of other worlds would be safe from the Taygetian power in Klingon hands. Having recognized all this, his only remaining duty was to remove the Klingon cruisers.

That the *Enterprise* and all her crew had to be sacrificed in the process almost gagged him, but he held firm to his duty. His only problem now would be tricking the Klingons into following him in this last dangerous gamble.

The second planet in the Taygetian system loomed up on the screen. Kirk sucked in a deep breath and held it for a moment while he took a last fond look about the bridge of his ship, and the people who had been his comrades for so many years.

"Mr. Sulu, drop all shields, and channel the power directly to the engines. Mr. Chekov, please do the same with the phaser banks. Then Mr. Sulu, build up full speed and take us right over the top of that planet, and drop us down the other side."

"But Captain," Mr. Scott began as he took a half step toward Kirk.

The Captain held up one hand to forestall him. "Please, Scotty, give me everything you've got."

"But it will horribly overload the crystals!" he said, his accent thick with distress. "It may even shatter them!"

"It won't matter once we clear the planet," Kirk said quietly, and Kor stared at him in amazement and admiration.

"The phenomenon. You are going to take us into the phenomenon, and like hounds after a hare they will follow us in before they realize what is happening."

"That is the general idea, yes." There was a murmur from the bridge crew, quickly silenced.

"Transfers complete, Captain," Sulu sang out after receiving a confirming nod from a white-faced Chekov.

"Full power on my command." Kirk tensely watched the screen, waiting until the Klingons were virtually within range and rushing carelessly forward, emboldened by the loss of their enemy's shields. "Now!" he shouted, and brought his hand down as if signaling the start of a race.

The *Enterprise* leaped like a startled deer, and raced for the planet. Sulu sent her skimming over the barren surface, not wasting speed or time by making a large arc. Then they were over the other side, and the luminescent tendrils from the space/time warp drifted about them.

Kirk heard a sound like delicate chiming bells, and in the next instant tasted the same sound. He shook his head, trying to keep his mind clear as it was overloaded with a barrage of bizarre and alien sensations. All around him people began to lose control. Some giggled and capered about the bridge, while others stared in rapt contemplation of something only they could see.

The instruments on the bridge began to glow with a pale, multicolored witch's fire that danced along the floor and ceiling in time to that strange and beautiful chiming. Everything was beginning to warp and fade, and Kirk realized he had lost touch with his own body. He could see it seated there in the insubstantial command chair, but *he* wasn't there.

"Captain," he heard Kor say softly. "It was a privilege to know you. You are worthy to be a Klingon." And then they were gone.

Chapter Thirteen

Spock stared down at the now blank screen. His shoulders and neck were rigid with tension, and his hands slowly tightened on the edge of the synthesizer, leaving deep gouges from the pressure of his Vulcan fingers.

Maslin instinctively reached out and, grabbing Spock by one wrist, tried to pull his hand away. This touch seemed to bring the Vulcan back to himself. He straightened slowly, almost painfully, and turned to face the white-faced landing party.

"Where have they gone, Mr. Spock?" Uhura asked, her voice small with shock and anguish.

"Who can say, Lieutenant?" He looked back at the blank, gray synthesizer screen. "Perhaps into an alternate universe, or perhaps they are still in our universe, but in an altered state."

"Any chance of your miraculous captain pulling the ship out of this one?" Maslin asked. The words were sarcastic; the tone wasn't.

"No," came Spock's blunt, hope-killing reply.

Kali stood off to one side of the humans, her arms wrapped tightly about her body as if she feared that if she let go she would fly into a million pieces. Her face was impassive, but her eyes were wells of anguish. Uhura stepped to her side, and placed a comforting hand on the other woman's shoulder.

"At least he did not die at Karsul's hands," Kali whispered, forcing the words past stiff lips. "He would have liked the way your captain lured them in after him. To die in such a heroic fashion would have . . ." Her control broke, and she began to cry in small, almost silent little sobs that nonetheless shook her slender body with their muted violence.

"Are they dead?" Maslin asked bluntly.

"I don't think so," Spock replied, but he forbore to give his reason for this belief. It was so illogical that he almost cringed when he admitted it to himself. Still, it could not be denied that somewhere deep within himself he believed that Kirk still lived. That powerful bond that held him to his captain was still there, and he believed, however foolish it might seem, that that bond would not be broken until death claimed one of them.

Maslin dug his hands into his pockets and, narrowing his eyes, stared up the glittering cliffs to where the Singers still continued their world-spanning song. He suddenly whirled, and sliding onto the bench began to bring up the synthesizer.

"What are you doing?" Spock asked, looking down into the small man's intense white face.

"The Taygetians have the power to manipulate matter, possibly even time and space in some way we don't understand. So let's get them to bring back the *Enterprise* for us."

"You cannot be serious. We have no evidence that the Taygetians possess such a power."

The composer shifted on the bench to stare challengingly up at the Vulcan. "And we have no evidence that they *can't*, so I suggest we try it. It's better than sitting here passively waiting to die."

McCoy stepped into the conversation. "You know what I told you in the tent. The disease is beginning to flare again. You try a stunt like this and you *will* die."

"Doctor, we're *all* going to die if we don't do something. That phenomenon is only a few hundred kilometers from the sun. If it goes we'll all die—you, me, the Taygetians, everyone!"

"What makes you think you can succeed now when every other attempt has failed?" Spock asked.

"Fear," Maslin said succinctly. "It's a pretty damn good motivator for a creative insight."

"That is not logical."

"Yes, and that's why I'm a musician, and you're not. In spite of your great technical ability you could never be an artist, because at base, once all the mathematics and the theory is removed there is only *art,* and that comes from the soul and the heart, not the mind." He made a few more adjustments with the synthesizer, and fed back in the Taygetian language program that he and Spock had so laboriously created. "I understand most of the basic grammar and vocabulary now so our only problem is finding a way to talk to them—to make them understand."

"Sounds like a mighty long shot," McCoy said quietly.

"It is, but Doctor, it's the only shot we've got." He began to play, a hauntingly beautiful improvisation based on the Taygetian song, and the cubs returned, drawn as he had known they would be by the heartrending music.

Uhura stood rigidly at Kali's side, watching the play of Maslin's long fingers across the keyboards, the way muscles and tendons tightened in his neck when he threw back his head and half closed his eyes as he concentrated on the music he was creating. She had seen McCoy remonstrating with the composer, and she knew with a deadly certainty what had been said. She had also seen Maslin's dismissive gesture, and her heart and mind were filled with an anguish so great that it was almost a physical pain.

No, please no, she thought frantically. She wanted to rush to his side, beg him not to make this effort, but she knew it was useless. Men like Kirk, or Maslin, or Spock followed only the dictates of their consciences, and acted upon their own driving codes of honor and duty. Pleas about love and need could distress and upset them, but never, never turn them from that sacred dream that they all served in varying ways.

"Sometimes I think it is a curse to love such men," Kali said softly. The Klingon woman had recovered herself, and now stood once more proud and controlled at Uhura's side.

"And you would know, don't you?"

"Alas, yes."

"And how do you handle it?"

"By loving and supporting him, and praying to the gods to return him safe to me when he has finished following his dreams."

"But why must our dreams always be so different?" Uhura whispered miserably.

"Go to him, give him what help you can," Kali said softly, and gave Uhura a gentle shove. Uhura walked quickly to the synthesizer and, standing behind Maslin, placed her hands possessively on his shoulders. He threw her a quick smile and returned to his music, and she stood quietly holding him as if by her very physical presence she could keep him safe.

Kali watched for several moments, then walked away to sit quietly staring out to sea while the song wove its mysterious pattern about her, and brought some measure of ease to her wounded heart.

"Respond! God damn you! Why won't you respond!" Guy suddenly shouted while beating his fists desperately on the edge of the synthesizer.

"Hey, take it easy, Mr. Maslin," Ragsdale said, placing a soothing hand on the smaller man's shoulders. "Here, have some tea, and take a break."

"No time. We have no time to take a break," Maslin muttered, but he allowed the security chief to assist him off the bench, and over to a camp stool.

The uninjured and ambulatory members of the landing party had gathered in an encouraging group about the synthesizer. Also joining the humans were the cubs. They sat in a polite and very interested circle about the synthesizer, but nothing Maslin tried drew any response from the Taygetians. They sat like cuddly little stuffed animals on a toy store's shelves, their mouths tipped in that never-ending smile, and their blue eyes happy and alert.

At sunset a mournful wind had risen which occasionally sent particles of sand stinging into their faces, and whipped their parkas about their trembling bodies. Only one moon was up this night, and it raced across the sky with the clouds scudding now and then across its pale, luminous face. It was terribly cold, and Spock had ordered that every available heater and all the lights be placed around the instrument. Maslin looked fragile, almost transparent, and the Vulcan had begun to fear that he would not live long enough to find the solution that might save the *Enterprise*.

Ragsdale thrust a steaming mug of tea into Maslin's hands, and Uhura wrapped her arms about his slight body, holding him close as she would a child. He sighed, and rested his head on her shoulder. His eyes were two hollows of blackness, and McCoy edged closer to Spock.

"I can't give him any more cordrazine."

"I know."

"He's dying before our eyes."

"We are all staring into that void, Doctor. If Mr. Maslin's efforts can save us then we must allow him to continue."

"Better one than all of us, huh?" McCoy grunted.

"It is the more—"

"Don't say it, Spock," McCoy said. "I really don't think I can stand to hear that word one more time."

"Why won't they respond to me?" Maslin asked, his voice small as he huddled within the folds of his parka. "I'm doing everything right, I know I am."

"I'm sure you are," Uhura said, stroking his hair. "Maybe they just can't relate to us."

"But music is music," he objected, struggling a bit to sit up.

"I know, I know," she said soothingly as she would to a frightened foal, and held him still, trying to force him to relax. "Guy, it's not your fault."

"Then whose fault is it?" he demanded. "I'm the big hotshot who was supposed to solve all the problems!"

"Without you we wouldn't even have gotten this far."

"I don't want to die on this ball of dirt," he suddenly whispered. "I want to go home, marry you, write my symphony."

Uhura swallowed the lump that had formed in her throat. "You won't, and you will."

"Then you will marry me?" he asked, his face recovering a measure of that devil-may-care expression that she had learned to love.

"Did you ever doubt it?"

"You wouldn't have married me that first night."

"No," she agreed with a laugh. "I thought you were abominable."

"And now?" he asked, his eyes pleading with her.

"I love you," she said simply, and then looked about with embarrassment, hoping that they hadn't been overheard. She noted with relief that the rest of the landing party had drawn politely away from them.

He reached up and cupped her cheek in one hand. She turned her head to press a quick kiss into the palm of his hand, and was alarmed and upset by the icy coldness of his skin. She quickly gathered his hands in hers, and began to breathe on them.

"No," he said, pulling his hands free, and sliding them around her body. "Give me that breath where it will do me some good."

She nodded, and they kissed. It was a desperate, clinging embrace, and in that moment she wished that they could just forget this desperate struggling to survive. All she wanted was to crawl away into their tent, and lie in his arms until death came to take them both. Tears burned in her eyes, and she could feel the warm trail as they overflowed and slid down her cheeks. He kissed away the salty moisture, then held her face between his hands, and stared at her.

"Don't cry, my darling. We don't have the time for that kind of self-indulgence."

"What should I do then?" she asked, forcing a smile to her lips.

"Sing for me."

"What would you like to hear?"

"Something I wrote—naturally," he said with a flash of his old sardonic humor.

"Naturally."

She cast about, and finally decided on a delicate little arietta that he had written for her in those first days when he had come aboard the *Enterprise*. He had used a bit of Italian verse from the seventeenth century for the text, and she loved the little song with a passion surpassing any other piece of music. She cradled him once more in her arms, and began to sing. The landing party gathered around to listen, and even the cubs ceased their constant warblings and joined in the circle, listening with the greatest of interest.

"Lasci ancore posare un stanco, un stanco." Her rich, warm voice reached a long sustained note, and the pure tone spun like a crystal ball supported by the arching waters of a fountain. There was a melodic sigh from the Taygetian cubs, and Guy's eyes flew open.

"My God! My God! My God!" he kept repeating as he struggled to his feet.

"What? What is it?" Uhura cried, alarmed by his agitation. She leaped to her feet and caught him by the arm, trying to stop his frenzied pacings.

"That's it, that's it."

"What?" Kali broke in.

"What's *it?*" came a chorus of voices.

"Please calm down!" came an order from McCoy that was ignored.

"Don't you see?" Maslin demanded, whirling on Spock and reaching out for the Vulcan with desperate hands. "We've been working instrumentally! Their whole orientation is *vocal*. They thought we were making pretty sounds at them, but it didn't have any *meaning*, couldn't have. After all, we weren't talking."

"Are you sure?" Spock asked cautiously.

"It has to be. Damn it! I understand that language, and every bit of logic and intelligence tells me they ought to be responding. So why aren't they? Simple. We weren't using the right medium. Besides, we've got empirical proof."

"Oh?" Spock raised a skeptical eyebrow.

Maslin grabbed Uhura, and yanked her over to face the Vulcan. "Her! They responded to Uhura's singing. They don't understand the words since it's another language, but they recognized it as communication."

"Come on, Spock," McCoy urged, moving in to join the debate. "It's at least worth a try."

"I was not hesitating because I doubted the efficacy of such an attempt, Doctor, but because I was trying to determine the most effective way to make the attempt."

"Simple," Maslin said, walking Uhura over to the synthesizer. "Uhura sings into the synthesizer. The machine translates her sounds and words into Taygetian, and . . . and well, we're home free."

"Perhaps. But let us not forget that the Taygetians are also telepathic creatures."

"Then we'll think real hard while she sings," Maslin said impatiently. "But what ever we do, let's for God's sake get on with it."

"Very well."

"I can't just sing cold like this," Uhura protested.

"I'll improvise," Maslin said, sliding onto the bench. "You follow. We've done it often enough before."

"Words? How about some text? It's a little hard to just start babbling in song about what's going on."

"True. Bear with me for a moment." He ripped a sheet of composition paper from the notebook that rested on the synthesizer, and began to scribble. "How about some help?" he called to the rest of the party. "Any of you good at jingles?"

"Dear gods what a task," Kali said, joining him and Uhura on the bench. "What shall we say?"

"We'll want to keep it simple since we'll just be speaking pidgen as far as they're concerned."

"Start with the phenomenon," Spock said, moving in.

"Then my people," Kali offered.

"The battle," Ragsdale suggested, becoming excited.

"And then the loss of the ships into the phenomenon," said McCoy, adding his bit.

"And finally we'll ask them to return our people," Uhura concluded soberly.

"All of our people," Kali added with a challenging look to the humans.

"But they'll just start attacking us again," Ragsdale protested.

"Not if my husband can get back to his ship and reassert control." She paused and looked about at the alien faces. "I have friends and companions on those ships. I would not have them all die because of a few evil men."

"Very well," Spock said, seeing that Kali was adamant upon this point. "We will ask for the return of all of the ships."

"Jesus, we may as well try explaining the ascent of man, the conquest of space and the founding of the Federation," Maslin muttered sourly as he stared down at his scribbled notes.

"What other choice do we have?" Kali reminded him quietly.

"Good point. Okay, let's get to it."

It took two hours, but at last they had something that basically scanned. Maslin read it over several more times, made a few changes, and then pulled a face.

"Yeats will no doubt spin in his grave, but maybe it will fly," the composer said as Uhura twitched the paper from his hands, and moved away to study the words in privacy.

"Fortunately this isn't an English comp class," McCoy said. "Besides it might sound better in Taygetian."

"I doubt it. You know how horrible things usually sound when they're translated."

"Mr. Maslin, at this time esthetics are not our major concern."

"You're right, Spock, I'm sorry. I guess I'm just being sensitive." He gave a self-deprecating little smile. "But you can't really blame me. This is the first time that my music has ever been given quite such a premiere."

"Let's do it," Uhura said, stepping back to the group. Her face was tight with strain.

"We'll use a simple ABA form," he said to her. "This will be the basic theme." He turned to the instrument, and played a quick, agitated melody that seemed to embody the desperation of their plight. "We'll then modulate into minor for the central section, and then back to the major key when you ask them for help."

"Play it one more time, please," Uhura said.

He obliged, and Uhura stood with her eyes half-closed, one

hand beating time on her thigh, and occasionally humming through a tricky or difficult section. They finished, and Maslin gave her an inquiring look. She nodded and, gripping the verses tightly in one hand, stepped to the side of the synthesizer. He handed her a translator that was hooked to the memory banks of the synthesizer. Her sounds would be routed through the computer, translated into Taygetian, and sent on to the listening cubs.

A hush fell over the assembled people as they waited for this final, desperate test of their theory. The sun was just beginning to rise, touching the peaks of the crystal cliffs with opalescent fire, and turning the wind-tossed clouds into billowing masses of pink and amber.

Maslin improvised an introduction, Uhura drew in a deep preparatory breath, and began to sing.

> *Hear oh Singers, gather near*
> *Heed and help us in our hour.*
> *For danger threatens*
> *And death draws near.*

There was a convulsive stir from the cubs, and they began an agitated yelping that had little resemblance to their usual melodic murmurings. Uhura faltered, then picked up the melody and went on.

> *In darkness, silent growing*
> *The rainbow colors dance and swirl*
> *All it touches are lost to living.*
> *Sun is threatened, soon it dies.*

She held out her hand, indicating the rising sun, and in the following verses tried to describe the phenomenon and its terrible power. She went on through the arrival of the *Enterprise* and the Klingons, the battle that had lost all the ships. By now the cubs were singing an agitated and complex counterpoint to her song that Spock was carefully recording on his tricorder. She reached the end, and made her plea for help with Guy and Kali joining their voices to hers.

Maslin, making one last desperate attempt for understanding, reached out in some unexplainable fashion, and there was a moment of disorientation as he felt his mind met and captured by the Taygetian cubs. Music seemed to be hammering into his skull. He felt the world spinning about him, and pain exploded behind his eyes, but he hung on because he *understood*. They were somehow communicating.

"People! You are people!" came a musical cry from a cub. Guy looked down to find one of the brighter, more aggressive cubs reared up next to the synthesizer with his front flippers resting on the bench.

Guy grabbed the translator out of Uhura's hands, ignoring her look of shock, for he was too busy searching about for the proper sounds. He had spent so much time with the Taygetian language that it was very familiar to him, and he had a very strong understanding of the tongue. Nonetheless, it was a very different matter to speak such a language, and he took his time, not wanting to make an error at this critical juncture.

"Yes, we are people," he sang while playing along with one hand on the synthesizer. *"And we have come to help you."*

"But you are asking us for help," the cub sang, puzzled.

"Yes, that is true, for we have lost our people to the space/time vortex. But I tell you now that if our people do not return to find a solution to this danger all of us will die. The vortex will eat the sun, and Taygeta will become a ball of ice."

"How can the sun not be? It would take the power of a thousand —— to remove the sun."

Guy puzzled over the unfamiliar sound, but he had no framework, so he gave up on the missing word. *"Nonetheless, it can be done. The vortex touches physical objects that exist in this space and time, and sweeps them into . . . otherwise,"* he finally said for lack of a better word. *"I myself have seen this happen. The inner world that orbits next to the sun is gone."* There was a howl of dismay from the cubs, and Maslin realized that whatever the Taygetians might be they were definitely not primitives where astronomy was concerned. They were obviously very familiar with their own solar system.

It took a long time, for there were moments when Guy simply couldn't understand, or times when he produced some odd sound that left the cubs totally bewildered. There was also the insatiable curiosity of the cubs themselves. They kept changing the subject and wandering far afield as they asked questions about the humans: how they lived, where they had come from, how they had gotten there. Guy could have screamed with frustration, but he forced himself to be patient, knowing this was not the time for him to display anything other than the most even of tempers. At last the cubs seemed satisfied, and willing to return to the subject of the *Enterprise.*

"So what is it you wish us to do?" the spokesman asked.

"Do what you do with the fish, and the deserts, and the rain. And bring back our ships."

"Show me what they look like."

Guy gaped at the cub, and then looked desperately at Spock. He had been virtually oblivious to the other members of the landing party during his exchange with the cubs, and fortunately they hadn't interferred with him, but now he needed help. He struggled to free himself from the grip of the singers, and they reluctantly let go. When the release came he almost collapsed onto the keyboard. Only Uhura's hands on his shoulders kept him from falling.

"They need to know what the ships look like," he gasped, his body shaking with reaction. "Hell, I don't know so somebody's got to take over for me."

"You were in a telepathic link?" Spock asked.

"No, I was asleep with my eyes open." Exhaustion had made him snappish. "Of course I was in a telepathic link."

Spock ignored the human's ill humor, and dropped down to kneel before the leader cub. He cautiously reached out for the creature's small, round skull, but the Taygetian displayed no fear. In fact it thrust its head eagerly into Spock's hands.

"Wait," Kali said, before he could begin the meld. "Show them Kor, and if it's possible have them return him to the bridge of the flagship. That will take care of this mutiny."

There was a burst of approving laughter from the humans. "Lady, I'm sure glad you're on our side," McCoy said with a laugh. "Because you sure are a devious little thing."

Spock got that faraway look that signaled his drop into the mind trance, but he was once again disturbed.

"Wait." This time it was Maslin. "It's going to take more than the mind meld. You'll need the music too. I'll play for you."

"Very well. Now, may we please get on with it?"

Maslin began to play. Spock sat in hunched concentration, singing in a pleasant baritone. It was a strange sight, the tall, slender Vulcan locked in close communication with a small, furry white creature with wise blue eyes. The creature suddenly trilled with excitement, and Spock released him and sat down in the sand. There was a moment of silence, and then everyone, even the most mind blind of the humans, was shaken by a powerful psychic call that went echoing through the corridors of their minds.

"What in the hell was that!" McCoy gasped while he clutched at his ringing head.

"Shing—that is his name—Shing," Spock explained, "has called for the leader of his people. It seems that the uses of the song are dictated by law and tradition, and our request does not fit within any of the guidelines. The cubs must therefore receive permission before they can help us."

Maslin had once more sunk back against Uhura's supporting body. His lips were almost blue, and his skin an unnatural white. She held him close, and looked up at Kali. "I've got to get him to—"

"Look," Kali interrupted, pointing toward the cliff face. Everyone followed the direction of her point, and there coming slowly down the cliff was an adult. Its silver coat shone like precious metal against the clear crystal of the rocks. In spite of its bulk it moved with curious grace, and everyone stood frozen as if in the presence of some great and powerful mystery. The cubs gave a cry of greeting, and flopped to meet the descending adult. The Taygetian paused, and caressed their heads with a rough black tongue before continuing on to the waiting humans.

"Mr. Maslin," Spock said, his eyes on the advancing Taygetian. "I will need you once again."

"Right." Maslin pushed upright, and laid his hands on the keyboard. There was a palsied shaking in his hands, and those who watched felt certain that he wouldn't be able to play. He seemed to draw strength from the keys, however, and the trembling subsided.

The adult, accompanied by a bevy of gamboling cubs, reached the humans, and regarded them out of deep blue eyes. Few of the humans could long endure that look. They quickly flinched and dropped their eyes, frightened by this one glance into eternity. Only Maslin stared with fascination into those fathomless wells of blue, and his laboured breathing began to ease.

Spock cautiously approached the Taygetian and, when he was in position, nodded to Maslin. He was preparing to speak, but before he could do so he was gripped by the most powerful mind he had ever encountered.

"Who are you that you cause the younglings to disturb the sanctity of the Great Song?"

"We are travelers who have come to save you from a great danger."

The matriarch seemed amused. *"We are in no danger. The Great Song protects all. And I believe it is you who have asked for help."*

"That is true. Our companions have been lost in a great rip

225

in time and space. We need your help to return them to our space."

"It cannot be done. Nothing must interfere with the song that protects the world."

"But the cubs have already said they would help us," Spock argued. *"It requires only your permission."*

The elder looked inquiringly at the cubs, and there was a burst of agitated singing from Shing. It was a rapid fire of song and thought, far too fast for Spock to follow. After several moments of listening to impassioned pleading from the cub, the older Taygetian sighed, a very human reaction.

"Very well, we will allow the young ones to help. You freed us from the hunters who were disturbing our peace. A favor for a favor," she said. *"But once your ship has been returned you must leave. You are a distracting presence on our world."*

"But . . . " Spock began.

"The discussion is at an end." She turned, and made her slow way back to the cliffs.

"Well?" McCoy demanded. "Will they help?"

"They have been given permission to aid us, but the matriarch has ordered us to leave as soon as the *Enterprise* is returned."

"Well hey," Ragsdale said. "It's a tough break for the Taygetians, but we can't force them to accept our help. I say that as soon as the *Enterprise* is back we haul our asses aboard, and get the hell out of here."

"Aren't we being a little premature?" McCoy said. "We don't even know if the Taygetians can return the ship. All we've seen are fancy tricks with fish and trees and such. That phenomenon is a whole 'nother ball game."

"An excellent point, Doctor."

Maslin lost interest in the conversation flowing about him. He felt horribly sick and weak, and all he wanted was the safety and comfort of the *Enterprise* sick bay. He looked down to where Shing was once more propped on the edge of the bench. He bent and rested his head on the cub's head, and was once more in rapport. It hurt less this time.

"Well, little one. All is well? You can help us?"

"Yes, Song Singer, all is well. And now we begin our song."

He slipped from Maslin's grasp and joined his companions, who sat in a tight circle about the humans. There was a tingling in the air as if great powers were being summoned into existence. Then the cubs lifted their heads and poured out their song. All those who heard the song—the few surviving Klingons huddled in their camp, and the *Enterprise* landing party—all bent under the assault to mind and body. People clutched at their heads and staggered about trying to find someplace to escape from the onslaught of sound. Only Maslin stayed erect. He seemed transported, his face alight with an almost worshipful joy. His hands flew across the keys accompanying the Singers in their momentous effort.

Deep in space the veils of alternate time and space that had separated the *Enterprise* from her own place parted. The ship was seized in a powerful force, and sent spinning from the heart of the vortex to come to rest once more in orbit around Taygeta.

The screams which had been halted in a hundred throats at the moment of penetration burst out, and the intercom echoed with their cries. Kirk staggered from his chair, and stared in wonder at the blue green water world floating serenely in the center of the screen. From behind him came a rush of air like the wind off the sea, and Kor vanished. The captain staggered up the steps, and reached out as if to snatch back the vanished commander.

"Captain!" He whirled at Chekov's anguished cry, and stared in bitterness and defeat at the three Klingon cruisers who had joined them in orbit about the planet.

He almost fell into his chair, shouting orders as he went. It wasn't fair, he thought with a tinge of regret, that they had to go through it all over again after just being given a second chance.

Chapter Fourteen

Karsul blearily shook his head, and commanded his eyes to focus and his brain to *work*. He was still shaken by that journey into otherwhere, that place where nothing made sense, and life itself seemed like a futile dream from some distant and unreal world. There were frightened mutterings from his bridge crew as everyone tried to cope with the suddenness of their return to their own universe.

Karsul stared at the main screen, and the hot light of battle once more glowed in his eyes, for the *Enterprise* lay helpless and foundering in the center of the screen. The young officer leaned forward, excitedly gripping the arms of the command chair.

"We have them now! They are practically dead in space. Obviously the Earthers do not recover as quickly from a shock as we Klingons," he said with smug complacency, addressing the bridge crew in general. "Khant, ready phasers.

Fire on my command." But the weapons officer made no move. Instead he stared with a white, sick expression past Karsul's right shoulder. "For the god's sakes!" Karsul exploded, starting out of the chair. "What's wrong with you, man? I gave you an order—now carry it out!"

"I think he's realized that your orders no longer have any validity aboard this ship," came an ironic and terrifyingly familiar voice from behind him.

Karsul whirled, and leaned back, panting, against the navigation and weapons console. "You!" he hissed, his lips drawing back in a feral snarl. But there was fear in his black eyes as he stared mesmerized down the barrel of the disruptor that Kor held leveled at his chest. "How can you be here?" Karsul babbled. "You were on the *Enterprise*. There is no way you could have transported here. . . ."

"Karsul," Kor said with almost gentle pity in his deep voice. "You should always demand to see the body of a commander you seek to replace. Otherwise you might never know when he'll come back from the grave to haunt you. You never were very thorough, though," he concluded thoughtfully, and squeezed the trigger. Karsul collapsed in a heap at the base of the chair, his uniform smoking from the force of the disruptor blast.

"Take him away, and see the body jettisoned," Kor ordered, indicating the corpse with the barrel of his weapon. The remaining bridge crew stared at him in shock for several more seconds, then two men leaped to obey. "Anybody have any problems with my resuming command?" Kor asked sweetly while Karsul's body was dragged ignominiously into the elevator. "No?" he asked, raising one eyebrow. "Good, then we'll consider that settled. Where is Captain Kandi?" Kor asked, rounding on the communications officer. "Has he been killed or merely detained?"

"Detained I believe, sir," the man answered with a quaver in his voice.

"See to it that he's released, and get the commander of that third ship on the line. Shibot, is it not?"

"I believe so, sir."

"Not too certain of anything, are you, Korax?" Kor asked.

"No, sir," Korax gulped.

"That's probably the safest," Kor confided before he swung down into his chair.

Seconds later the screen flickered, and the heavy features of Captain Shibot stabilized on the screen. "Kor, my old friend," he cried jovially, after the initial shock of seeing the other commander wore off. "Good to see you."

"Surprising too, no doubt."

"Ah, well . . . as to that . . ."

"Never mind," Kor said, cutting him off. His tone was suddenly harsh. "As you can see I have reasserted control over my ships, and since your services are no longer required, I suggest you get back to your scheduled route."

"But the *Enterprise* . . ."

"Will do very well as she is."

"But—"

"Shibot, don't make me give you a taste of being out-gunned three to one," Kor said wearily. "We have more pressing problems than the presence of one Federation starship. So please, just get on your way."

"This will have to be reported."

"By all means report it, because at this point I truly don't give a damn about high command. I'll either return a hero because I've solved the mystery of the phenomenon or I'll die here making the attempt."

"Ah, yes, I see. And either way my report won't make much difference."

"An excellent bit of deductive reasoning, Shibot."

The other captain fidgeted momentarily, then looked up with a smile. "I think the log can be suitably altered."

"Good."

"Oh yes, my congratulations on your marriage," Shibot said as he signed off.

"Thank you," Kor muttered quietly at the now-empty screen, and he felt his chest constrict with fear as he contemplated Kali. The phenomenon be damned, he thought. The first thing he was going to do was get back to Taygeta and check on his wife. He wondered what he would do if he found her killed by the mutineers, and for one moment he wished he hadn't killed Karsul so cleanly. If anything had happened to Kali he would have liked to take it out of the other man's skin.

The ship-to-ship hail came whistling through the bridge, and Kandi's face appeared on the screen. He looked tired, and there were several bruises on his face, but overall he looked unharmed.

"Everything back under control?" Kor asked.

"Yes, sir. I wondered if you had any orders for us?"

"Yes, when you've finished with your mutineers, hold on the edge of the phenomenon. We're running out of time, and I don't want to be surprised by anything."

"Executions are already underway," Kandi said tonelessly. "But where will you be?"

"Joining the *Enterprise* in orbit around Taygeta. I want to check on the status of the landing party."

"I hope everything is all right," the younger man said softly, and Kor read the concern and affection in his friend's eyes.

"Thank you. I hope so too."

Kor had barely settled back in his chair when the hailing frequency was opened again. This time it was Kirk.

"I'd hoped I'd find you there," the captain of the *Enterprise* said without preamble. "But I'd sure like to know how it happened."

"You are not alone in that. Frankly I have no idea, but when I realized what had happened I seized the initiative."

"What did you say to that other ship? They lit out of here like a gargoola with its tail feathers on fire."

"I just pointed out to them the decided drawbacks and disadvantages of being outgunned three to one."

"He should have called me. I'd have given him a testimonial," Kirk muttered ruefully.

"I am bound for Taygeta, and you?"

"The same. I'll see you down there."

"My landing party remains mute. Have you heard from yours?" Kor forced himself to ask. He hated to betray his anxiety in front of the human, but his concern for Kali was too great to remain impassive.

"There seems to be some strong interference which my communications officer has been unable to break through. We'll just have to hang on and hope."

Kor grunted in response, and they broke connection. It would take only minutes to transport to the surface of Taygeta. Then they would know the worst.

"Stop! Tell them to stop!" Spock shouted over the massive chorus that rose and fell around them. "If anything were going to happen it would have happened by now, and their song is interfering with my communicator. I cannot ascertain if the *Enterprise* has returned or not with all this racket."

"Mind if I'm a little more tactful," Maslin yelled back. "After they've busted their asses for us it wouldn't do to call their music a 'racket.' "

"Do as you see fit, Mr. Maslin, but get them to stop."

"I'm tired," Guy said to Uhura. "Can you sing it for me while I play?"

"Of course," she replied from where she sat next to him on the bench. Guy kicked up the amplification on the synthesizer, and Uhura sang loudly into a microphone. One by one the cubs faltered and subsided as Uhura's voice reached them.

The quiet was startling to the humans after having been in the center of a barrage of music for the past twenty minutes. The adults were still singing their song, but after the shock of two full choruses singing at full voice it seemed almost restful.

Spock flipped open his communicator. "Spock to *Enterprise*. Come in *Enterprise*. Do you read?"

"We read you, Mr. Spock," came Kirk's voice from behind the Vulcan. Everyone whirled, and even Spock did a momentary double take, for Kirk stood only a few feet behind them. With him was a full security force.

There was a hum and a flicker, and then Kor was there also, accompanied by armed guards. Kali gave a sob of joy, and flung herself at her husband. He caught her in his arms, staggering a little under the impact, and pressed her into a passionate embrace. The humans politely turned their backs on the reunion, and moved in on Kirk.

"I'm pleased to find you here, Mr. Spock," Kirk said. "I admit I had my doubts when I realized Kor had lost control."

"We were able to fight off the Klingon assault. Unfortunately we lost two crew members and Yeoman Chou was wounded during the fighting."

"Sorry we didn't get back in time to prevent that. By the way," Kirk said with an almost comical look of puzzlement. "Do you have any idea how we did get back?"

"Yes, Captain. We managed to convince the Taygetians of your plight, and they sang you back into existence."

"Then you've broken the language?"

"Yes, but only the cubs will have anything to do with us. We have had one brief conversation with one of the adults, but—"

"Jim, Spock," McCoy suddenly interrupted. "It looks like the old lady is coming back." The two officers turned and surveyed the cliff face, and as McCoy had said the matriarch was returning.

Kor, his arm around Kali's waist, walked over to the three officers of the *Enterprise*. "What is happening?"

"I think we're about to be granted another audience," McCoy said quietly. "I just wonder what she wants this time. She seemed very reluctant to approach us the first time so why do it now?"

"Speculation without facts will accomplish little, Doctor. I suggest we wait."

In a short time the matriarch had arranged herself on the top of a hillock of sand, and with a stately inclination of her head indicated to the intruders to approach. The cubs had gathered about her like a court about their queen. There was some melodic murmuring, then silence fell as the Singer began to speak.

"We have done as you requested," she sang, and Spock, frowning a bit with concentration, translated. *"But now you must leave. Your presence, beginning first with the destructive presence of the hunters, and now your own internal squabbling, has disrupted the Great Song."*

"Great Song? What's the Great Song?" Kirk whispered.

"Apparently the constant song that the adults are singing," Spock answered.

"But what does it? . . ." Kirk began, but the matriarch was once more speaking.

"Nothing must interfere with the sacred work which protects our world, and you have begun to interfere. Therefore you must go."

"But the space/time rip," Kirk objected. "Spock, we've got to make them understand the danger. We've got to stay in order to discover a way to remove the phenomenon."

"It will be difficult to pursuade her given that the Taygetians apparently view our presence as interfering with a ritual of religious significance."

"Well try, we've got to get through to them."

"Lieutenant," Spock said with a glance to Uhura.

"Yes, sir," she said. She drew in a breath of air, but Maslin was not there to provide the melody. Instead he was staring off into space with a rapt expression.

It was the first time Kirk had really taken a look at the composer and he was shocked with what he saw. The man looked shrunken and frail, as if he had aged twenty years in the past few days. His skin was drawn tautly over the bones of his face, and his eyes had sunk to dark hollows. Uhura touched him gently on the shoulder. He gave a start, and slowly focused on his surroundings.

"Yes?" he asked hoarsely.

"I need music."

"Okay."

"Great Lady," Uhura sang. *"There is a danger in the sky that surpasses the danger caused by—"*

"Silence!" the Taygetian ordered with an imperious shake of her head. *"We are a peaceful people wishing no harm to any living creature, but I tell you now, if you will not leave our world we will destroy you. We have the power to restore. Do not doubt that we have the power to remove."*

"So what do we do now?" Kor asked with a grimace.

Kirk spread out his hands in helplessness. "I don't know. Recommendations?" he said, looking about the circle of anxious faces.

"Leave," Ragsdale growled. "What else can we do?"

"But that won't solve the phenomenon," McCoy protested.

"Oh, yes it will," Maslin said suddenly from the bench. Everyone stared at him as if he had lost his mind. "The solution is so obvious," he said, sliding off the bench, and walking painfully over to Kirk. "I should have seen it days ago. The rip exists because the Taygetians are singing with missing voices. The disruption in the harmonics caused the rip. It will go away if the Taygetians quit singing."

"But it is unlikely the Taygetians will voluntarily stop the song, given its significance to them," Spock said.

"They're not going to have much choice," Kor muttered dryly. "Once that phenomenon hits their sun they will all die."

"An expedient solution, but one I am not fond of," Spock replied. "These are a highly sentient race. They deserve to live."

"So how do we get them to shut up?" Kor demanded somewhat belligerently.

"By convincing them that there is no longer any reason for the song to continue."

"But if the song is a religious—"

"It is *not* mere religious formula," Maslin stated, his voice rising in anger. "Don't you understand yet? They believe they have to keep singing or be destroyed by the radiation wave from that nova."

"What?" came a chorus from the listening people.

"An interesting theory, Mr. Maslin, but what do you offer as empirical evidence?" Spock asked.

"Look, we all wondered at the destruction on the other planets, and wondered how Taygeta could have avoided being fried with the rest of them. There had to be something on this world that protected them against the radiation wave. Well, the only thing that's here are the Taygetians, all of them busily singing from birth until death. What could possibly require such an immense effort except a life-threatening crisis?"

"But that wave passed through here three thousand years ago," Kirk protested. "No race would keep on after the danger had passed."

"Wait, Captain. Mr. Maslin's theory has a great deal to recommend it. We know that the Taygetians have the power to manipulate their environment, so why not extend it out to the fabric of space that surrounds them?"

"But the time, Spock, the time."

"It would have taken years for the wave to pass fully beyond their world. By then the true purpose of the song might have been lost, and the action taken on a purely religious significance."

Kirk rounded on Maslin. "Can you translate the song, find out if we really are on the right track?"

"I was trying that earlier, and it's just too damn complex. It would take me weeks, and I gather we don't have weeks. I can tell you that in form it closely resembles the manipulative songs that the cubs sing to bring in fish, or create forests, or whatever, so it's clearly an environment-affecting song."

"Only it's the granddaddy of all of them," McCoy muttered with a glance up at the cliffs that surrounded them.

"My God," Kirk murmured, also gazing incredulously up at the cliffs. "How terrible. An entire race has devoted all its energy to defending against a threat that no longer exists. All development in art and science has been stunted because there was no time to spare for them. What these creatures might have accomplished if this had never happened," he concluded softly.

"And think of the young ones," Uhura said, dropping to one knee and stroking one of the cubs. "How horrible to grow up knowing that once you reach adulthood you will have to take up a life of endless drudgery. There's no choice, no opportunity."

"Ideas? Recommendations?" Kirk said, looking about the assembled people.

"Why don't we just tell them the danger's past," Maslin said with a flash of his old impatience. He began moving back to the synthesizer. "We know the language now, it seems fairly obvious to me, but maybe there's some reason why we need to be complicating matters," he concluded, and dropped heavily onto the bench.

"It would seem logical, Captain, but since the Taygetians are a highly telepathic race it might be best if I melded with the matriarch. Our grasp of their language is as yet imperfect, and this is far too important to run the risk of a misunderstanding."

"I couldn't agree more. So how do we start?"

"You make your plea, Captain, and Mr. Maslin, Lieutenant Uhura and I will try to insure that it reaches the Taygetians intact."

Kirk moved away from the assembled people to marshal his thoughts. His eyes were focused intently on the glittering cliffs, and occasionally one hand would tighten into a fist. It betrayed his nervousness.

"So, the humans are once more going to sweep the field," Kor murmured to Kali.

"I don't begrudge them the victory," she replied, her eyes moving from Maslin's slender, pain-racked body, to Uhura's beautiful face, and on to Spock, where he was cautiously approaching the matriarch. "They have earned it, while we have done little but hinder them."

"Imperial High Command is not likely to share your view."

"So," she said with a little shrug. "We will have to give them a tale that will make them happy."

Kor chuckled, and pulled her tightly against his body. "Such a cunning little Klingon."

"Sometimes I wonder if I am a very good Klingon, Kor," she said, looking seriously up at him. "I *like* the humans."

"Kali, my darling, so do I. Or at least I like these humans," he added after a moment's thought. "I don't know how I would feel about them if I had to live among them."

"Then by all means let us make sure the High Command doesn't find out about our collaboration or we *will* find ourselves living with the humans."

Kirk walked back to the group, and took up a position near Spock. "All ready?" he asked tensely.

Spock nodded. "The matriarch seems undisturbed by my physical contact, so I see no problem."

"I see lots of them," Kirk muttered, and glanced over at Maslin and Uhura. "Ready?"

"Ready, sir," Uhura replied. Maslin said nothing. Instead he stared blankly down at the keyboards, and pulled in great breaths of air as if preparing himself for some final, mighty effort.

Spock reached out, and spread his long fingers over the rounded cranium of the Taygetian elder. She lifted her fathomless blue eyes to meet Spock's brown ones, and suddenly the four people, Spock, Kirk, Maslin and Uhura, gasped and became rigid at their places. McCoy started forward only to be pushed back by Kor.

"Leave them! It is apparent they are in the Taygetian's hold now. To interfere might do irreparable harm."

"But what about harm to *them!*" McCoy raged, but Kor maintained his implacable grip on the doctor's arm.

Suddenly Maslin began to play. It was haunting, desperate music that rose in sweeping waves into the silver sky. Kirk, his eyes seeming focused in eternity, began to speak, and seconds later Uhura's voice rose in song. Spock, who was the focal point for all of this energy, jerked as if he were a puppet whose strings had been pulled in random directions, and his face twisted in pain.

Kirk felt as if he were once more trapped in the phenomenon. Colors twisted and swirled about him, and music was all about and even within him. He began to lose sight of who he was, and what he had come to do. The very awareness of self that was the core of all humans was slipping from him, whirled away in the fantasy of music that comprised all reality for him now. He longed to spread open his arms, and spin away like some chip carried on the maelstrom of sound.

Suddenly he became aware of other presences that inhabited this strange silver overworld with him. He felt a strong and beloved touch, and knew Spock. That familiar contact brought back his own identity, and he once more knew himself. Next there was an impression of warmth and beauty, and he knew he had found Uhura. Then there was the other presence. Quicksilver and mercurial, it danced just beyond his reach. But there was something wrong with this presence. Its fire was dimming, and it flickered feebly while the others who were with him burned with a solid light.

He sensed another presence behind him, the way a blind person could sense the position of the sun by its warmth and light. He slowly turned, although such a mundane word could not fully describe the movement that he made, and there was the Taygetian. He knew it was she from emanations that flowed from the glowing white-and-gold form. Kirk suddenly realized with a thrill of shock that he was seeing the Taygetian as she would appear to other psychic beings. He warily approached the creature. Not so much out of fear, because there was nothing threatening about the feelings that washed about him, but out of respect for the awesome power that was embodied before him.

"Lady," he said, and was startled when his voice rolled away from him with a mighty echoing sound.

"Speak, human."

"Lady, the danger that you guard against has long passed."

"How shall I know that you speak the truth? Your kind has done little to recommend itself to us."

"We are very sorry, lady, for the harm that was done to your people by the hunters, but I beg you not to judge all humans by the acts of a few evil ones.

"As for proof, on my ship there are very sensitive devices that can scan the heavens, and read and analyze what is found there. When we first arrived on your world we discovered the passage of the nova, and have traced it far beyond

Taygeta. The traces of the radiation wave are now very distant, for it passed through here some three thousand years ago."

There was a long pause during which Kirk tried to cling to his identity and not become lost in this strange, silver mind world. As he drifted he suddenly felt a delicate touch on his mind, as if gentle fingers had explored through his memories and emotions.

"I have searched your mind, and it seems that you have spoken the truth." Kirk could feel the Taygetian's distress and confusion, and he pitied the creature. "Still, I cannot see that this alters matters. The Great Song is a sacred trust passed down from the time of Nasul, the leader who taught us to blend our individual powers to save our world."

"But surely this Nasul would not have wanted to condemn his people to endless drudgery for no purpose," Kirk desperately cried, for he could sense the matriarch withdrawing from his mind. "Nor would he have wanted his people to destroy themselves. Please, listen to me! The song is no longer an instrument of protection. Instead it has become a weapon that has turned against you! That rip in space and time is caused by the loss of voices in your song. If you don't stop now it will destroy your sun, and with it your entire race! Surely the fulfillment of your duty doesn't require you to go down into death and darkness."

"Show me this danger. I would look upon this vortex. Take me there."

"But," Kirk began, then speech became impossible. There was a moment of gut-wrenching nausea, and then he found himself floating above his collapsed body. He watched with detached interest while McCoy raced from his side, to Spock's, and then to Uhura and Maslin. He wanted to call out to the doctor, to tell him that all was well, but even though he formed the words and heard himself speaking McCoy took no notice.

"Come. We will go now," the matriarch ordered, and Kirk found himself traveling through space. Even though he knew intellectually that his frail, physical body was not being exposed to the deadly cold and airlessness of space, he still found himself cringing in on himself.

"Fascinating," Spock's voice came from the glowing entity on his right. "Some form of astral projection. But obviously limited in range," the Vulcan added when they all came to rest some distance out from Taygeta.

Kirk found that he could see very clearly and to a much greater distance than his human eyes would have permitted. He could see the *Enterprise* orbiting the planet in close formation with Kor's flagship, and he felt his chest squeezed tight with emotion as he gazed on her perfect lines. Beyond the two ships he could see the second Klingon ship looking like a toy as it hung before the phenomenon. The phenomenon itself shimmered and glowed with iridescent fires as it hung like a prismatic curtain across the fabric of space. The Taygetian sun was only a faint yellow glow behind the shifting colors of the space/time rip. Even though Maslin's and Uhura's physical bodies were slumped unconscious over the synthesizer there was still music swelling and ebbing all about Kirk. He realized that he must be "hearing" the music that was in their minds, and he found it more beautiful than any earthly music he had ever heard.

"So," the matriarch said quietly, and her thoughts fell bleak and hopeless upon Kirk's mind. "I behold our doom."

"But it doesn't have to be!" the captain insisted. "It is your doom, in the sense that you created it, but you can also stop it. Just stop the song!"

He could sense the indecision in the elder Taygetian, and he cast about desperately for some other argument, some plea that would reach and convince her.

Suddenly a group of cubs came flying past like a bevy of

glittering comets. If they were awkward and ungainly on land here in the dark sea of space their astral bodies darted and spun with the grace of dancers. They whirled about him and his companions, playing at intricate games of tag while the distant stars formed a glittering backdrop for their antics.

Like children of any world, Kirk thought. *But what children! They can have the stars as their playground. Or can they? Once adulthood is reached such games are put aside in favor of their duty—a duty that is pointless and wastes their potential.*

And it was then that he knew what to do.

"Lady, if not for yourselves then for the sake of the children. Stop this song before it destroys you all. For generations your children have only been able to look forward to a life of endless toil and drudgery, and a toil to no purpose. Trust us and we can give you the stars. As members of the Federation the resources and learning of a thousand worlds will be available to your people, and your great powers can be used for the benefit of hundreds of races. Lady, I beg you, don't deny your children a future!"

The music which had been maintaining a quiet counterpoint to his words suddenly rose in a joyful crescendo. It mirrored Kirk's sincerity and desperate hope, and it seemed that a hundred orchestras overlaid by one lone voice wrote a tone poem of a future so beautiful that only the most callous of creatures could have ignored its vision.

There was again a moment of nausea and dislocation, and then Kirk found himself rising shakily to his feet. Sand cascaded from his parka, and he brushed the last clinging particles from his pants.

"Jim! Jim! Are you all right? What happened?" McCoy gripped him by the shoulders, and there was a babble of confused voices all about him. Then the matriarch emitted a long piercing cry that went wailing up and down the tonal scale, and the song ceased. Silence fell over the silver-and-crystal world of the Singers. For the first time in three thousand years there was quiet. The only sounds were the hiss and boom of the waves on the beach, the sigh of the wind through the rock cliffs and the sound of a woman crying.

Chapter Fifteen

Kirk set McCoy aside, and moved to Uhura. She had slid off of the synthesizer bench, and was now sitting in the sand with Maslin cradled in her arms. The composer's face was a pale waxy white, and the air rattled in his throat with each breath he drew.

McCoy came barreling past Kirk, and ran his tricorder over Maslin's prone body. He then looked up at Kirk, and gave a small shake of his head.

"Can you do anything for him?" the captain asked quietly.

"Make him comfortable, maybe try a few tricks, but it's doubtful," McCoy replied in the same low tone. "Let me get him back to the ship."

"No." The single word was very weak, and followed by a paroxysm of coughing, but it still held a vestige of Maslin's old command. The composer drew back his lips in a travesty of a smile, and looked up at Kirk. "No," he said again. "This seems a very good place for a musician to die."

"Guy, no," Uhura whispered, and her face was a mask of agony.

Kirk suddenly became aware of the curiously watching security team that had accompanied him down from the *Enterprise*. "Thomas," he snapped to their leader. "Take your team, and track down those last Klingon mutineers."

"Aye, sir."

"You go with them," Kor said suddenly to his own guards, and waved them away.

"Don't cry, my heart," Guy was saying to Uhura when Kirk returned his attention to the couple. "Life is very rarely as we wish it to be."

"If only you hadn't come," Uhura cried, and her words were like a whip to Kirk's already sensitive nerves. He braced himself for Maslin's reply.

"And if I hadn't come I would never have known you." He took one of her hands, and lifted it weakly to his lips. "Also," he paused, and for an instant an expression of almost transported joy crossed his face. "I wrote my greatest piece here. This time my music really did speak to the heavens."

"Oh, Guy—" The whistle of a communicator cut through her words.

"Kirk here."

"Scotty, Captain. Just wanted to report that the phenomenon has vanished, as well as the subspace harmonic that was wreckin' the dilithium crystals."

"Very good, Mr. Scott. Secure the ship, and wait for my call."

"Aye, sir."

"So, Kirk, we did it," Maslin gasped painfully.

"I would say rather that *you* did it."

"What's this? Modesty from the great captain of the *Enterprise?*" Maslin said with a touch of his old raillery. "Come, come, Kirk, don't ruin my image of you."

The captain dropped down on one knee next to the dying

composer. "You ruined my image of you," he said, taking one of Maslin's limp hands. "And I want you to know that I'm sorry. I never intended it to end this way—"

"Please, Kirk, don't become maudlin," he said with an impatient gesture. He cast the captain an ironic look. "Besides, it is true, what you once said: Some things are worth more than our own selfish little lives. I wouldn't have wanted to miss the Taygetians." The cub who had been Guy's constant companion seemed to sense that something was happening for he suddenly flopped forward, and placed his head beneath Guy's hand.

The composer's lashes fluttered down onto his cheeks, and McCoy once more stepped forward. "Come on, Jim, let me take him back to the ship."

"No." This time it was Uhura who spoke. "Honor his wishes. If he must die at least let it be here."

"That's it, Madam Star Fleet, you tell them," Guy rasped out, and managed once more to open his eyes. He studied her face, and slowly smiled. "Did I ever tell you how much I love you?"

"Not enough times," Uhura said with a catch in her voice.

Kali suddenly spread open her arms, and shooed the circle of watchers away the way a housewife would herd a flock of recalcitrant chickens.

"That's our Kali, ever sensitive," Guy murmured faintly, and Uhura saw that his green eyes were beginning to wander unfocusedly.

"Guy, don't leave me."

"I won't. We've . . . learned that much . . . haven't we? I'll . . . be close . . . always," he murmured disjointedly. "Best I go. Otherwise . . . you might not become a . . . captain. Show them all how it's done, love. . . ."

Uhura gently closed his eyes, and then from all around her the cubs began a sorrowful, minor-key lament. The small cub who had lain with his head beneath Guy's hand suddenly lifted his head and, looking directly at Uhura, shed a single sparkling blue tear. Reaching out she caught it on the palm of her hand, but instead of spattering in salty rivulets it lay smooth and cool on her skin.

And now the tears came. Hot and violent they ran down her face as she sat bowed over the body of her love.

"So this is it then," Kor said as he, Kali, Kirk and Spock walked through the corridors of the *Enterprise* toward the transporter room. "Once more we are denied our warriors' duel."

"Now don't blame me for that," Kirk said, holding up a restraining hand. "As I see it *you're* the one who opted not to fight, but rather to work together."

"And we did pretty well, didn't we?" Kor asked with a grin.

"Yes, I think we did. So, what do you do now?"

"Go home and face the music—please forgive the pun."

"Will it be bad?"

"I hope not. After all, Kali and I will have several weeks in which to concoct a story that will make it appear that we emerged victorious while you slunk away with your tail between your legs."

Kirk raised a hand and covered his eyes. "Oh my reputation, my poor battered reputation," he moaned.

"Your damn reputation doesn't need any further inflation," Kor stated bluntly. "You're already a damn living legend." Kirk looked sheepish. "And furthermore, I once again have to leave the field to you."

"Fortunes of war."

"But this time it wasn't a war. Think about it, Kirk, this time we stopped fighting ourselves; it didn't take the Organians to stop us."

"So, maybe we are all becoming wiser," Kali said.

"Unfortunately we are only two ships," Spock said dampeningly. "Your Empire and our Federation are still standing eye to eye and toe to toe on many fronts."

"Don't be negative, Spock," she said, making a face at the Vulcan. "I am not saying we have solved all the problems, but we have at least demonstrated that it can happen."

"Speaking of problems," Kor said with a hesitant clearing of his throat. "Once you get the three Taygetian ambassadors back to the Federation, and formal relations are established, I don't suppose we could *borrow* a few of them to improve some of our problem worlds?"

"You head the trade delegation to Earth, and I'll be there to assure that it works out."

"All right. It is a deal." They had reached the transporter room, and the foursome paused at the base of the platform for their final leave-taking.

"I won't say good-bye, but rather farewell, for I think we will be meeting again," Kor said, gripping Kirk by the upper arms.

"I hope so, Commander. And about the matter of the Taygetians, you get the changes made so that there can be trade between our people, and I'll see to it that you get what you want."

"Your hand on it?"

"My hand on it."

"You realize what you are asking me to do, don't you, Kirk," Kor said as they shook. "You are asking me to take over the halls of power, and redirect our Empire."

"Commander, if there's any man who can do it, I think it's you. I would say that you're well on your way to being a living legend too."

"Captain, please," Kali said, placing her hands in the middle of Kor's back, and pushing him toward the platform. "He is already vain enough. Please don't add to it."

"Ah, but my darling, I will always have you there to deflate my ego, so all will be well."

"As if I have *ever* tried to diminish you!" Kali gasped angrily. "Why you—" she began, but Kor picked her up in his arms, and pressed a firm kiss on her lips to silence her.

"And that is how you handle women," he said with a wink to Kirk as he deposited his wife on one of the transporter disks. "And now, farewell until the next time."

"Good-bye, Commander," Kirk said, lifting one hand.

"You better hope you're still *alive* by then," Kali said threateningly to her husband as the transporter took them.

"A highly volatile people," Spock remarked when the platform was clear.

"Yes, Mr. Spock, but I like them."

"I have also never understood human taste," the Vulcan added dryly as he and the captain walked out of the transporter room.

"I suppose it's a case of like to like."

"Undoubtedly."

They walked in silence to the turbolift, and Kirk called for the bridge. "Well, we have quite a load of passengers for the trip back, what with the Taygetians and the hunters."

"Yes, but it is unfortunate that we could not return with our original passenger."

"Yes," Kirk agreed, and fell into a thoughtful silence as he considered the simple burial ceremony that he had conducted for Maslin on the shores of that silver sea. "But no man ever had such a requiem mass sung for him."

"Yes, he would have enjoyed it."

Kirk stood silent for several more moments then abruptly asked, "Do you think Uhura is going to be all right?"

"Given my lack of understanding of human emotions, Captain, I am perhaps not the best person to ask. Dr. McCoy considers himself a delver into the secrets of men's souls. You might better direct your question to him."

Kirk grunted a reply as the doors of the turbo lift whooshed open. The bridge was humming with quiet activity, and the captain stood for a moment at the top of the steps reveling in the familiar sights and sounds. All of his number-one bridge crew was in place, Sulu at the helm, Scotty at the engineering console, Uhura on communications and Spock moving smoothly to his place at science. It felt good to have them all back, and Kirk realized that he had missed the comfort of their familiar presences. He hoped there would never again be an occasion when he would be left isolated aboard his ship.

Settling into his command chair, he half turned so he could study Uhura's face. In the days since Maslin's death she had been very quiet, frighteningly quiet, and her usually serene and gentle expression had been replaced with an indecipherable mask.

She reached up to adjust the monitor in her ear, and the motion set something at her breast to swinging. Kirk looked closer, and saw that she was wearing a crystal tear. It spun and sparkled like frozen blue fire on the end of its chain. Kirk shivered slightly, and wondered how she could wear the thing. He would have thought the memories it roused would have been too painful.

He continued to stare mesmerized at the jewel. How strange, he thought, that something so small could have been at the heart of their entire mission.

"From out of the greed of men," he murmured to himself.

"I beg your pardon, sir?" Uhura asked, swinging around in her seat.

"Just thinking aloud, Lieutenant."

She regarded him thoughtfully for several moments, then said, "I wear it as a reminder, sir."

Kirk started a bit, and wondered if her continuing close contact with the highly telepathic Taygetians was rousing some dormant esper powers within her. He shook off his unease and, rising, moved to her side.

"I had wondered," he said quietly, leaning in on her. "But wouldn't it perhaps be better to put this behind you, and try to forget?"

"Grief and loss aren't necessarily bad things, Captain," she replied in a low tone. "Oftentimes we grow as the result of such experiences." She lifted the gem and, allowing the chain to slide through her slender fingers, watched the tear flicker and sparkle in the air between them. "Besides, this is a crystal tear, one of the tears of the Singers. . . ." She lifted her head, and looked into his eyes. "I consider that somehow appropriate."

He gripped her hand and gave it a hard squeeze before returning to his position in the command chair. He took one last look around the bridge, then nodded in satisfaction.

"Mr. Sulu, set a course for Starbase 23. Warp factor three."

"Aye, aye, sir."

The muted roar of the engines rose in intensity, and Taygeta, cloud-wrapped and mysterious, dwindled and fell away behind them. For one brief instant he heard a chorus of farewell echoing in the corridors of his mind, then it was gone as the *Enterprise* leaped beyond range of the Singers. He would probably never hear their music again, but someday, with the help of the three Taygetians who traveled with them, a multitude of worlds would ring with their particular brand of music that sang to the spheres.

The Novel STAR TREK® Fans
Have Waited Twenty Years For . . .

STAR TREK®

SPOCK'S WORLD

by
Diane Duane

Ever since 1966, when the very first episode of
the original STAR TREK television series aired,
casual fans and devoted Trekkers alike have been
captivated by the alien Mr. Spock and his home
planet Vulcan.

Now, for the first time anywhere, you can have
an in-depth look at both.

SPOCK'S WORLD . . .
A September 1988 Hardcover Release
from Pocket Books.

THE
STAR TREK
PHENOMENON

THE

STAR TREK

PHENOMENON

_____ **STAR TREK– THE MOTION PICTURE**
64654/$3.50

_____ **STAR TREK II– THE WRATH OF KHAN**
67426/$3.95

_____ **STAR TREK III–THE SEARCH FOR SPOCK**
67198/$3.95

_____ **STAR TREK IV– THE VOYAGE HOME**
63266/$3.95

_____ **STAR TREK: THE NEXT GENERATION:
ENCOUNTER AT FARPOIINT**
65241/$3.95

_____ **STAR TREK: THE KLINGON DICTIONARY**
66648/$4.95

_____ **STAR TREK COMPENDIUM REVISED**
62726/$9.95

_____ **MR. SCOTT'S GUIDE TO
THE ENTERPRISE**
63576/$10.95

_____ **THE STAR TREK INTERVIEW BOOK**
61794/$7.95

_____ **STAR TREK:
THE NEXT GENERATION:
GHOST SHIP** 66579/$3.95

_____ **STAR TREK:
THE NEXT GENERATION:
THE PEACEKEEPERS**
66929/$3.95

**POCKET
BOOKS**

Simon & Schuster Mail Order Dept. STP
200 Old Tappan Rd., Old Tappan, N.J. 07675

Please send me the books I have checked above. I am enclosing $_____ (please add
75¢ to cover postage and handling for each order. N.Y.S. and N.Y.C. residents please add
appropriate sales tax). Send check or money order--no cash or C.O.D.'s please. Allow up
to six weeks for delivery. For purchases over $10.00 you may use VISA: card number,
expiration date and customer signature must be included.

Name _____

Address _____

City _____ State/Zip _____

VISA Card No. _____ Exp. Date _____

Signature _____ 118-05

For more information regarding

STAR TREK®
THE OFFICIAL FAN CLUB

please call or write to:
STAR TREK: THE OFFICIAL FAN CLUB
P.O. Box 111000
Aurora, CO 80011